THE PALISADES

This book is a work of fiction. The characters, incidents, and dialogue are drawn from the writer's imagination and are not to be construed as real in any way. Any resemblance to actual events or persons, living or dead, is entirely fictional.

THE PALISADES

 For information, send inquiries to Cascadia Publishing, 4007 Cascadia Ave. S. Seattle, WA 98118

ISBN: 978-0-615-34789-9

To the memories of my Mother

and

Joan Weiss Hollenbeck

THE PALISADES

Nicholas

In Big Sur there is a cottage that sits at the edge of a palisade. It is the last refuge before the high mountains that rise up like sentries to the rest of the country. When the air is clear you can see the coast run its length to the horizon, but when the fog rolls in it is masked and hidden as if a magician had waved his hand over the earth to erase it.

It's 1992 and fall is coming. The mornings have been slow to warm. The air is crisp and an icy breath blows over the landscape to chill the leaves and ground. The sun has risen and a deep mist overtakes the road and tall grasses that are summer browned.

I've driven away from my mother's home and am now sitting in my car at the bottom of the cottage road. On the seat next to me is a letter I found on her kitchen table. She'd carefully written my name, Nicholas, on the envelope. Next to it was a tiny leather satchel that was outlined with bright blue beads sewn at the edges. I've left them both unopened out of fear, but now I take them up and put them in the breast pocket of my shirt, get out of the car and reach down to pull the zipper up on my coat to cover them.

I can barely see the shake-shingled roof of the cottage from where I stand at the far edge of the road. There is a wall about thigh-high made up of loose stones edging the drive. Grasses have sprouted between the stones making the wall softer as it cuts the overgrown thicket off. The sweetness of the sea air is cut by the citrus smell of cypress when I start up the steep incline and see the cottage come into view.

Stepping onto the road makes me tremble a bit and the pit of my stomach begins to flutter. I stop midway to take in the curving coastline, the jutting peninsulas, the pines that have hung to the cliffs for hundreds of years and the sea.

When I turn back to the cottage I am instantly transported back in time. There is my brother, Peter, on the porch at dusk and dim lights from the cottage windows haloing his small head. A dilapidated van is in the drive. Its muted color and form shape shifting as the light evaporates. Stands of eucalyptus trees are to the side of the outbuilding where monarch butterflies feed and let the sun warm their wings. There is the collection of sea creatures: anemones, starfish, crab, sand dollars and mollusks drying in the sun.

I remember my brother's shouts as he and I ran down the hill to the cove where we spent whole days beach-combing and tide-pooling. My mother's spirited pull of our arms as we dashed into the woods behind the cottage where she told stories and led us to a "secret" pool of black-glassed water and the way we'd play hide and seek in the fog needing only to separate ourselves by ten feet some days to disappear. There was a constant dampness. Two minutes outside made our skin and the hair on our arms sparkle. It was a place of mystery to me and a place where I discovered independence though I tagged onto my brother because he was older and less enchanted by our new surroundings than I was.

At ten, he could brood hard and motionless for hours. Some days I'd see him outside; his shoulders humped, his face sullen, working his hands deep into his pockets as he sat on the edge of the porch leaning against a roof support. He'd stay like that until our Mother finally noticed him and took him a sweater if the wind came up or the sun went down. There wasn't much conversation between them because they understood each other. The two of them knew what the other was thinking, but stayed clear of the thoughts. He kept his distance from both of us and disappeared for hours without saying where he'd been. Big Sur fitted him as sure as an otter to the sea. Now, more than twenty years later, he lives not far from here, but he has been as remote from me as if he lived clear across country.

The cottage is probably a fine home to someone now or maybe a summer rental as it was when my mother, Peter and I spent a season there. I have very little memory of that summer - I was six - but the one recollection that remains clear is of my father, my brother and me driving away from the cottage in the dark, heading back home to Los Angeles and watching my mother, her wild black hair caught in the wind, chasing us down the hill screaming after us.

Her story is inextricably entwined with mine, though I had not seen her in twenty-two years. I am nearing thirty and it has taken me the better part of those years to come to the place where I was before my mother re-entered my life. She has lived here in Big Sur all these years, been in and out of institutions up near Monterey, given so many chances to make good, but she had finally settled into her vagabond life - a life I was ashamed to be linked to until now.

I can't understand how she came to live in a van on the streets and in the mountain parks of Big Sur, how she made a life out of this and retreated from people and moving away from them if they tried to help her. She's lived off government checks that came to the post office in town. And as a miser would, lived from cans of food she bought from the small market next door to the bank, which was next door to the post office. She'd simply walk from storefront to storefront in a routine that she vigilantly kept up. Now her life has consumed mine.

As I began to investigate her, my own routine was cast aside - getting up early in the morning, making coffee before walking my dog and then getting ready for work. I'd be in the office by nine to be greeted by Patty, my boss and friend, with rolls she'd picked up on the way in. Sometimes the routine was broken by a touch from Matt every time welcomed, but now his light touch is gone. Now I'm cold and feeling anxious having come to the cottage to find out what it is I've forgotten. However remote this place seems to me now, it is a place of beginnings.

I work the letter out from under my jacket where I've kept it from the damp and look at it. As my mother has folded the pages together, I'll combine my life with hers. Only then will it make sense. I'm optimistic that I'll be able to sort everything out, compile the details so that they'll be clear to me. It's all I can hope for. If I were to scatter the pages in the wind, throw them from the bridge just down the way and let them float down into the pines and river I would probably come to some conclusion about my mother: that love would have been enough for her, would have moved through her as surely as the ink through the pen that marked these pages. But from a certain point in her life the possibility of love stopped existing. A bright clear bowl of light was turned off.

Maybe the life that I've constructed about her is simply wrong; the facts gathered from the people in our lives were only stories made up to appease or protect me. Her absence has wanted me to make her the enemy of this story. Why haven't I come to this cottage before knowing that here is where it all started?

I walk slowly around its perimeter. The windowpanes reflect the sky. The shingled sides are wet to the touch and moss has grown at the corners of the eaves. I sit on the edge of the porch where Peter sat. The sun burns through the fog. I think of Matt waking up warm in his own bed wondering why I've let him go and if I'll ever return. How do I give myself over to him?

The letter is thick and full. There is much to read, much to understand. I open it, look out across the palisades to the sea below and back. I begin reading. How would you start a life not your own? How would you start your life over again?

Marjorie

Dear, dear Nicholas...my son. When I saw you standing silently against the wall of the police station, a jumble of emotions running across your face, the years of my life rushed at me with such force that I was speechless when I looked at you. You're a man now. Deep eyes dark as olives judging me, jaw squarely set in mistrust. You held yourself tightly, shoulders and arms bunched together as if forming an army. And I stood looking like a criminal - maybe I was - feeling that the time I've missed with you is lost.

As I look back on that moment - and though my body had been badly beaten - I couldn't help feeling that our life together had the chance to begin again.

It is strange, but my mind has cleared. It's worked softly out of where it's been for several years. It has taken a long time, but maybe it takes an event like this to show me that I have lived my life badly. I can't make any excuses. I have treated you and your brother badly. I have been knocked into knowing this and yet I have questions for you. So many questions, but it may be too late for them and they probably don't matter now.

Thank you for putting me in this small guesthouse. It is the first place I have lived in for many years that doesn't have wheels, white sun-drenched hallways or bars covering the windows. I'll start a garden in the spring. It'll be a pleasure.

The ranch itself is beautiful and only miles from the sea. Frank, the owner, has taken me to the beaches I love; the green stones of Jade Beach, the private coves and waterfalls that spill into the ocean over mossy rocks. They are places of magic and wonder. There is every shade of green and blue and when I can't tell one color from the other, it makes my head dance and my heart open.

I've cherished the last few days here for their simplicity and sense of beginning. You may catch glimpses of them in these pages. But for every one of these days there have been hundreds of disappointments, which I will try and spare you. I'm afraid that once I start, they will come back like a flood knocking everything down that was in its path.

I want to spend my time writing down the true story of my life. But I can only write when my mind is clear, which is more and more now. In the afternoons when I'm tired, I have to put down my pen. Then I go out and walk among the pastures and fields and look back to the mountains where, on the other side, the ocean waits. Further down the road, if the sky is clear, I can imagine that across the flat plain of the Central Valley I can see to the Sierras beyond. I can make out their faint shape and believe that another life exists there.

Now, the matter of my history. I want you to pass this information to your brother so he may judge me fully. My only wish is that you will come to find out about me and understand what really happened so long ago.

PART ONE

1.
Nicholas

I'm being chased down river on a floating boat of splintered wood. I make every effort to escape the boat, but the water churns around me with such force that to jump into it would be my suicide. Then the skies clear, the water abates and the boat, splintered down to its last floatable self, comes to a sudden halt against a bank that opens out to a vast landscape. There are fields upon fields rimmed by soft green hills, but separated by a sparkling chain link fence. I tumble forward when the boat hits the bank and comes to rest at the fence. The sun is bright and hot and the land is an abundance of detail: trees, rocks, shrubs and natural cuts where the earth slipped. When I look up there is a car racing toward me on a road that is desolate as night. The windows are blacked out. I hear the engine race. Suddenly, it fades into a slow rumbling idle. The driver's side window rolls down. My mother's smiling face appears from out of the darkness. I stand up to go to her, but she slowly closes the window and disappears.

I stand frozen there and then run to the fence, climb over it and go headlong into the fields never looking back.

The phone rang and rang again. It was early morning. I stretched across Matt and picked up the receiver.

"Nicholas Welch?" An official sounding voice spoke at me through my haze.

"Nicholas Welch?"

"Yes?"

"Sorry to disturb you." The voice didn't sound apologetic to me, "but we have your mother, a Marjorie Welch, down here at the station. Roy Halpern, you know Roy, anyway, he said he was a friend of yours and also knew this woman was your mother."

"My mother?"

"Yes, he said you might want to come down and pick her up. She's in awful bad shape. It looks like she's been beaten up." The voice said, and added, "She could use some medical attention."

I pulled away from Matt, hot and dripping sweat down the middle of his chest. His breathing, which was labored and heavy, began to catch in his throat. Matt turned over and squinted at me, his body curved in to my side and was barely covered by the crumpled sheets. Matt slipped a hand up under my leg and squeezed my thigh. I motioned for him to go back to sleep.

"But I haven't talked to my mother in years."

"That's what Roy said." The voice lowered into a whisper. I pictured the man turning his back away from whoever was listening. "But I think you should come down and see her for yourself. She was out of it when she came in, but she's calmed down a bit now."

"I can't," I said, "call my brother."

"We did."

"You did?"

"He said to call you."

When I entered the police station there were small notices hanging on the wall with fingerprints and WANTED photographs. They were hung carelessly, as if the effort of it was far greater than finding them. Their surprised photo-flashed faces were dim and lifeless. I pictured my mother on one of them - her tangled curly hair as I remember from my dream, her small mouth smiling down at me. I imagine her photograph against the wall, same hair, and same small mouth. It wouldn't surprise me.

The clerk motioned me down a too-bright hallway to a waiting room with four chairs lined up against a wall. They were the stiff metal kind, with soft foam rubber cushions torn down the middle by too much weight. I sat in one of them, my nerves caught up in their own misguided whirlwind.

It *had* been years since I'd seen her, but I knew she was around town living in a van and moving from place to place just in time to avoid fines. Big Sur isn't big enough for someone to get lost in, but I knew she tried. Local legends become just that over time and she became one for her eccentricities. You can watch her in the town square summer evenings stretching on an old Indian blanket in the waning sun. I have stood across from the park on the sidewalk, watched her tilt her arms up and out, then down her leg to her toes. She stretches every body part to music that only she hears. She is oblivious to anyone passing by or stopping to stare at her because her movements are truly beautiful and have a tai chi quality.

During winter she'll sit wrapped up in the same blanket on the bench in front of Seastrand's Bag and Laundry where students, who commute to Santa Cruz for school, wash their clothes, meet and buy cigarettes and Coke. She bums quarters as they come out of the store or wait for their clothes.

I suppose you never imagine that your own family could be one of the homeless who now fill the streets in cities and towns with their hands out or with cardboard signs. As I avoided them, I avoided her. Guilt by association wasn't what I wanted, but I was curious.

Since I moved back to Big Sur, I watched for her. At times, her van was parked out on Highway One, disappearing in and out of the early summer fog. Once, I pulled over and saw her disappear over the side of a cliff. When she was out of sight I got out, crossed the highway and peered down into the half-light. I watched her scramble over the rocks clutching a stick and using it for balance. She wore a cape that flew up in the wind and made her look like a witch. She was agile and seemed to dance from flat to flat. She stood as a conductor would over an orchestra while the water swept furiously under her. She'd stand for long periods of time in the fast moving fog catching the sea spray that billowed up as if from a geyser to cover her and make her shimmer.

Sitting in the police station's holding room, I wonder how she will react to seeing me. I am much older now. I count the years on my fingers since she abandoned us. Has she wondered about me? Has she stolen around town like I have trying to catch a glimpse of me? I don't know for sure. Sometimes I felt eyes on me, as I'm sure she'd felt mine on her.

There were years she disappeared without a trace, the familiar sight of her van gone from the streets. Her comings and goings were as sneaky as the fog that slips around the Coast Ranges. I was caught up in my own life, drifting from job to job, untied to anything or anyone for many years. Now it seems I have finally settled, put down the urge to get up and leave the moment comfort sets in.

I've preserved myself, held on to the tenuous shreds of my life as if for no other reason than to extricate the loneliness I'd felt and the self-hatred that plagued me in the course of being left to fend for myself. I built up enough armor and thickened it to the point that I could withstand almost anyone or anything that would dare to penetrate it. All the forces of Napoleon could have stood at my door. But I have slackened a bit with age. Matt has been a part of that.

There were footsteps in the hall and, once again, I snapped closed the buckles, tied the sheeted metal ribbons and strapped on the shields that have protected me so far.

My mother came in restrained by handcuffs, her hair a tangled web of black. Her eyes darted around the room then came to rest on me. In that moment something gave way inside me. Maybe it was pity on her or the loosening of my armor. I gazed back at her in wonder. I was still determined to do what I had to do. But she just stood there, no reaction or expression. It seemed as if she was still in shock from the beating.

"Nicholas?" The police officer compared the two of us, then said, "of course, you must be." He looked at me as I looked at the cuffs. "She was a little wild earlier."

"Then you can take them off now." I stepped back, took my mother in all the way. "How long has she been here?" I asked.

"About an hour. They wouldn't take her at the hospital. No insurance or next of kin." The policeman let go of her arm, removed the handcuffs, and then unconsciously wiped his hand across his leg. "I expect you'll be taking her now."

"Most likely," I said, examining my mother, "most likely."

"That's that, then," the officer said. "There's some personal things of hers at the front desk. All you need to do is sign for them. I expect Roy will be calling you in the morning to see how you're getting along. He had to go home earlier."

Without taking my eyes from her I said, "Thank you."

The policeman bent over close to my mother's ear, "Marjorie, you're free to go now." She just stared straight ahead at me. The policeman turned and walked out of the room.

"Do you want to sit down?" I asked. She shook her head. "Then let's go."

I turned expecting her to follow me. When I realized she hadn't moved, I turned back to her and said more strongly than I intended, "Let's go."

I put my jacket over my mother's shoulders. She kept her hands clasped together at her stomach as I led her to the car. I opened the door and guided her in, then closed it. My jacket caught in the jamb and I opened the door again, pushed my jacket through the space then slammed it shut and caused my mother to flinch.

I went to the driver's side, climbed in and started the car. The radio came on loudly. "Sorry," I said automatically and looked over to her. She just sat there and quietly wept.

I sat in a waiting room after admitting my mother to the hospital. I could hear the whirring of the air conditioner as it blew in cold, clean air. Nurses walked by like ghosts through the white; the fleshy color of their arms and necks provided the only human link in the impersonal space.

A doctor came through the single white door, nodded at me and said, "Your mother, I'm afraid, has had a bad time of it." His forehead was scarred with lines running horizontally across it. "She has a number of contusions and bruises including a bruised rib. I'm sure she'll be fine, but I'd like to keep her overnight and possibly one more day. I think it'll do her good. We gave her a little something to keep her steady."

"All right." I said.

"Do you want to see her?"

"I suppose so." I got up, shouldered my jacket and followed the doctor through the door into a future I knew was irretrievably altered.

Her body was still under the sheets, only her arm and head poked stubbornly from the white. An eye had begun changing colors and was puffy and blue. In fact, her whole head had taken on the shape of a knobby gourd. Her face was weathered and dry, the skin under her eyes and jowls billowed like outdoor laundry, loose and fragile when her face moved in her dream.

The only picture I have of her more vivid than that is the one given to me by my Dad that I've carried around for years. She stands profiled in black and white, her summer dress loose over her shoulders holding me up high over my brother Peter, who looks at her with his hands up begging to be taken up. In the background, the ocean and a perfect horizon cut the photograph in half. Stretched across the foreground is the long, thin shadow of my father.

I watched her sleep for a moment and touched her arm as if to see that she was really real. I bent close to hear her breathe. Part of me wanted to pull her up and hold onto her, but I stepped away, turned around and headed out the door. In the hallway, my body shuddered letting loose a loud sighing sound. I felt the hole where I had put the pain, hurt, loss and betrayal open up and then I felt the need to go home, put my head to Matt's chest and take him into me just to be filled up again. Instead, I sat back down in the lobby and stared unblinking at the blank white walls in front of me.

2.
Marjorie

I woke to a nurse fussing around my bed, her hand cold on my arm, my vision fuzzy until I slowly focused on her.

"I'm sorry," the nurse said, "I didn't mean to wake you. I just need to change this dressing." She was efficient about her work as I looked around the room. I knew where I was and knew how I got there. You had brought me, Nicholas; your face was pinched and angry. What would I tell you? That I'd finally paid for this life I led? That I had to hang on to the last thing that was mine? How would it seem to you? You didn't know me.

"Your son is here to see you," the nurse said, "He's been here for a while. He just went out."

"That can't be," I said, "I can't see him."

"He wants to see you." She said, her voice fluttery and high-pitched. She pulled my arm up and reattached a white bandage. She laid my arm gingerly down between the bed rail and me. A clear tube with a needle ran up in the air, a drop of medicine dissolved into the liquid that filled it. She checked the level in the bottle feeding into the wires, and then injected another needle into the receptacle, which fitted into one of the lines. I felt warmth travel up my arm and through my body and knew, from so many times before, that I'd soon be lost to sleep.

You walked in clutching your jacket. You said, "Hi." I wanted to cry. I wanted you to touch me, but you kept back away from the bed, your face drawn and puffy, your clothes hanging off your body.

"You have to leave," I said. You shook your head, held tight to your coat, the muscles in your arms tightened and knotted up.

"Well, I got a call from the cops and Peter couldn't come."

"He wouldn't..."

"Well, I don't know much about that..." You looked away.

"I didn't ask for you to come," I went to move up in my bed, but my muscles had swollen and made it too difficult, "but Roy..."

"I talked to Roy this morning, he called." You moved over to the window. "He told me what happened. That your van was stolen."

"It's gone? But I tried to get him."

"You shouldn't have done that."

"What was I supposed to do?"

"Let him take it," you said.

"Then where would I have lived?" You were quiet then as if put down by what you already knew. The long fingers of my heart unclenched themselves, but I tried to do everything in my power to keep them tight, close. You looked hurt standing there, but there was something open about you because your eyes were rimmed in a golden sliver of light, expressive and otherworldly and I needed that. Best of all, you were now before me and my past opened to the possibility of making amends. I didn't know this at the time, writing this now with my head clearer, I knew what you were feeling though you couldn't say it.

In the hospital room, hushed as a cathedral, I told you what happened about the thief - his short, stocky body, the cap he wore low over his eyes - I tried to describe him best as I could, but there wasn't much I remembered except what I felt when I fought with him.

The attack, I suppose, was inevitable. My mind had been fitful and trembling through the day like broken water. That was how it was for me the past few years out of the state hospital in Monterey. There, my mind floated, a constant dizzying waterfall, the straight line of it tumbling and clouded. The daily battles I endured after I was released tired me and so I climbed into my blankets in the back of the van early every evening to escape into sleep.

The man came late. I woke to someone testing the handles on the van. I listened as he moved around it from one handle to the other. I thought I had locked every lock, but as he moved to the front passenger side I looked up and saw that it was still up. As I leapt up and lunged for it the door swung open and I came face to face with the thief. There was something faintly familiar about him, but he wore a worn baseball cap, which partially hid his eyes. He looked young, maybe thirty; it was a little hard to tell. He grabbed my arm and twisted it away. My legs slipped on the blankets and my body fell over the divider that separated the front and back of the van.

He moved over the passenger seat into the driver's side. I lunged back over the seat and grabbed him around the throat. His body slammed back trying to shake me off, but I held him to the headrest and pulled. He grabbed a piece of my arm and twisted it with such force that I cried out and lost my grip. He turned and came over the divider at me then stopped.

"Don't fight me."

"Get out. Get out." I cried. I knelt on my knees away from him. The pain in my arm pierced through my chest.

"Get out of the van." He moved to the sliding door and opened it. The air blistered with cold. The wind swept around the inside. "You got about thirty seconds." I crashed against him and pushed him through between the seats. He hit his head on the dashboard and screamed. "Goddamn it." I fell over him. He grabbed and hugged me against his body with such force that I couldn't breath then flipped me over and slammed my head against the dashboard. Everything went black. It was all I remembered because, when I woke up, I was lying on the side of the road, my legs bent up, my arms angled out with flashing red lights bouncing over me and the trees along side the highway.

When I came into the room and saw you at the station my heart skipped a little and seemed to shut. The last time I saw you, you were a little boy, independent as a released balloon floating away. I tried to bring you into me, but you had a curious way of winding away from me and edging out of my grasp. Now you look as singular as ever. I can sense that my absence has taken its toll on you.

Even then, during the worst of the pain from the accident, I couldn't understand what made you search out the corners from which you watched people. How you retreated to them as if trying to find a safe harbor so that you couldn't be buffeted by a chance wind or storm.

You'd turned into a good-looking man like your father, but with my black hair and your own dark gleaming eyes. I took your shape in, thick around the chest like him, but with a long torso and short legs. Your face is round and less angular than mine, a face that can't stop your emotions from being found in it. My father used to say that my face lacked dishonesty, which is why I could never tell a lie to him. You are the same and it is a quality that I love. Your body, however, folds and unfolds chameleon-like as your moods change and the way in which you talk shifts tones and brightness.

When you were small you'd list about as a rudderless sailboat slipping sideways into things rather than moving headlong into them. Just as easily, you'd slip out of things that held your interest however fleetingly and gave up found objects where other children held onto them tenaciously.

Peter was demanding. He'd take things from you and make you beg for them back. He was impatient. He'd work himself into a frenzy when things didn't come his way. I'd separate you two sometimes because you were quiet and loving in small ways. I didn't want you to learn how to be angry or insolent from him. I suppose he had reason to be. He was old enough to hear your father and me fight - those long nights of anger and days of desolation towards the end.

You learned quickly though, moving onto the next problem, sorting through things and making up your own ideas about them.

I wondered if you had attached yourself to anyone, whether you drew women in as your father had with me. I couldn't speculate though, because when I saw you, you looked so angry, so oblivious. How are you with someone? Do you take them in and cast them out after you've learned all you need to know? I can't picture you married for some reason. Even after all these years, I felt your detachment around people. Lying there staring at you, I didn't know whether I was the cause or victim of it.

Unexpectedly, you moved over to the side of the bed and bent over me. I wanted to touch you. I could feel your warmth come down over my face like a blaze of sunlight from a bright window. You whispered, "I don't want to know much," your voice cracked, "I don't know you. You don't know me. I'll see you through this, but that's all," you said. "I've got to go." You stood up, shook a hand over your eyes and through your hair.

"Don't leave me again, Nicholas. Please." My voice broke and my face collapsed. My battered eyes stung closed. "Not this time."

"What do you want me to do? What could you possibly say to make things right for me?" Your voice was sharp-edged yet brittle and caused me to reach up and grab hold of your hand though my own pain was fierce.

"What can you say, Nicholas? What can you say to never searching me out to find out the truth?"

"What truth?" You said, wrestling yourself from my grip, but I closed my hand around your wrist and dug in. "That you abandoned us? That you were so selfish you never thought to come and see us? I think you are mistaken to think that I owe you anything. I hardly know you."

"Is that what you were led to believe all these years? That I just easily let you go? You were taken from me. Your father took you from me."

"Because he had too," you hissed.

"Do you believe that?"

"I don't want to talk about it anymore," you said, prying my fingers from your arm. "I've spent too many years trying to forget you. Now I'm fine and happy." You looked away. Your face was ashen and diminished.

"Are you?" I asked.

"Yes."

"How can you be? You knew I was here, didn't you? You knew that I'd lived in that van for all those years. You knew! I didn't even know what you looked like. What kind of person you turned into. Except Ray told me about you and Peter last night. He told me that you two have been living here for quite some time. So tell me how you're happy. Tell me that you never thought about me."

"I never had to. Lydia, my stepmother, was there and you were never discussed." Your eyes slid away from me. "She made up for you."

"Don't try to hurt me with that." I said angrily. "Don't try it." I was hot now and moved up in the bed again to fight the sleep. "I know what I see. You're as lonely as the last time I saw you."

"I am not." Your voice had a whisper of petulance. It was good to see that not all the child in you had disappeared.

"Then how could you be happy?" I said forcefully, "I want to know."

"Because I thought that you didn't need us or didn't want us." You visibly shook, but your body began to fold. "Even Peter doesn't want to talk to you." There were tears around your eyes when you met mine.

"Peter betrayed me," I said soberly, "I have no reason to speak to him." I was filled with regret. It was clear you had been lied to. I felt like I'd have to start from the beginning, coax my past from the recesses of my mind like water coming up from a wellspring to cover a cracked desert floor to smooth over the cuts and wounds that had hardened over so many years.

My body loosened and slipped into the bed. "There is a lot that you haven't been told, Nicholas, but first you have to understand how to be something you've never been." You moved over to the side of the bed again. The door to my room opened and the nurse came in. A cool rush of air from the hallway swept past us. You bent down over me and asked, "What's that?"

I said to you, "I'm your mother."

My mind gave way to disarray again as I closed my eyes. You touched me. Your hand rubbed my shoulder. If the clear vivid pictures became blurred inside my head, the touch of your fingertips was as sharp and painful as the memories that came flooding back to me in the days ahead. But the liquid that was shot up my arm spread through me and took me casually into sleep and dulled your touch.

3.
Nicholas

When I got home from the hospital, I sat at the kitchen table with only the window light exploding through the room. I pulled the photo from my wallet and looked hard at it. I wanted to see what her face looked like unlined and youthful. But the camera only caught the side of her, the upturned smiling lips and the new lines at the corners of her eyes and thin neck. I studied it to see if there was any hint in her that belied her unsettled mind. All I could detect was happiness. I could almost feel my small body being swung upwards, shaken gently, me laughing at the thrill. It is one of my clearest memories I had of her because of the photograph, though it is being erased by the image I have of her now.

On my way home, the morning sun angled through the town defining the buildings and raking, like light from open doorways, down the streets. I felt tired in the car, but also, in an odd way, exhilarated with possibility. I felt that something had happened, that doors had been swung open and a cacophony of sounds, smells and people were echoing down a hallway toward it. Though I was frightened, I needed to remember the details of them and begin to stitch them together so that they'd make sense.

Matt padded into the kitchen wearing my robe. There is always something sexual about the way he moves, puts on his clothes or takes them off. Maybe I just feel this. Many of the mysteries of our new relationship are edging away after almost a year; we make love easier, less strong unless we are both tired and our emotions raw from fatigue.

For me it is good love, satisfying, except for some part of it that I can't put my finger on. I still feel needy and self-obsessed, wanting to continue by stroking his body or holding onto some part of him that will add weight to our sex. He only takes me in his arms and goes soundlessly to sleep causing me to lie there, crumpled up next to him, eyes wide open.

"Did I wake you?" I ask.

"I heard you drive up." He goes to the cupboard, pulls down a coffee filter. He looks at me, I nod my head. His eyes are normally hazel, but today they're darker, almost a deep green. He wears his hair down past his shoulders, has a habit of putting a pinch of it between his thumb and forefinger then placing the front locks behind his right ear. "So, how'd it go?" He looks at me with a concerned expression, his face re-inflating from a crushed pillow. Matt sleeps hard.

"On a scale of one to ten?"

"I'm serious, Nick. It's not everyday someone gets to meet his mother." Matt holds up the coffee can. "You want some?"

"I'm going to try and get some sleep."

Matt measures out a scoop. "It was odd, really, but okay too," I say.

Maybe it should be here that I talk about Matt, the uncomplicated way in how he loves me. Maybe I should describe him to you so that you have a picture of him. I think that right now, though, it is enough for you to know that he loves me, cares how I am. I can't be as forthright in telling you that I love him. I think I'm working towards it, but it is harder for me; to profess love for another is something I've never done, have only recently come close to.

Now that Matt has moved in, it has been easier for me to avoid the actual words because our daily lives move us through it and just by coming home every night to him, a thing that I have come to enjoy, I assume he knows how I feel. Moving him in was a bit like throwing myself into a body of water that I know is cold, but I'd been standing at the edge of it for so many years that made the plunge necessary. I was glad that I was still able to come up for air.

I get up from the kitchen table and go into the bedroom. I peel my clothes off slowly, feeling exhausted and weak. I climb into bed and pull the covers up which are still warm. I think of my mother handcuffed, how she wore them as if she'd been used to the way they felt on her wrists. It makes me ache, causes me to bury my head in my pillow. I want to remember her happy.

The sun is full now on the cottage. Wind comes up the hill and keeps the air cool. The highway below is busier; daily traffic has begun. I can't see the highway from where I sit, but I can hear the cars push the wind around the bend. The ocean's color is changing, becoming lighter as the sun flattens out the detail of the waves. Here is where my memory begins to work.

That summer, when Peter and I lived here with our mother we would stand on the bluff and look over the jagged edges of Point Lobos and the curving shoreline. This coast is different from the one we were used to. It is colder, windier and covered by pine and cypress trees that look as if they'd fall over at any moment. The beaches are like small coves that don't sprawl any kind of length, but seem to close in on them because of the constant roil of water. At high tide, the waves snarl up against the rocks sending towers of white above the shoals over and over again until the tide recedes or the wind settles down or shifts.

The coves attract wildlife of all kinds; sea otters, natty-feathered birds, seals and the migrating whales that swim close to shore. The creatures seem more weathered and browbeaten than the sea life at home, as if they lived a harder existence, as we did after we left our father.

The last day I saw my mother was wonderful. We had woken early. Peter got breakfast for both of us: cereal and milk, some scraps of bread. We ran down the hill toward the beach and took the trail that snaked under the bridged highway and emptied out into the cove. The tide was way out and the tide pools were revealed far out into the water.

Our mother came down after us as we explored the tide pools. She always watched Peter and me from her perch on a rock almost ten feet in the air. She climbed up the backside of it, spread her blanket to soften the rough edges and sat there while the wind whipped sea-spray around the shoals. We could barely hear each other above the crashing waves; it was as if we existed in a silent movie, the organ taking the part of the waves. Only the yelps and bellowing of the sea lions could be heard as they sunned themselves, or slipped off the islands of rock into the water.

My brother picked starfish out of the pools. He swooped his hand down and plucked them right off the rock before the starfish could suck themselves to it. He did this all day long to the lazy ones, then took them by the arm and flung them across the water trying to skip them along its surface. I thought it was cruel and remembered protesting to my mother about it, but she only waved and smiled at me to carry on.

I found a small squid trapped by the outgoing tide in a tiny pool. I chased it around the small bowl of water and finally caught it. I brought it up and cupped it in my hands. It squirted black ink and I dropped it in disgust onto the rock. Peter, who had come up behind me to watch, laughed and threw a starfish he caught onto the squid.

"There," he said," that'll get him."

"Peter!" I shouted.

"Go tell Mom, then. She won't do anything." I almost went to her again, but I knew he was right. I knew that if I said anything, she'd only give that little laugh and wave her hand at me again as if it was the most natural thing to do.

If we were in the cottage, she was almost always in her bedroom, leaving Peter and me to watch TV. Sometimes at dusk, she'd emerge, fix herself a drink and go outside. She'd disappear into the woods behind the cottage and be gone for an hour or so.

We followed her once, stole into the woods after her. We knew we shouldn't have done it, but Peter was more curious than I in what she did there. At dusk, the trees seemed to blend together into a dark black. Once your eye opens and lets in the remaining light, the details worked together like magic. I imagined a fairy-tale forest at that age, and its wonders and danger. The smells became more dense and complicated. It was hard to tell where they came from, the damp ground or the trees and shrubs: ferns dangled from the redwood trunks, mushrooms sputtered from the ground in great clumps, upended roots sprouted bright orange growths like abscesses.

I followed Peter a few steps back, sometimes clinging to his shirttail. As it got blacker, I grasped him harder until he'd swing his hand back and bat mine off him. When he stopped, I peered around him and saw in a clearing our mother standing in a small circle of rocks that she'd obviously gathered at some point. She held a palm out as if waiting to receive something, her head bowed in supplication. Once in a while she'd take a drink from the glass in the other hand, choking it down. She murmured something to herself, tilting her body forward as if to look at her shoes. Peter just stood and stared at her. I could tell he was baffled by her behavior and it worried me. I always looked to him to try and figure her out, and when he couldn't understand her it frightened me.

On the way back, Peter broke and started running down the trail and disappeared in the blackness. I called out to him, but he wouldn't answer back. I just stopped and started crying and then I sat down right in the middle of the trail and began to shake. He must have realized that I wasn't going to follow him and came back to collect me. He hadn't gone that far, he said, calling me a baby, but it was far enough for me.

When I stopped looking up to him comes later, but during those days at the cottage our relationship was like that, the broken cords of communication, the misunderstandings, of him exacting vengeance on me for the mere fact of being born. The results were that I lived in fear of most everything: from learning how to tie my shoes (I always tied the laces in knots) to entering into relationships (not unlike going into the woods). It was all wrapped up into the separation of our parents and which sides were we going to take or how we would assume each other would act. For me, at six years old, I was on the side of whoever was closest, and though our mother was, at best, distant and wrapped up in herself, she was there. Looking back on it now, I believe he was taking revenge on the fact that Mom paid what little attention she gave to us, to me.

When I got older, I began to exact revenge on Peter. I played cruelty like a card shark. Lacking the physical prowess to best him, I reduced him to fits of anger by putting words together that sliced gaping wounds into his psyche at the most inopportune times.

I flung words at him. I waited and watched as he recoiled from their sting and would be full of myself. I worked him like this for years until he moved from the house when he went away to college. But, because of what happened between our Mom and Dad, we were caught up together in some strange, symbiotic relationship that had more to do with binding together to withstand our parent's mercurial relationship than the fact that we really liked each other. In reality, Peter was more independent than I.

But that day we were on the shoals jumping over tidal pools. At the time, I often mimicked him, so I began hunting down the starfish and poking at them with my stubby, little fingers. In the water, the starfish were bright orange or matched the color of the purple rocks. Since I wasn't quick as my brother, I was never able to free the starfish from their moorings. Instead, I pressed my fingers into them or tickled the ends of their arms in hopes of peeling them off. They fascinated me, how they could remain there hard against the angry, swirling waves, their bodies firm and supple, vulnerable only in one spot.

We played there for hours until the tide started to inch in and fill the pools. My mother came down from her watch and led us back up the beach and then the trail that switch-backed up to the cottage. In the grove of pines that covered our way up, the air was cool and wet. I pulled up clumps of grass from the sides of the trail and threw them back in Peter's face, baiting him to do something in front of Mom. He wouldn't retaliate, of course, but I knew he'd store each offense up in the back of his mind and save them for one, really mean recourse of action.

When we got back to the cottage, she made us toasted cheese sandwiches and spread mustard on them before smashing them in some tongs she had that you could place right on the burner. Since the metal sandwich holders were round, I peeled the overlapping crust off the sides. The edges flared up and caught fire so a perfect round circle was left inside the toaster. My brother liked the crust. He stood there next to Mom and toasted it over the other burner and his fingers would burn before he'd realize it.

Having put our dinner on trays we sat down in front of the TV. Mom disappeared into her room with a glass of coke.

"We can't watch this," Peter said, flipping the channel. Gilligan was turning the crank on a bamboo camera for Thurston Howell. Peter spun the dial around which he called 'TV Roulette' and came to "Wild Wild West." Artemus Gordon was explaining something to James West and then they were off, riding towards something in the black and white desert. We sat for a while eating our cheese sandwiches, letting the blue light of the TV wash over us as it got dark outside.

There was a knock at the door. We both turned around. We saw Dad looking into the cottage through the square panes of glass in the door, his breath left round circles of mist. Peter got up and ran to let him in. Dad came in wearing jeans, a coat and smiled at us. He was worn out, his smile a little weak. He was flustered too, as if he had trouble finding where we were.

"Hi boys!" He moved into the room and looked around. "Where's your mother?"

"Why?" I asked. I was unsure of him; Mom had said that he wasn't a good person, that I should be careful of him.

"Where's your mother, Peter?" he asked again.

"In the bedroom." Dad walked up to Peter and gave him a clap on the shoulder.

"Mom," I shouted.

"Go get your things now... both of you." Dad said.

"Where are we going?" I asked.

Dad said, "Don't ask questions, Nicholas, just do as your told."

"But Mom said...." I went over to where he was standing feeling defiant.

Mom came from the room, shouldering her housecoat; it floated around her legs, which seemed unsteady as she came into the living room.

"What's this," She sounded frightened, but her voice was thick and her words buttery and soft.

"What's going on? Peter, Nicholas?" She had a cigarette in her mouth and her eyes were unfocused and heavy.

Peter called out from our room, "Dad's here!" I was still confronting him, my three and a half feet to his six, hard as an animal defending its territory.

Then she saw him. "Oh," she said startled. The cigarette fell to the floor leaving a smoky trail after it. "What are you doing here? You're not supposed to be here."

"I'm here to take the kids. You're not taking care of them properly."

"How would you know?" she asked, pulling the belt of her robe tighter.

"Nicholas, go get your things because if you don't we'll just have to leave them here." I could tell that he meant it. I thought about my stuffed bear, my favorite overcoat and all the things I'd collected on the shore. I wanted them, I knew that, but I still held my ground.

"Look at you," he said to Mom, then looked down at me, shouting, "Nicholas, we're leaving here in one minute." I knew he meant it this time and no amount of interrogation on my part would stop what was happening. It put an urgency on whether I wanted my things or not. So I ran back to our room where Peter was throwing things into his red-striped duffel bag. He was acting as if he was glad to be leaving.

"Peter, I can't believe you."

"Believe what?" he said. "You're such a baby."

"I am not."

"What's he doing here?" I went after him and knocked him over.

"Oh boy," he said getting up, "now you're gonna get it." He started punching me hard in the stomach. I fell to the ground and tried to cover myself. He tore into me and then I started crying loudly.

"Get off me. Mom!"

"That's right, call to Momma, Momma's boy!" He kept punching me. I could feel him checking off all of the transgressions I'd made against him as if he'd been keeping a list.

"Mom," I cried. I got hit again. Both of them rushed in, Mom all hysterics and Dad yanking Peter to his feet. Mom grabbed me and held me close. She blanketed me with her body that was flushed and damp. Dad held Peter back from me. Peter was enraged, but then he stood dumbly off to the side. My shirt buttons had popped off and were strewn about our feet like marbles and Mom bent down to collect them. She was sobbing now. She couldn't see clearly to pick them up, so I reached down and helped her gather them.

"Why, Eric? Why are you doing this?" she cried. I looked at my father and for just a split second I saw him unsure of himself. Just as quickly his mind shifted and I could feel him stiffen and prepare.

"Look what they're reduced to," he said. "They never fought like this. Never."

Dad picked up the duffel bag, "Nicholas, where's your stuff."

"I don't have it." I cried, still stooped over on the floor.

"Peter, get Nicholas' coat. We're leaving now." Mom grabbed my arm. Dad grabbed the other. "Marjorie, let go of him now. You had your chance." He looked back at Peter who was searching the closet. "It's on the bed there, Peter." He glared down at Mom who was kneeling against me like she was praying with her head down.

"You can't do this, Eric. You can't."

"You've made a mess of it, Marjorie, don't you see?" For a second there was a trace of warmth in his voice, but that too disappeared. "Let go of Nick. C'mon Marjorie, do as your told."

"Don't talk to me like a child, you bastard," she said, her face finally coming up. "Your mother put you up to this....

"Mom had nothing to do with this."

"Bullshit," Mom said. I'd never heard her talk like that.

"Peter, go out to the car." Dad said, as he handed the duffel bag to him. My brother just stood there looking at me and I could tell that he was sorry. He walked over to where my bear was and picked it up and buried it in my coat. He nodded at me then left the room. My eyes were wide now as I watched him go.

"Listen here, Marjorie, I don't have a lot of time."

"That's always been your excuse, you son of a bitch. Always sneaking off to one place or another."

"Don't go too far...." he said.

Mom got to her feet though she was still clutching my arm.

"Don't tell me how to act, Eric. How many times.... How many times was it?"

"Was what?" Dad was now red in the face. A shiny little vessel appeared along side his right eye. Mom was hysterical, her face deep red as a beet, her eyes full of hatred.

"How many times did you fuck her while I was pregnant. How many times!"

At that, he slapped her so hard she lost her grip on me so that I flew against Dad's chest, my arm twisted as something gave way in it. There was an audible snap and a pain as sharp and true as a knife as I screamed. I thought I'd forgotten the rest because the next thing I remember of that night was waking up at home with a cast on my arm.

Except now, I remember being pushed into the front seat next to Peter, cradling my arm and looking back over my shoulder to see my mother running down the hill after us, her arms flailing and her mouth open as wide as night with the lighted cottage growing smaller behind her. I watched her disappear into the dark and out of our lives. Then my Dad yanked me back down in the seat and turned my head forward with the big palm of his hand.

4.
Marjorie

Your grandfather and I lived in South Pasadena, a little enclave of craftsman styled homes and stucco, Spanish buildings just east of Los Angeles. It seemed a great distance from the ocean and was much warmer. If you drove down the streets, you could detect that small lives were being led: each of the houses were butted up against each other with ten feet of side yard between them. Driveways circled up to the door or were straight lines to the garages. Since the houses were built after front porches went out of fashion, you didn't see much of the neighbors, even on Sunday afternoons.

My father was a city worker who laid pipe for the water district. He'd come home, his back bent as a broodmare, with his coveralls greased and dirty. I'd sit and listen to him talk about the day as he took a shower before fixing us dinner. It never occurred to me to cook for him and he never asked. His dinners were ordinary, simple. I'd clean the dishes just as soon as we finished because we never stayed at the table since we knew all there was to know about each other.

Mother died when I was four. Polio had worked through her just after she had me, had made it hard for her to hold me and I was pulled from being nursed by her after it was discovered. I was lucky. The doctor had told both of them that I had developed immunity from it. I imagine that she spent most of her energy pushing me from her womb and caring for me during those first few good months as I have little recollection of her. I don't remember her suffering, or being away in the hospital. But I have a connection to the whiteness that exists in them; if I had a map to chart their hallways and rooms, I would have steered clear of them, moved surely away as animals have second senses about territories.

I regarded my father with gentleness. I believe now that it may have been to our disadvantage: he never got over the early death of my mother and there was so much left unsettled and undiscovered between them. He never remarried and rarely went out; his mistrust of the world was solidified by anger, frustration and the long, slipping away of his wife.

I inherited my skin from her. Mine was paler than my father's, which was dark and leathery as an old shoe. From her pictures, I could see my nose and the deep inset of my eyes, which gave me an almost gaunt appearance. Her features were more defined, however, as if a light hung constantly at a right angle above her face. I sometimes questioned my father's devotion to me because of my looks.

His life had a quiet intensity, though I knew he tried his best to lighten his mood around me. What remains with me are his big hands and how he used to draw pictures in the air - large unencumbered figures that swam and flew as he spoke. He also had a way of talking to one side, as if including another imaginary person, perhaps my mother. I almost expected her to answer or join in on our conversations.

I always dressed older than I was - makeup was taught to me early by our neighbor who watched me until my father came home. Mrs. Jorgenson attached herself to me by way of feminine things: perfume, body oil, clothes and casseroles. Her sense of style was borne from television. It was always on, even when the stations had signed off. We could hear "America the Beautiful" from her living room on summer mornings when we kept our windows open. From her programs, she learned style and grace and tried to teach me to curtsy and pirouette, apply molten lava red lipstick and paint my nails cherry blossom pink. She showed me ways to dress that would accentuate the curves of my body that might or might not develop. But mainly she expressed herself elegantly and had such an effect on me that my father began to come home early some days to rescue me from the clutches of "that woman next door." She was all there was in the neighborhood to care for me after school. We didn't have the money for clubs or lessons of any sort.

Every afternoon, I heard my father's car pull into the driveway, the pistons knocking like hollow, old pipes. I'd run from the woman's house to where my Dad collected me in his arms, then we'd be back in our house, a jumble of things, nothing belonging together, but a worn out Indian man and me, his hapless daughter.

Our neighborhood was a mixture of cultures. If Los Angeles is regarded as a melting pot, we were positioned in the center at the top of the swirling mass about ready to be pulled under. Besides Mrs. Jorgenson, who was Norwegian, there was the Almaraz extended family, which was so large that there seemed always to be a steady stream of people exiting and entering their front door. The Shimaros, a quietly intense family, emigrated from Japan, set up in business by family here, were never home save for Saturdays which they spent in their garden, clipping at the same bushes for long periods of time. There were the Whites, quite literally so, whose blond hair and white skin transformed them into ghosts in the evenings. They'd flash by their front windows directly across from us. Unlike the Shimaros, we almost never saw them outside except for the quick dashes they made to their cars.

The difference in our cultures never caused us to mix as children. The other kids attended different schools and participated in activities that had little to do with being children, but more with their opposing heritages and beliefs. There was a separateness that was palpable in the neighborhood, an almost eerie quality that befitted a ghost town on the edge of a desert. As I grew up, I came to believe that there was no room for assimilation, no desire to come together, but still, when we passed by, we smiled as if we had something in common, as if just by surviving in this world, we were beating the odds without ever meaning to.

When it came time to go to college, I wanted to go locally so I could be near my father. We settled on the city college in Santa Monica. I commuted the first year. My Dad set up a car pool with a friend from work. My classes were every other day, so that left Tuesdays and Thursdays for my father to have the car. If I needed to get there on those days, I bused there, taking a circuitous route across the city.

College was expected of me in a peculiar sort of way. I wasn't really expected to achieve, but rather to "fit in" finally. We agreed that a college too close by would be of little use because I'd see many of the same people from high school.

After the first year ended, I took a job near school that I found on one of the bulletin boards. I had to be there early to begin answering phones and start the coffee so it was determined that, with the money I was making and my father pitching in, we'd look for a place one Sunday for me to live close by.

We found a small studio in the back of an apartment complex; the single room seemed as if it was added as an afterthought and built out haphazardly. The door to it opened out onto the garages, but it was cheap.

When the second year began, I sat, just as I had done the entire first year, with a spectacular array of writing tools and an ever-present pad of notepaper, waiting to diligently take notes from my instructors.

I tried desperately to have order in my life. The summer job turned into a between classes job filling in for sick or vacationing people and doing the odd chores. Finally, I had stepped out of myself for the first time to take care of my own needs and I felt liberated in a way. Only on weekends, when I went home to my father, did I give myself over to him. Our roles changed a bit. I began to cook the meals when I was home. We ate healthier - vegetables, rice and chicken. I cleaned up after him around the house. He seemed older to me, yet it had only been a couple of years since I'd moved out.

That part of my life changed quickly, however, as I turned more towards the pressures of school and what was going on around me.

On a Friday afternoon in the spring, a boy, not much heavier than a floating feather, walked up to me as I was heading for class. "Do you have a joint?" He asked.

"A what?" I asked.

"A joint." he glanced around feverishly. I looked at his Converse sneakers. They were ready to tear where his toes left an impression in his tight shoes. It dawned on me what he was asking me for.

"Well no, I don't smoke it. I don't think it's right, my..." I became flustered, but I boldly pressed on because, in the first two years I'd been at college, this was the first boy that had voluntarily spoken to me. I wasn't about to let him get off that easy.

"Shut up," he said, "people can hear you."

Then I furtively looked around as if I'd conspired in an illegal act, but one that had gone nowhere. "Don't tell me to shut up." I said. I stopped and looked at him. His hair gathered at his forehead in tight curls like a poodle.

"Sorry," he said, "You wanna get high?" He reached into his jacket pocket and produced a dilapidated cigarette. "I've got a little left." I wondered how on earth could he think that I would want to alter myself, irretrievably pull myself down the path of the beatniks and hippies that littered the lawns of the school. But then I looked at him again and he smiled this wan little smile and, instantly, I felt lighter.

"Sure," I said.

This boy and I sat for hours talking. Every once in a while he'd light the joint and pass it over to me. He asked me where I was from and when I told him Los Angeles, he asked where I was really from because I didn't look like I'd grown up there. He asked how I got my coloring, my eyes, my skin, which he said was dark and smooth, like the surface of a new, wood table. I couldn't tell him because I didn't know. In comparison to him I was darker, though I'd always measured myself against my father.

When I went home that weekend I sat with my Dad at the kitchen table under the cheap, bright table light. I considered him. I began asking him about our ancestors.

"So what tribe are we from?" I asked. My Dad was sopping up water that had spilled from the sink. He was bent down on the kitchen floor. He sat up on his haunches, squeezed water from the sponge into the sink. I stared at him.

"The Tlingits," he said, curiously looking back at me.

"The who?" I sat on the counter watching him, studying his dark hair, the lines across his neck.

"The Tlingits. They're a tribe in the Northwest. Not too many left anymore."

"You've never talked about them."

"That was a long time ago. My father's father moved his family down here in the twenties. The fishing had dried up for two seasons in a row and he needed money."

"Hmmm. Well, what about you?"

"What about me?" He stood up and stretched out his back, the sponge was full and dripping. He squeezed it out again in the sink and I watched the water run through his fingers.

"It's just that you never talk about it much. I remember a few times, but mostly I don't know much about our history."

"I never thought it was that important to you. You never asked." He put the sponge up next to the spigot after a last wipe around the outer rim of the sink. "Why are you so interested all of a sudden?"

"I'm not really. It's just that I have no sense of where we come from."

"We're from Los Angeles."

"I know that. I meant our history."

"Well, there's not much to tell and get off the counter. You know you're not supposed to sit up there." He waved his arm at me and I obeyed. "You've certainly become a curious thing." He switched off the light over the sink and walked out of the room. I stood leaning against the counter. He walked away; his body slope-shouldered and hunched a little, shaking his head.

Through the rest of the semester I stopped putting my hair up. I let it grow. Soon it began hanging down over my shoulders straight as an axe blade. I wore sandals and beaded moccasins, long dresses that cascaded down to my ankles and tied with a leather strand at my chest. I replaced makeup with a tan I'd achieved by lying in the sun for long periods of time. I wanted to become dark like my father. I wanted to carry a feeling of otherworldliness like a halo around my body that he managed just by being. I wanted to be Indian.

My father began to assert himself in this part. He didn't like me changing - or changing as fast as I did. But because he didn't like it, it became an obsession for me. I collected baskets and beads and scoured the stores around Venice for anything that was woven, etched or carved by any tribe of Indian. I practiced chanting and drum beating, the sounds echoed off the walls. I read one history after another of the Northwest Tlingits. I switched my major to History. My apartment became a shrine of baskets, stone pottery, colored rugs, woodcarvings and a fishing spear, which hung at an angle over my bed.

I smoked pot regularly with Randy, the boy with tight shoes, during and between classes. When we were high, my senses dulled, but I was acutely aware of my body; it loosened, a slight tingle worked its way from my legs through my torso and then out into my fingertips. I could feel Randy watching me as I watched him.

The last time we smoked together, I allowed him to feel me up and in turn he allowed me to touch him. For the first time I felt the touch of a man. His hand reached under my skirt and he pulled my panties down, wrestling me up and over him as he removed them. I floated over him; my hands on his chest supported my weight. I rubbed against him and felt sensations just outside of myself. I shut my eyes, imagining us on the earth, on wet leaves, the night air running up my back, tribal dances, the heat of a blazing fire, but the groans and twists he made brought me back to him on the colored rug, in the middle of my living room. I looked down and he had exhausted himself over his belly. He was embarrassed for having done so and quickly turned over on his side away from me. I pulled him over on his back again and looked at him. He shifted his eyes to the right of me, but I continued looking at him, his chest heaving.

"Get off me," he said, "Get off. I can't breathe." He pushed his hips up to knock me off. I tied the front of my dress up and fell back against a chair. I was clear-headed, able to take in what had happened. Randy buttoned his shirt, re-buckled his belt and wiped his belly with his shirttail before tucking it into his pants. I sat against the front of a chair, my arms and legs splayed out like an abandoned marionette.

"Why'd you do that?" he asked. "Why? We were getting along fine."

"You didn't want to?" I asked as I thought for a minute. "I don't know. You started it." I said, feeble as a newborn.

"Why didn't you put it in?" He asked, bitterly.

"I don't know," I said. I think I had forgotten to really. It never occurred to me that that was necessary.

"Jesus," he said. He got up to leave.

"Where are you going?" I asked, not wanting to be left alone just yet.

"Up the canyon," he said.

"What canyon?"

"Topanga." He was almost out the door.

"How're you going to get there?" My voice grew shrill, panicky. I felt abandoned.

"Hitchhike," he said.

"I'm going too." I was desperate.

"I'm leaving right now." He walked out the door quickly as if to be rid of me. I stared dumbly at the door wondering what I'd done, why the sudden change in him.

I caught up with him outside on the curb in front of my apartment building. He looked at me and shook his head. I'd grabbed a denim jacket and a leather backpack. Not knowing how long I'd be gone, I threw in a box of crackers and a couple of day old rolls Mrs. Jorgenson had given me.

She too was disappointed in me. I'd forsaken the road to glamour. On weekends at home she'd made offhand comments like, "Oh, your nails were so lovely once," and "I could do your hair up like we used to." She'd look at me with those wilted eyes of hers, damaged by years of heavy eye shadow. "Not just now," I'd say, accepting her gifts and backing out the front door.

I followed Randy down to the corner of Lincoln and Venice boulevards. He went into a liquor store and bought some cigarettes, a large bottle of beer and some chips. He came back and stood with me on the corner. I didn't know what to do, but he stuck his thumb out and then a car came by, slowed. The driver asked where we were going and Randy told him. "Get in," the driver said, and I crawled into the back with Randy. I remember feeling a bit sick to my stomach, a little hot and clammy. The nervousness I felt made me shiver and Randy was no help.

We were let off at the mouth of Topanga Canyon on the coast highway. Randy crossed the road and I followed him. It was early evening and the light was dissolving into dusk.

"How far up do we have to go?" My eyes were big as olives.

"Halfway up," he said. He was concentrating on trying to get the next ride.

"Are there other people there?" I asked.

"Yep. A few."

A van pulled over, its front lights beaming at us. A small dust storm kicked up under its wheels. The driver, bearded with dark eyes, smiled and looked at Randy.

"Hey Randy, you on your way up?"

"Yeah, man." Randy said.

"What about the girl, she coming to?"

"I guess," he said, climbing into the back.

I looked at the driver, but then quickly averted my eyes. We kneeled among rakes, shovels, clippers, fertilizer and pots of flowers. The air in the van was thick with the smell of soil and marijuana. I was intrigued.

"You from around here?" the driver asked, watching me from the rearview mirror.

"Yes," I said, "I go to school at City College."

"With Randy?" he asked.

"We're not in the same classes, well, yes. We met there." In the space of one hour I'd gone from being on the verge of womanhood to a little schoolgirl again.

"I went there," he laughed, "name's Michael, yours?"

"Marjorie," I said. He turned in his seat.

"What?"

"Marjorie," I said a little louder, "There's a lot of noise back here."

"I've never heard that name before," Michael said. The disquiet I felt before was now gone. Randy sat back against a large bag of planting soil, quietly staring at the side of the van. I pulled my jacket over my shoulders. Michael had the window open blowing his smoke to the rushing wind.

We made our way up the canyon slowly, the van sputtering, only catching speed on the downhill. I looked out the small back windows and saw a line of headlights forming. The engine noise was impossible to talk over, so I relaxed, sat down, and in the artificial lights from the angry cars to the rear, took up one of the books he had scattered across the floor - Jack Kerouac and Allen Ginsberg, Shakespeare and William Faulkner, Henry Miller and a heavily studied volume of poetry by someone named Wallace Stevens. At the time, I'd never heard of these names save for Shakespeare, but I could tell by their bruised and battered shapes their importance to him. It seemed odd to me that Michael would butcher words hopelessly when they spilled from his mouth. Words such as 'poignant' came out with the 'g' solid as concrete.

"Do you do that on purpose?" I shouted.

"Do what?"

"Mispronounce certain words," I said, "Hasn't anyone noticed before?"

"Mispronounce what?"

"What you just said. The 'g' is silent in poignant." I tried to contain myself.

"I know that."

"Okay, just letting you know," I said.

As we pulled into a campground, his way of speaking had me laughing to the point of losing my breath.

When we stopped I saw small fires and lanterns glowing down the dark gully. Tree limbs from the oaks danced in the diffused, smoky light. Huddles of people spoke in whispers with an occasional shriek while they moved in pairs, silent as secrets, from group to group. I was startled at the amount of people, their shy shuffles as they walked, their clothes and muted blankets worn over their shoulders.

I could hear music and singing, the sounds of a flute floated through the air. Two women danced, their arms undulating in their own rhythms. They seemed to step like herons, their feet lightly tapping the damp and rocky ground. Oak leaves were scattered among mounds of new spring grass. Dogs skittered by, tails between their legs like scolded children. Sometimes they skirmished over bits of food and debris, but halfheartedly. Some of them just lay by their masters uninterested in getting involved.

I saw bright red buttons of light glow brightly then disappear sometimes accompanied by a muted cough and then silence.

Randy slipped into the cloudy hillside without a word. He'd been reticent in the van on our way up, refusing to acknowledge our earlier sex by never looking at me. I watched him go, his shoulders and head bowed down, almost ashamed.

Michael, on the other hand, was very attentive - his interest in me was studious and sexless. When he touched me it bore no intent, no expectations. He had a kind smile. We were like two people who had met after a long absence, big-hearted, open.

He led me through the tangled forest and negotiated a path between sleeping bodies and makeshift tents where, from some of them, you could hear whispers and shuffling and soft cries of pleasure. It seemed as if all of my senses were magnified, stretched beyond their normal level of casual awareness and if I were startled, I would have exploded in millions of electrified particles.

5.
Nicholas

I came back to Big Sur after college before my mother reappeared in my life. This stretch of coast had fascinated me from the time my brother, mother and I stayed here - on one side held the woods with their tangled trees and hidden canyons and on the other, the wide sea that changed daily. The landscape could open me up or close me in at any moment depending on my mood. Some days I'd hike along the beaches and on others I'd navigate the wet trails that smelled of moss, decomposing leaves and bark. It seemed that everything was always wet; the rocky cliffs and shrubs glimmered and seeped water, which sometimes pooled at their bases and mirrored the sky adding to the shimmer.

I knew my mother lived somewhere in town. Maybe part of me wanted to find her, ask her all the questions I'd kept in my head. I'd wondered what became of her. Part of me wanted to search her out like an adopted child who has nagging questions about his origins. But I was angry at her abandonment of us. All those years I - no, we (Peter and I) - waited for signs of her arrival or interest in how we might have turned out. I didn't delude myself into thinking that I could live here without seeing or hearing something of her. When

I found out the truth of her existence, the first time I saw that van out on the highway and her disappearing down into the fog and mists, my feelings of detachment from her became muddled. I still resisted our meeting again, which I knew would eventually come.

I found a job working for a woman who owned a computer typesetting service in an old office building downtown. I rented a room in a house through Peter who'd been living here since quitting college after a couple of years. The owner of the house was never there except for a weekend now and then. He lived in San Francisco, worked all over the country and rarely found time to use the house that had been left him. So I took care of the place, fixed it to my liking, changed the furniture around and began adding the things that made it my home.

Peter built his house up a canyon down the coast road. When he left home for college, his involvement in my life became a series of visitations, mostly of his own convenience. He had a knack for showing up on my doorstep with the most incredible news. He hadn't been to my new house yet, but just after I moved in, he showed up and just looked at me and smiled. "I got married, Nick." he said.

"You what?

"I got married a couple of days ago." Peter stood there on the front steps, hands in his pockets.

"Christ, Peter, why didn't you tell me? I would have liked to have been there."

"Linda and I just decided, that's all. She, well she looked at me the other morning and we just did it."

"Congratulations, I guess. Did you call Dad?"

"No." He said flatly. "He doesn't have to know."

"Why not?"

"Well, you tell me, Nick. He hasn't even met Linda." He came past me through the door. "Why don't you tell him next time you talk to him?" Peter shrugged the last comment away and I watched him take off his jacket and sit down. We hadn't seen much of each other once he left our Dad's house. He rarely came home for holidays and his calls were infrequent. He'd chosen college upstate at Humboldt - as far North in California as he could go and still stay close to the water and afford tuition. Dad had told him he could go anywhere he wanted, but he refused his help and was paying his own way. It seemed that when he left, he broke from almost everything he knew.

I drove up there once when I was a senior in high school. He had recently met Linda and was living with her in a small apartment that was part of a six-unit brick building. When he opened the door I saw that he'd let his hair go long, pierced an ear. He smoked too - smoke curled out of from behind him. Between the two of them, they must have gone through a carton of cigarettes during the weekend I was there. He invited me in - their apartment was spare, very little clutter - a magazine here, a forgotten book there. You could hear the street through the windows and the music from the neighbors. It was loud but Peter didn't seem to notice or care. He just continued with conversation like nothing was going on. Not being used to that kind of noise, I continually turned my head at each new sound.

I was curious about Linda. She mostly sat while Peter and I caught up on Dad, Lydia and our half-sister, Catherine.

"Not much has changed," I said as I watched Linda breathe life into her cigarette. Her thinness, short hair and nervous manner weren't like the kind of person I pictured Peter with after the constant string of beach girls he went through when he lived at the house. "Dad's not home at all anymore and Lydia and I just sort of hang out together and do stuff." Our stepmother, who was always at the corners of Peter's life, was central in mine. She'd made a point of trying to raise me. I was still young enough to accept her, where Peter never much paid attention to her.

When we woke the next day. A bank of clouds hung low over the clapboard houses and hazy hills that make Humbolt bone chilling and a study in grays. We climbed into Peter's brown pick-up; the three of us crammed into the front cab with steaming coffee cups, trying to hold them up as we slipped off the vinyl bench. Linda obscenely straddled the gearshift, but took no notice of it as he drove us through the wetlands that curved the land into the mountains. Sand and dirt mixed with grass-covered stretches of ground that veered off into ponds, which rose and fell on the tides. Egrets, Blue Herons and tiny shorebirds flew up in bunches when he swerved off the road in his pick-up and drove along the water's edge. He went fast over the bumps through patches of water where if we stopped, we would have gotten stuck. But he gunned the truck through them, took them blindly as I held hard to the dash and pushed my feet against the floor so I wouldn't hit my head against cabin's roof. He screamed and laughed over every wild bump, every piece of earth that gave way under our weight. He hollered when he felt the car lose touch with the ground. Linda just sat quietly in her seat, but I could tell by her fingers digging into the dash that she was scared and I knew that for some reason she'd resigned herself to the ride, that Peter had found someone who'd be there during his changing moods, his storms and squalls - and would love him all the way down to his source.

When we came to a stop back by the highway, I looked at Peter, his face. What was etched there was a dark pane of glass and a mirror of myself in my moments of rage, but he was smiling, his grin reaching ear to ear like it was cut from a pumpkin and that scared me more.

"What's up, Nick? It's a bit of a shock about us getting married, I know that, but I thought you'd be happy for me."

"I just had something in my head, Peter."

"What was it?"

"Nothing. It just came up and disappeared." I came back to him slowly. "Yeah, Peter, I think it's great. I'm happy for Linda and you."

"I know I should have called you, but it was something we just did."

"Can I at least take you guys to dinner to celebrate? I feel like I have to do something." I kept thinking of Linda, who I run into once in a while. I'd always catch her darting into a store or from it, perpetually in a hurry about something. I couldn't imagine what it would be. Peter wouldn't let her work and they didn't have any kids. I wondered what she did all day. She was pleasant enough and our short bursts of conversation between hellos and good-byes were limited to where Peter was or what he'd done on the house.

"Are you okay?"

"Yeah, I'm fine. Linda must be excited that you finally made it legal."

"Yeah, I pretty much didn't want her to up and walk. She's good to me, you know." Peter got up from the chair. "Hey, Nick?

"What?"

"Look in on Linda in a few days, would ya? I'm heading out to the platform tomorrow and I just want to make sure that she made the right decision. I'll be out two weeks this time. Just go say hi. She'd really like to see you." Peter put his jacket back on and moved towards the door. I walked away a bit trying to raise my spirits about his marriage.

"Peter?" I turned to him and looked at him. "Where's that cabin we stayed at when we were kids?"

Peter's face was like light disappearing. He stared me down. "I don't remember."

"I was just curious. I wanted to see where it was, that's all. See if it's the same as how I remember." His face stormed over.

"Don't go there, Nick. You're getting into things better left in the past."

"You know where it is, I can tell." Where I had been light and just mildly curious before, the real reasons for going back began coming up to the surface. "What's the big deal?" I asked him pointedly.

"Leave it alone, Nick. Please."

"Just tell me where it is, Peter. I want to see it again." I was wondering why Peter was trying to keep the memory of the cabin from me. I hadn't counted on the cabin's location coming out of him easily.

"Why don't you wait until you've been in town longer. We'll go when I get back."

"Christ, Peter, what's the big fucking deal?"

"The deal is, is that I don't want you fucking there." He came up to my face, "Now leave it the fuck alone, will you? God, I come over here to tell you something great has happened in my life for a change and you bring up all this past shit. One time, Nick, just once let me be happy."

"Peter, I've got to go. I don't know why, but it's my shit too."

He looked closely at my face. He took a long moment. The words came out syllable by syllable - so slowly they seemed to melt from his lips. "Pinecrest Road, down by the Point."

"Thanks," I said and watched him. In my usual way, I'd taken his moment from him and I felt sorry I done that as I watched him leave, but it became important that I knew where the cabin was. All these years it had stuck firmly in my mind and was the beginning of Peter's wild swings between happiness and despair, love and anger, which had come to life so clearly that weekend in Humboldt. I believed also that my reasons for coming back to Big Sur, and the history of our family lay locked inside those walls.

I drove up past Point Lobos and found the road. I saw the cottage that Peter and I had been taken from. It was perched on a hill up a long drive. No one was there so I walked around it several times, stopping to look in the windows. It had changed very little over the last twenty years. Some of the appliances had been updated and there was a new TV where the old one used to be. Instead of the hardwood furniture, there was soft patchwork fabric covering the sofas and overstuffed chairs. The large fireplace, the polished wood floor and stools that lined the counter that separated the kitchen from the living room remained.

I sat on the porch for a long time looking out over the sloping foreground and the ocean that extended from the grassy hillside. The cottage was transparent in some way, a window from which I could look back, but it made me uncomfortable and I felt loose and slippery as sand.

I tried to imagine how my life would have been here if we'd been allowed to stay, how it would have played out in such natural beauty and quiet, idyllic days. How we'd spend the nights listening to the winds whip through the high trees and over the shrubs that crowded the landscape. I'd become a force of independence, a man strutting over the beaches and casting low under outcroppings of rocks when the tides settled down for a few hours and the restless waves retreated in the summer doldrums.

My mother would have snapped out of her melancholy. She would have returned to the way she was a few months before we'd moved North, all light and breathy laughs, her mutterings a bundle of jokes and tiny gasps of pleasure as we tried to please her then. She'd lead us through the forest on days after school, winding her way through thickets to secret places where we'd swim afternoons in the pools under waterfalls.

She'd sit with us at night telling us stories of Indians and weave for us small toys made of pampas grass and broadleaf skunk cabbage that grew in the ravines between the mountains. We'd have dances on the beach and beat shells as she fluttered her arms in the firelight. But mostly, we'd just hang together, the three of us - Peter, me and our Mom - and move out from our actual daily existence into a world that would have gleamed under a light so warm that to behold it would have made everything right.

I allowed these thoughts because, as I sat there lazily day-dreaming in the heat on the porch, I wished for a different childhood after she left - one of mutual need, of tenderness and love. I also knew that I'd been a part of it, that there were things I allowed to happen, especially when Peter and I left Big Sur. Another son might have asked questions earlier or demanded to know what had happened for her to disappear from our lives. Instead, I was the kind of son that just shut down, became silent and watched from the corners of my family and tried to take in everything I thought I understood.

The roar of the trucks slammed by on Highway One, the only throughway that held Big Sur and the rest of the seaside towns together.

During the winter there was a landslide that knocked hell out of the highway and sent it rolling down the steep mountain and crushed itself into the water. Months went by before neighbors on either side of the slide were able to make the short trip to see each other. News was sent over quickly constructed wires that had been lost.

I imagined my brother loving this - keeping people away, making it impossible for them to wander aimlessly through what he called "his town." It gave his life purpose to avoid community because he thought that people trashed Big Sur. The landslide put into perspective just how fragile we were in the world. He said that, “by sucking everything out of the earth and cutting things away to accommodate ourselves, we'd put ourselves in danger. I could see him laughing by the side of the road, looking over the vast landslide with a certain amount of satisfaction because he and Linda lived simply.

In the past year, visitations were limited to ceremonies of weddings and graduations, births and deaths. Sometimes the casualness of getting together forced the long drive around the winding mountains to take the interstate far down out of the way and come winding back up or down the highway to spend a few hours or a day before making the trip back.

I wondered how hard the sudden change would have been - I hadn't arrived yet - then I thought about it for a moment more and realized that would've been less time fooling with people and more time to spend by myself too, looking out over the water, watching it crash and wash against the rocks, watch the cars skid past and the people ogling the view as if they were the first ones to see it.

In the time I'd been in Big Sur, I'd gone down to the beach when no one was around. I reached into my shorts to feel myself, try and masturbate, but the effort was too great and the risk of it put me down and I'd take my hand out, turn over and think of anything but that. Sometimes, I'd wish there'd be a man to lay there with me. We'd make love and carry on like two men after something they really wanted, like kids, a family or just the comfort of knowing that there wasn't some deadly virus, smaller than the human eye could see, passing between us. Instead, I jumped up and went off to watch the sea lions and pluck starfish from the pools like my brother used to do. I hated myself for doing it, but I continued trying to get at that one spot, that one place where the starfish's existence hung and floated under the control of my hand and the thought of being alone that might or might not force me to cast it like a disc as far away as possible.

On some days, I'd hike back into the hills and follow rivers up jumping from boulder to boulder. There were distances I'd cover that took me deep into the forests. I'd overcome my fear of them so that the deeper I got the more at home I felt. I took off on long day hikes never using a map. I wouldn't see people at all.

When I was young, and had been taken back to my father's house, I pretended to be in these forests by walking around his large house late at night without the lights on. I felt my way around on the blackest of nights when the fog was so thick off the ocean it seemed like it sucked itself against the windows. I memorized every room that way, even the living room with all its chairs and knick-knacks, the long lacquered end tables and the hearth that jutted out obscenely in front of the fireplace. I made a game of it by moving through each room losing points for things I ran into and shaving off half points for a simple brush. I did this every so often as if needing the sense of danger at being caught or the simple thrill that it was my own time encased in the freedom of black.

The cottage. It stands there dark-wooded, plain as day. Nothing special. But I can see through to the TV from the pane of glass my father looked through. I can see past the kitchen down the hallway to the bedroom Peter and I shared. I can imagine now my mother, behind her closed door, smoke billowing from her lips, liquor stashed under her mattress and her coming out of her room every so often to get something to mix with. I can smell her now because I'm old enough to know what that smell was: whiskey and the sick, sweet odor of flat coke.

There's Peter at her door screaming, "I want to go home!" because he'd had enough, and me running up to him, tugging on his arm pleading with him.

"C'mon, Peter, let's go. Leave her alone." I tug at him some more and he shakes me off.

"It's boring up here," he says, "there's nothing to do. She's crazy."

"Let's go outside. C'mon."

Peter pounds on her door and shouts at her again, then he turns to me. "Let go of me, you little shit," as he shakes me off again.

Her door yanks open. Mom comes barreling out, glass in hand - she grabs Peter's arm hard like she's trying to hold a wild horse.

"Do you want to go?" She screams at him as she bends into his face. "Do you want to go?" She pulls Peter to the front door and tries to open it, but her hands are full. She throws her glass against the wall where it shatters and the drink splinters off and ice shoots across the wood floors. She drags Peter out of the cabin and into the dark. I'm following behind, half afraid and a little happy that Peter is finally getting his due for pestering her like he has.

It's raining- the drops are falling hard and fat. It is so dark. They lurch down the driveway. Peter is pulling back from her, but Mom has him good, "Do you want to go down and be with your father? Is that what you want? I'll put you in one of these Goddamn cars heading down."

We get close to the highway. Mom's barefoot and by now we're all soaking wet. The rain has slicked us down. I'm crying for her to let him go as we reach the highway. Cars speed past us, the wheels run the rain through their treads, and their engines are loud like rushing trains.

Peter gets away from mom's grip, but she just keeps going across the road. Lights, rain, noise. She's yelling at the top of her lungs, waving at the cars to stop. She keeps walking down the road, her dress stuck against her, dripping water at the sleeves and edges, light silhouettes her body when headlights catch her out of the black. Peter and I stand at the edge of the road. I'm wailing. Peter is silent. We watch her head off down the highway and into the black. Her arms flail around her body, all bony and squid-like. She screams the whole way down, her voice getting lost in the sound of the rain and cars.

Peter pulls me around and up the driveway, but I call after her. "I'm calling Dad," he says. The rest of the night he's quiet. There's no phone and neither of us know how to drive. There's no way to a phone until morning so we sit up and wait for her to come back, but I fall asleep, curled up next to my brother. I'm warm because he's helped me change into my pajamas, but he stayed in his wet clothes and just sat there by the heater, the blue light of the television washing over us.

She came back in the night at some point, but she stayed in her room all the next day. We could hear her crying. At some point she pounded on the wall and wailed at the top of her lungs. Peter took off early to find a phone. That night, Dad showed up. It was the first time I saw her come out of her room. I'd run into the woods after Peter left to that secret pool and looked into it to see my reflection. I threw a rock into the water to erase it and watched it slowly ripple away.

The amazing thing about those days was her silence - as if there was nothing left for her to say. She'd run out of words when we left Los Angeles. Mom just took it all in giving Peter and me directions with a point of a finger or the nod of her head. She'd see to our needs before losing herself. She'd get us dressed and fed, take care of the laundry, take us into town to buy food. I was content, but Peter began getting angry easily. He balled his fists up like little hammers, slamming doors shut. He moved around heavily trying to get her attention when she'd lock herself in her room. I believe now that she tried to hide from us when she began to lose her balance, which only infuriated Peter. He made good on his promise to call down to Dad and that's when he lost himself. We were never the same.

Now I sit here on the porch, in the iron blue light of the fall afternoon, wanting desperately to regain what was lost of the days I remember loving with all my heart - all their freedom, their darkness, and their danger.

6.
Marjorie

I spent the night up in Topanga Canyon. Michael brought me to his camp where he built a small fire and because I thought he needed it, I shared Mrs. Jorgenson's crusty rolls and crackers with him. He'd managed a bottle of wine on the way up, stealing it from a liquor store at the mouth of the canyon. We spent the evening talking and nodding people away as they approached us.

Michael spoke quietly, his voice rising and falling beneath the snapping of the fire. I leaned towards him. "This is a nice place to be," he said, "On weekends it's much more crowded. During the week most of the people go back home. Those who are here during the week tend to be more genuine anyway." He spoke fast and animated, " When I finish work I come up here. It's great... no pressure... no rent... and when it starts raining I jump in my van."

"You're not from here, I mean California are you? The way you talk..." I asked.

Michael pulled a leg up, one over the other. "New York." he said, "Where I come from people plant their gardens in windowsills and on rooftops. They go upstate or out to the country on trains. There's hardly a gardener in New York, yet these people talk about the country and the land as if they get some spiritual thing out of it, when the most they see of it from day to day is in a book on their coffee table. It's bullshit." Michael reached into his tent, pulled a gray blanket out, "Here, take this blanket." I pulled it close over my shoulders.

"You sound like you don't like the city too much."

"It's not the city, it's the people. They're hypocritical. They move out here from the East and all of a sudden they have this garden, somewhere to plant things, and they haven't an idea of what to do with it."

"Isn't that how you make your money?'

"Yes."

"What's the problem?" I asked.

"No problem, it's just that I quit a job today because this lady couldn't figure out why she couldn't grow lilacs out here. She'd been bugging me about those stupid flowers since I started with her. She doesn't seem to realize she's in a different climate. I couldn't take it anymore so I told her to find someone who could grow them for her."

"Sounds to me like you're a little temperamental,' I laughed, stretched my legs out. The air on my back was cold and damp. The fire let out a hiss and then it popped sending splinters of heat onto the blanket. Michael bent over and brushed them off.

"Do you want to trip?" Michael reached into his pocket and produced a handful of multicolored pills, like a collection of marbles thrown together from various sets. "They come in international flavors and colors. Just pick one."

"No." I said flatly. I did not need to feel myself sent over the edge. My senses were still acutely vibrant and to dull or enhance them would have felt like a cheat.

"You'll have to excuse me," Michael said, "I'm being self-destructive today and I don't mean to bring you down with me." He picked a blue and white one out and then took a drink of the red wine.

I looked at him as if seeing him more clearly than I had before. His face was smudged with dirt, there was a line extending from his cheek to his neck giving his face a lopsided look. He wore his curly hair long to cover the scar and to make up for the fullness that was missing on the one side of his face. His eyes were cloudy and distant, spread out over their sockets like two eggs with their yolk just broken. Yet there was something about him that was handsome. He had a dark complexion and the shadowy remnants of a beard. Most of all, he was hypnotic in a mysterious way and I could sense that he always seemed to be on the verge of telling me some great piece of information like a snippet of history or an anecdote relating to someone famous. But I also felt that there was a part of him I would never know, as if there was a fragment of him kept under the surface of visibility.

I watched him, though, in the next fifteen minutes, slip into a state of outward confusion and inward bliss. His eyes watered over and if they were cloudy before, they were downright stormy now. His face became opaque and gentle, the scar twitching almost imperceptibly.

"Marjorie, I have spent the better part of the past two years unraveling everything that I thought I was supposed to be. I was supposed to be a lawyer and all I can do is bring myself to someone's garden everyday and plant flowers or rip out the old and dying. Most everyone I know thinks of me as a failure, so I've stopped going back home and pretending to be something I'm not. I can't stand to be in the same room with my family and their faces looking at me and judging me for something they thought I would become."

Michael began rocking back and forth in a position that had to be uncomfortable. His legs were folded together like pretzels and I thought that it would take a group of people to unwind them.

"We are all shaped by the images we see when we're young. I don't think my family had much to do with what I've become. I seem to be a product of many other people and many other things." He looked at me with those glassy eyes. "What about you?" he asked.

"I don't know, really. I guess my father... well, he raised me by himself since I was four, but he worked mostly." I tried to think what I could say, but I stopped a moment and for that little while it was silent save for the night sounds.

"I spent a great deal of time with him, you know, my father. But there was also this lady who took care of me after school and when he had things to do." Again, quiet settled over us. I began to think of my father at home cooking dinner like he always did, but alone now. I wondered if he worried why I'd changed so much so fast. I loved him, our vacations to the mountains in summer and to the ocean on weekends and holidays.

We'd camp in the big national parks, always in their off-season. We felt as if we owned them, that we were given the use of the land by gods and spirits. Father brought out his ceremonial feathers and beads at night around the campfire. As he shook them to make sounds he'd bring me to dance with him, my feet placed firmly over his. He'd make his voice deepen and screech and whisper and echo as he told his stories. It was during those times that I think he was indeed magical, as if his own spirit would rise up out of him and take us far away. I believe that he felt this too, because he would spin his tales and it would seem as if we would never come back.

My memory finally filled, remembering then how he tried to instill in me the memories he had of his ancestors, their ways. I was receptive to it when I was small, yet as I grew older, I let those stories fall away liked dropped pennies.

Michael and I talked through the night and fell asleep as dawn crept up the canyon. When I woke, the sun was beating down on us. My forehead and body felt clammy and the heat made our waking much more difficult. We'd slept close and the sweat from his belly and my back sent shivers through me as he pulled away from me. I lay there a moment taking in his scent. I've always loved the smell of men, dark and oppressive as night.

Michael groaned as he stretched, his arms reaching out above his head. I turned away from him in my embarrassment, but I felt safe too. I looked at him. His torso was tight and trim, the muscles across his stomach stretched like pulled rubber bands bunched together. He wasn't quite thin, but I could tell that he needed better food, but that it wasn't a concern he bothered with.

"Good morning," he said, "I hope I didn't talk your ear off." He laughed a little. "It's my tendency."

"Oh, no. I was in my listening mode."

"Well, we'll have to talk about you today." He sat up, smiled at me and pulled his legs in tight to his chest.

"There's not much to say, really," I said, "Not much at all."

When my eyes focused, I could see down the camp that turned out to be on the side of the canyon, precariously nestled in like a bird's nest under an awning. The oaks were less ominous and extended their muscled limbs over the ground. White-barked sycamore trees and wide-leafed bays lined the creek bed that slowly flowed water. Armies of low shrubs and outcroppings of rock populated the hillsides. The camp seemed deserted, but for a few people. The smell had changed to a dusty oldness, and the air felt heavy and dry.

"Where did everyone go?" I asked.

"They're probably not up yet, or they went down the canyon to the beaches or probably just went home." Michael stood up, his knees and bones crackling as they straightened. "Most people only come here at night to get high."

I reached down and pulled my dress around my legs; there was a breeze coming up the canyon and I was still shivering off the sleep. Michael stepped away from our site into the bushes up the hill. His back faced me as I stared at him through the bushes. I decided to treat the morning as an adventure.

Michael made his way back somewhat embarrassed. "It was a long night. I couldn't wait." His face broke into another grin. "There's some outhouses down the way."

"Be back in a second." I said as I leapt to my feet. My own body steadied, the joints stretching their way back after having adjusted to the hard ground.

I saw the small oblong houses in a clearing. There were two of them, stiff as sentries; a small gathering of people stood by. They were bunched together like the night before as if they were afraid of something. I would learn that they seldom did things alone, treating the outer world like a villain that would descend on them if one felt a desire to be separate. Their discussions were always private and short. They sat together for long wordless stretches of time as if conversation was forbidden. I knew I could easily fall in with these people.

When I returned Michael had slipped into shorts and a clean shirt. He'd rolled up the sleeping bag and folded the blankets we'd shared.

"When are you going back?" he asked.

I hadn't thought of this yet, but said, "I need to find a ride back to town."

"I can take you, but I'm not going there until tomorrow." He gathered everything up in his arms. "You could come to the beach with me if you want?"

I followed him, expectant-eyed, slow to learn, yet devoted to the moment. I helped him carry the blankets, tripping over an errant end that I finally gathered up and held awkwardly under my other arm.

We drove down the canyon and up the coast highway where several other cars were parked along the cliffs. We pulled in to a stop at the bluff and when I got out I peered over the edge and looked side to side. I saw how the land gently sloped to the ocean or veered sharply downward. From where I stood the beaches looked far away, people tiny as pebbles walked along the edge.

We scrambled down; the way was treacherous where the trail disappeared from a fallen piece of the cliff. At some points I lowered myself by inverting my body into a crab-like position, my hands splayed out, my chest pointed upwards, the leather backpack cushioning my back against the chalky rock. Michael went below me to catch me if I fell. He tumbled down in control locking his feet against outcroppings to stabilize him in case I might come bouncing down the path. I stopped to catch my breath and it was then that I was struck by the blue panorama in front of me. All different shades of it blended into each other. It was one of those days that seemed to sparkle as cut glass, where the reflections of light angled into your soul to fill you up and make you forget everything else.

When we reached the sand I had to stop and catch my breath. Michael adjusted the backpack on my shoulders and took the blankets from me.

"We'll go up a ways," he said.

"Is this where you usually come?" I asked

"Most of the time," he said, "but the other places are too far up and we got a late start."

Reaching a part of the beach that was clear of driftwood and seaweed, Michael threw a blanket out in the air and let it settle on the warm sand. I pulled off my pack, removed my sandals and waited to see what Michael would do next. Without looking at me, or regarding the fact that I was there watching, he removed his shirt and shorts and stood casually naked in front of me. It was the first time I had seen a man wholly nude and quite unconsciously so. I saw how the lines of his body intersected the various parts, the way his neck stretched and pulsed. I watched the muscles in his legs expand as he moved about shaking off the sand that had covered the edges of the blanket, and how his torso folded and unfolded as he bent over. I felt the possibility of sex with him, the burgeoning feelings I had towards him. My stomach tightened. He could tell I was looking at him, but he simply turned and headed to the water.

As he turned, I pulled my dress over my shoulders while facing the cliffs. I removed my panties and stood laughing, feeling as if I could float above the ground. In that sudden rush of freedom I turned around and exposed myself to the world as I'd never done before. I threw my arms back and pushed my body out.

Michael turned, smiled and waved me down to the water. He looked at me, eye to eye, without even looking at my body. This confused me, but it allowed me a freedom I wasn't expecting. I walked down to the edge of the water sure of myself, my body, but then I stopped at the shock from the cold.

"Go slow," Michael shouted then laughed.

When he came down, I splashed water at him, his skin instantly goose-bumped. I wanted him to see me, become aroused by my playfulness, but he jumped into the water and came up yards away from me. We ended up thrashing around, jumping the small waves and coming up for air when we were pulled under.

When we finished swimming we lay on the blanket together soaking in the sun. I kept watching him as he lay on his back. I looked at him as I had before, but after a while I turned over on my side because I couldn't keep my body from shaking. After several moments I reached over and touched him, then ran my fingers lightly over his arm. He turned his head and looked at me.

"I'm sorry," he hesitated, "but I can't."

I pulled my hand back. "I didn't know how to start," I said.

"That's O.K.," He went up on an elbow. "I appreciate that."

My body relaxed, the nerve endings finally numbed to some deeper understanding. "I thought perhaps you'd be interested." I had nothing to base this last comment on, but I rolled it around in my head so long that it came out perfunctory and unintentional.

"Normally, I would," his voice was shaky, "but... well, I don't normally sleep with women." He lowered his head back down on the blanket.

It was a long moment before either of us said anything. When we did say something, we spoke at once.

"Michael..." I said.

"I don't mean to disappoint you Marjorie," his voice was soft and hesitant, "and I was thinking that last night I would give in, but I couldn't really, you know, in the long run, do that to you. You seem too nice."

"You could of." I turned my head to him. "I would have let you."

Then I felt like I wanted to save him, pull him into me, but I stood up and went down to the water.

He joined me there. "Are you upset?" he asked.

"Not really, just a little confused." I couldn't quite look at him.

"It's not you, you know, I mean, I've slept with other women, but nothing ever happened really, emotionally that is. There wasn't any connection."

"You don't have to explain," I said.

"I just want you to understand, that's all. You seem like you don't quite know what to say and it's important that you know." There was desperation in his voice and then resignation - almost as if he'd let a part of himself go.

"Why is it so important?" I asked. "I just met you."

"Because you're hurt and I'm tired of disappointing people."

There was a long moment as if the ocean had flattened out and the waves ceased to roll into shore. He was right. I didn't understand and I wasn't sure that I wanted to either so I moved away from him and left him standing there.

I walked up to where we had laid out our things and slipped my dress back on. Then I started walking up the beach never looking back. When I returned he'd packed his things, but left the blanket and a smattering of pills were strewn across it. I looked up and down the beach and then up the cliff we'd climbed down. I saw him two-thirds of the way up. A dark, tanned figure against the bright, beige colored sandstone cliff. It seemed as if all of the deafening sounds of the ocean, the birds and the chatter and shouts of other people, gathered and echoed back at me from the wall.

In a panic I shouted up to him. "Michael!" There was no response. "Michael!" I called again. He turned, looked down and saw me standing and waving my arms back and forth. A shale of rock loosened and cascaded down. The air filled with a soft billowing cloud. I saw his foot temporarily grab at the air and his hands flail back at the cliff. I screamed once more at him as I watched his body leave the trail and tumble down over a ledge, hitting it hard enough to break loose the nose as it crumbled after him.

I froze. The long moments of his falling held me there. The sounds came crashing towards me from all sides. The people on the beach were turning towards the noise to see Michael and his body outstretched against nothing but blue and the falling cliff side.

When he landed, his bones shattered and a free fall of rock and sand covered him, then silence as people stopped for a moment to take in what had happened. After a pause there was the terrible, terrible sight of Michael, the noise, the shouts, and the sound of my own screaming.

7.
Nicholas

I'm channel surfing and I end up on one of those Christian stations where they're talking of love as being this huge miracle. The Miracle of Love! Love Between Two People is God's Plan! It's a miracle by God! Some perfectly coifed white man - dressed in a tailor-made suit, a whole sea of echoing, black faces atop purple tents behind him, begins singing the praises of God. I wonder how it is that he understands love singing like that, but stranger still he was dressed like he himself were God. How could he know that love comes at you naked, as complicated as a newborn, just wanting you to take it up and hold it? I'd resisted letting someone take hold of me. I've been afraid that I wouldn't know what to do, that I'd bruise my ego. No one had instructed me on how to behave, how to think of love as being tender and the finest gift.

I've often wandered through town with my head down. I'd relegated myself to my daily life: the work, the drive home, fixing dinner by myself and eating it out on the porch on good days or staying in, slopping up food over the kitchen sink. Single people don't set places for themselves. They drink out of jars, pour spaghetti sauce straight from its bottle into the bowl and light it on nuclear fire for a couple of minutes until putting the noodles directly in it. There is no attempt at presentation: the joyful arrangement of vegetable, starch and meat. All of this becomes habit and habits turn into insidious routine and before you realize it a month goes by, then two, then a whole year.

I'd been alone so long that it took someone like Matt to wrestle me down and make me see what I'd been doing. Matt, who is bookish and handsome, had rescued himself from the dull ache of those passing days. He took it upon himself to make me his project. I gave myself over to him. I let myself be taught how to set a table for two, pull the bedspread over so that there were equal covers, place two towels on the bathroom rack. Though these things took some remembering, the adjustments came surprisingly easy for me.

On a Saturday in June, a month where the fog hangs heavily in the trees, I started doing some inside repair on the house. I'd gone to the hardware store for bolts and screws, tools I'd need to fix molding that had peeled from the joint of the wall and ceiling in the living room. Matt was standing at the entrance to the store. I could feel him watching me, holding his gaze as I went down the aisles. It's like being in a grocery store, but the feeling is different – something intrinsically male happens – your body puffs up, you do the verbal dance with the helper, you pretend you know more about hardware and tools and fitting pipe together than you actually do. You have this momentary camaraderie with a total stranger based on hundreds or maybe thousands of years of hunter/gatherer genes that, in most gay men have been squashed by the pursuit of other things. But there I was doing that most male of rituals being cruised by a guy I'd never seen before.

As I moved through the aisles, going from one end of the small store to the next, I kept glancing back to see if he was still watching. He was harder looking

than I, which intrigued me because I thought I' cornered the market on that. I'd hate to use the wor rugged, but there it is. He wore khaki work shorts, worı and covered in dust and paint. He had on a t-shirt anc an over shirt. Thankfully, it wasn't plaid, but a dull blue – the ends of it un-tucked. His hair would be wavy if he'd let it grow out, but it was trim and newly cut.

I could feel that sensation in my body when I meet someone whom I think I'll end up with at my home or his. It's a strange combination of nausea, cold shiver and butterflies that courses from my legs and down into my arms. I collected my things and turned back to see if he was still at the front of the store. He'd disappeared and I was disappointed.

When I came out of the store, the fog immediately began wetting my arms and clothes. I quick-stepped to my car and was juggling my bags to get out my keys when Matt stepped up behind me.

"Hey." My keys clattered to the pavement. He dove for them and we fell together, hitting our shoulders hard. I became annoyed at my clumsiness. I always do something in these situations that embarrass me. Once I left my car in gear and got out while it slammed into the back of the guy's car I was trying to take home.

"Sorry," he said.

"That's all right," I took my keys from him and went to unlock my door. By now I was getting soaked from the fog's heavy condensation. I glanced at him. His hair was wet and his shoulders were dark from the falling drizzle. He was smiling.

"What are you smiling for?"

"I've been wanting to meet you for over a year. I'm Matt." He extended his hand, but I made a motion to show him my hands were full. So he put it on my shoulder. His touch was heavy and thick, his fingers squeezed my collarbone and it felt good.

"A year?"

"I saw you at the beach one day - the nude beach. It was hot and there were a lot of people there. I

was with friends, but you were alone. You had a killer smile – when you smiled anyway – which wasn't often."

"It has a mind of its own."

"You should smile more, it reminds me of my mother's smile. I watched you all day and never got up the nerve to go over and say hi."

"What gave you the nerve today?"

"I wanted to see you smile again."

"Here." I gave him a fake one.

"That's not it. You had a big grin when you were at the edge of the water and not a stitch of clothing on."

"It's that kind of beach. I like being naked." I said.

"I'm a little more modest," he said and put his face in mine. "Smile, goddamn it." That forcefulness gave him a big grin because I had to laugh.

"There, that's the one."

"You waited a full year for that?"

We had lunch. Beers and Sloppy-Joe brisket sandwiches. The restaurant was deserted, but people came and went quickly – only in the late afternoons did they settle in and sit down to watch sports and talk about the tourists and weather. Those are the two main topics in Big Sur – tourists and weather. Mainly weather because when it isn't any good, there aren't any tourists and Big Sur survives on their comings and goings. In '83, when the landslides hit, people worried about their businesses – some even shut down fully, laying off their workers until the road re-opened. The area has a transient labor force – summer comes and jobs spring up all over the place. The bulletin boards are full with notices of work around town, but winter takes those jobs away. The kids head back to school leaving the hardcore locals to take over their jobs to keep them busy through the lean months. I wondered if Matt was one of those who had come for the summer.

"Don't you have to go back to work, or something?" I asked. We'd been sitting there for a little over two hours. Either something was going to happen or I needed to finish the ceiling at home.

"No. It's Saturday."

"People work on Saturday," I said.

"Not this one." He mopped the juice from the beef up with the end of one of the restaurants famous breadsticks. Then he popped it in his mouth.

"Do you like people?" he asked.

"Rarely," I said, only half-joking.

"You should."

"You work at a hotel, right? The Post, wait.... No... Ventana."

"Wrong." He stared me down and tried to will me the answer.

"Customer Service something then."

"No way." Have you ever worked with the public at large?" He shook his head. "No, thanks."

"What then?" I was growing impatient, not liking the guess-what-you-do-for-a-living game.

"I'm a student."

"A student?"

"I'm in grad school up at Santa Cruz. I live with my sister down here and commute. Saves a lot of money, really, but sometimes it's a tough drive depending on the weather." He sat back and watched as I took a sip of beer.

"What are you studying?"

"Philosophy. I specialize in Kant and ...... "

"An academic."

"Scary?" He asked.

"Not really. You just don't look like one. I mean, you have hair on your legs and your fingers are thick and rough." I took a couple of them in my hand and turned them over to look at the creased swirls of his fingerprints. He pulled my hand into his and held it there. I looked around the restaurant to see if anyone was watching.

"Nervous?" He paused, brought my whole hand into his fist, "About this?" He squeezed.

"As a matter of fact..." I gave up my hand to his and then he let go. "Yes." He reached under the table and lightly touched my leg. "How about this?"

To me, that was less intimate. "No."

I began to fall - tumble away from myself - I wanted everything to be quiet. I wanted everything to fall away. I wanted to bring my lips together and say "Shhhh. listen. Hear that? Hear that music playing across the road, down the highway, through the trees?"

He grabbed the check and went to the counter, paid the bill when the lady came out from behind the window. He came back to the table and said, "Let's go to your place."

On the way there, I couldn't understand how I'd gone from buying hardware to having an almost total stranger follow me home. There was a danger to it, a palpable sense of dread on my part – not from any malevolent thing that he may do, but what I might do – like give myself into him. I kept checking the rearview mirror to see if he might have changed his mind and swung down another road, but his compact pickup truck was stuck behind me and I felt like some dog that just follows you because he's got to, because he exists on the swell of duty.

We came into my house. For the first time I truly didn't know what to do, but he sensed my hesitation and asked to use the restroom I think more out of breaking the tension than by his need to relieve himself.

"The bathroom is that way," I said. He took off down the hall. "Now make a left."

This gave me a couple of minutes to check myself in the mirror. Vanity isn't one of my traits, but I wanted to see what he saw. I think disbelief at my luck at attracting a guy like him had a lot to do with it. I'd never considered myself box-office draw, more like character actor material, "Oh yeah, he's the guy, what's his name? He's the guy who was in that movie, can't remember the name of it."

He came back in the living room. Came up to me and put a hand on my chest, kissed me. "On the way here, I was thinking that I wanted to come in here and tear your clothes off and take you down. But then it'd be over and we'd be embarrassed and that would be the end of it." He kept his mouth close to my ear.

"Probably," I said, not wanting to hear what he was saying.

"So I was wondering..."

"Yeah?"

"Could we have dinner? Do this right?

"I don't have a lot of experience with that. I'm sort of used to doing what you were thinking before."

"Me too, but I think that would be bullshit in this instance."

It intrigued me that it'd been a year that he'd been wanting to see me again. I was still working on the possibility of sex with him, but then I pulled away and got a good look at him, how he studied me. I could see that he was willing to risk more than a couple of hours, and though it was a new feeling for me, I was willing to risk more, too, because it was what I needed.

How to act? After he left the house, I wasn't sure. Should I beat off to make the horniness go away? Maybe I'd think more clearly, call the number he'd given me and weasel my way out. I've been a professional at that. I had no idea how to behave, but I didn't want to simply excise the feeling I now had by easily getting rid of it. I wanted to savor being wanted.

In the intervening time between Matt's leaving and returning for dinner the following night, I'd wondered how my Mom and Dad had met, how they loved each other enough to marry and how they caused as much pain to each other as they did. Do other children of divorced parents have as much trepidation about the possibility of two people coming together as I did? I think that it depends on where in the marriage the split takes place. My brother and I were never shuttled between them. We had no knowledge even of where one was.

I grew up watching my stepmother and father co-exist together, never believing that they were just more than two people thrown together in an odd sort of way. I believe there is love between them, but it is one of caution. I don't want to watch what I say or do around another person. I'd spent my whole life doing that around my Grandmother and sometimes my father, whose moods shifted like winter wind. If I was going to be with someone it had to be a natural coexistence - no pretenses or unfounded arguments, which is probably too much to ask for.

I'm twenty-eight! He's chasing me! He has been waiting for me! Maybe it's time to see what it's like. If Peter can have Linda, my father, Lydia – then why can't the name Matt roll off the edges of my tongue as easily as their spouses' names must?

A panic set in. I went to bed early that night. But in the middle of it I woke and stared up at the fan above my bed. I'd turned it on because it was muggy. The air from the swirling blades washed over my face and I tightened my body to prevent myself from giving into the needs of my cock and then I rolled over.

Not being able to sleep, I went out to the porch and watched the clouds of fog move up the hillside. It comes in so fast and envelopes the land in such a way that I imagined a ship out on the water losing its way along the coast and running up onto the rocks.

I was lost in time before I realized that I'd gotten cold. I went back inside, turned on the TV and fell asleep.

When I woke, it was still gray, but the fog had lifted and hung off the tips of the mountains like bed sheets strung from line to line, the light filtering through them and casting a white glow everywhere. My panic had abated during the night and had left me with a quiet hopefulness that carried me through the day.

When Matt arrived for dinner that night, I relaxed into a mild concentration of watchfulness and helplessness and decided that the best thing for me to do was to just go through it. Matt had dressed in jeans and a heavy shirt. He had such a strong presence, and I was overcome a bit by it. His eyes were a clear bright hazel and focused on me when he stepped through the door. He set down a brown bag stuffed with what appeared to be groceries. He bent to kiss me hello and I met his lips with mine. Then his hands and arms were on me and mine on him. Then we were on each other, removing clothes, stepping back to look at one another's bodies, touching, moving our hands up and over our skin, feeling everything while dinner waited for us to finish.

While he slept, tangled up against my chest in the sheets, I was wide-awake. I am not a person who is sentimental about sex. It is a forthright thing. I am rough during it and push through to get to the point where we lie in each other's arms, feel the weight and texture of our skin, the softness of his breath on my neck and the wetness that lays like shiny kelp over our bodies.

Up until that night I hadn't been with very many men, but each man that I had slept with caused me to compare the differences between sleeping with him or with a woman. I tried envisioning the curves of a woman's body versus the angles of the man's, the purpose of her soft belly against the hardness of his or the difference between entering either of them. With Matt, even this one time, made me realize that I couldn't compare them because the actual experience of the sex was much the same, but the emotions were as foreign to one another as two countries on opposite sides of the world.

When he woke up, he pulled away and took my hand into his mouth. Then he swung his body up and got on top of me. He smiled and bent towards me and lifted my face to his. "That last time was too quick," he whispered.

"Yeah?"

"We're going to go very slow this time."

The following day was a Monday and he left at six in the morning to run by his sister's house to change and head up to Santa Cruz for an eight o'clock class. I was left to lie there in the sheets and take in the new smells he'd left behind.

He told me he'd call after his lecture so I waited for it like a teenager. I tried to envision the future, but I couldn't. I knew that I was heading off into new territory.

When he did call, I was smiling to myself all the way through our conversation; a smile I didn't realize was there until the very last. When we hung up, I hurriedly got dressed and went out into the day that had opened up to me – the smells and touch of the wind, the warmth and the sunlit views out to the ocean because now the fog had lifted up over the mountains and disappeared.

8.
Marjorie

"You should come home now," my father said. I'd called him late that afternoon from a gas station at the junction of the canyon and the coast highway.

I'd gotten a ride from a sheriff who'd seen me at the beach and had come back after his shift to find me and take me back home, but I'd told him I was okay.

I spent the remainder of the day watching everything. They lifted Michael's body up the side of the cliff by tying him into a stretcher and yanked him up by a winch strapped to the back of a fire truck. It took over an hour to pull him up. The basket they put him in swung back and forth, sometimes hitting the side of the wall hard. When he disappeared over the top of the cliff, it looked as if nothing had happened, that Michael's accident was just a minor hiccup in the normal events of the day.

"I need to be picked up. I have no way to get back to town now," I said into the phone, my voice plain and uncolored.

"I'll come get you. You just stay where you're at. Honestly...," he said, pausing a moment, "just stay put." I hung up the phone. As I stood there a group of people

I recognized from the beach pulled up in a car. A woman poked her head out a side window.

"We're having a fire down at the beach tonight to celebrate Michael. Why don't you come?" I looked at her, but didn't say anything. She was smiling at me, though the corners of her mouth turned down and her eyes were doleful. Another woman joined her in the window.

"That happened to another guy last year. It's sort of an annual event here," she said, her voice shrill and scattered as frightened birds.

"Maybe you'll think about it?" the first girl said.

"I will," I said and walked away.

After another hour I saw my father's car lurch into the gas station from where I stood by the bathrooms. I knew he had it in first gear and that the clutch and his foot seemed to work independently of each other. The only time he could stand to let me drive was when he didn't want to go to the store in need of something himself. All other times he drove and I suffered along with the car his driving and his inability to navigate bumps, curbs and other obstacles that seemed forever to be in his way.

He pulled up next to me and I got in the car. Our old Dodge tilted to one side under the weight of him so that as I climbed in I slid sideways on the worn seat more than I wanted to.

"Close the door, honey," he said. "We'll go by your place and pick up a few things you'll want at home, Okay?"

"Okay," I said, repositioning myself against my door.

"Then you'll come home for a while." He put the car in gear and headed toward the highway.

He asked me what happened and I told him. I told him about Michael, about our conversations and about the fall.

"You should be home with me. You are not ready for this. It was my mistake." His eyes filled with tears, "I could not help you with this."

The last time I'd seen him this upset, he'd been talking to an old woman friend of his in our front room. She was a woman whose voice barely rose above a whisper yet she walked so hard our porch always belied her appearance at our door. Her dresses were printed with floral designs and her feet exploded from the straps of her sandals.

That day she came with news that the husband she'd left years before had finally died and their son was coming to live with her which meant that my father could no longer come to her house during the early evening hours and during days on the weekend.

Their times together had lasted as long as I could remember, but was never spoken of. The only thing father would say as I got older and could take care of myself was that he'd be gone for a bit and don't wait up. But he'd be there in the morning like nothing had happened as I sat and ate my breakfast. It was a few years before I understood what they were doing, but I never asked him about it.

That woman was the reason my father never remarried. She took care of the part of him he needed and never pressured him into marrying or moving in. I suppose that both of them felt like they had already done it and by marrying they would just be taking a step back.

When she sat there and told him about her son I knew that he loved her more than he was willing to admit, that the adjustments he'd have to make would be intolerable and lonely. With me going off to school and his mistress letting him go, I believe that it was far more than he wanted to handle at that moment.

From my hiding place behind the wall in our dining room I could hear them talking. Once in a while I peeked around the corner to watch.

"Henry...Henry...listen to me. Paul is coming home in a few days." She stroked his hand, "It's been a good run, hasn't it?"

My father didn't answer back. She went on, "It's not the end of it. It's just that we have to be a little more careful...that's all."

It appeared that he didn't see it that way because he held out his hand to her and bent his head down to the crook of her arm.

I stood there watching them, two old people who shared secrets from their children. As they moved into each other's arms, and as they hugged their big bodies together, I ached deeply for my father.

Our car rattled towards Santa Monica and as we drew closer I felt panicky. My forehead grew hot and I moved continually against the imitation leather of the car seat. My father looked over at me.

"Be still," he said."

"I don't want to go back," I was looking out the window watching the off-ramp signs sweep past.

"You don't have anything at home now. You're going to need some things." He put his hand on my shoulder as if to steady me.

"I don't want to go there either."

"Well, we're going." He took his hand away. "You need some rest and... and look at you, your face is all withdrawn like you haven't eaten."

"No I haven't."

"Maybe we'll pull off and get something to eat. That's what we'll do. You'll feel better." He turned the blinker off and turned down into a part of town filled with signs, gas stations and all-night stores.

"Remember where we are so we can get back on."

Night had come. As we drove down the streets looking for a place to eat, the signs and streetlights flickered on and slowly glowed bright. We found a small diner and sat down in a booth. There was nothing that drew us in to that particular place, but we ended up agreeing on it because it looked inexpensive and seemed as if no one was there.

We said nothing until we ordered. I knew I was hungry, but I couldn't bring myself to order a large meal so I opted for soup and a salad. The waitress wore jeans and a blouse that fit her haphazardly around the waist. I never looked her in the eye, but I felt her disapproval of me.

I excused myself and stepped out from the booth, went to the bathroom and locked myself in. I stood at the sink and looked in the mirror. My face was streaked from the corners of my eyes and there seemed to be a cut on my cheek I didn't remember getting, but I wiped at it and it disappeared with my hand. I realized it was blood from Michael when I had brought my face to his on the beach. I moved my hands up the sides of my face and through my hair. I tried to finger the matted strands, but my hair felt slack and lifeless and hung dirty down to my shoulders. I splashed water from the spigot against me. Tiny rivulets hung from my cheeks and nose, slipped down from my neck into the collar of my dress. I retied the strands of leather into a bow at the front and shifted the dress over my shoulders. Then I dried my face clean.

When I looked back in the mirror, I had re-envisioned myself. It was the most unexpected thing. In the midst of the day I took on a weight and now felt that my life had developed meaning and resonance, that the shared moments with Michael were not lost, but a part of me.

I returned to the table where my father had started his meal. I called the waitress over and ordered more food. In addition to the soup and salad I ordered chicken, green beans, several slices of bread and a large helping of mashed potatoes.

My father looked at me oddly. Then he went back to his dinner and stole glances at me between bites. When my dinner came I ate hungrily and fast. The food felt good and when I finished, I sat back in the booth, gorged, and smiled at him.

He looked up at me and pulled from his vest a small weathered packet of leather. He opened it to reveal a thin pocket and slipped out a feather wrapped at the end with a piece of worn red velvet and outlined by tiny, brilliant blue beads. It was slightly beaten, as if a sudden gust of wind had undone its zippered flanges, but its beauty was simple. Dad held it up above the table.

"I've carried this many years in my pocket." I watched it turn in his fingers. He went on, "This was your mother's. I'd given it to her before I married her and took it back on the day she died. When she got sick I pinned it to her shirt so that she could survive her death." The overhead light shone along the feather's back and glinted off the dark stem. My father continued, "I've saved it for you all these years. You need protection and now this feather belongs to you. It's grown too heavy for me to carry." He reached across the table and gave it to me as I put my hand out to accept it. I held it in my palm and rolled it around.

"Dad," I said, "I don't want to go home."

"I know," he said. I saw him letting go, realizing that I didn't want to be held, as if the bonds so tightly held for so many years were finally loosed from their moorings. I felt this, but a part of me grasped at him for a moment. I wanted to take away what I'd just said, but the feeling slipped away.

Dad let me off in front of my apartment. He didn't say anything so I reached over and lightly kissed him on the cheek. I imagined him going home, the dashboard lights of the car illuminating his heavy eyes, pulling up in the driveway and sitting for long minutes in the car like he did on bad days before going into his empty house.

It made me pause outside the car door, but then the Dodge lurched forward as it always did down the half-circle driveway and out to the street where it joined the other cars as my father headed home.

9.
Nicholas

Perhaps there are things that one associates with a father - smells like smoke, leather and soil that recount days or nights huddled with him on the deck or out in the backyard. Maybe there are clothes that other people wear that remind you of the way he bent down to look at you when you were young. Or there's a glance you catch from someone that jogs your memory of his moods and temperament.

My father's hands intrigued me: how the fingers extended moving constantly, strong and gentle, performing a caress, an act of violence, causing pleasure or pain. The fleshy pads of his palm could be warm or cold as I'd trace its lines with the tiny fingers of my hand.

When I moved away from Dad's house after high school, I didn't think of him often. I pulled the white shade of memory down. What scared me was the snapping up of the shade - as if someone pulled it down real quick then let it loose and the easing of the grip I thought I had on the shade coming faster than I could control it.

So on this night I slid away from Matt out of bed, wide-eyed and cold like I just stepped from a warm shower into bristling arctic air. The blankness of sleep shut out of me like an electric-wired fence that shocked if you came near. I pulled on a pair of sweat pants. I surveyed Matt and reached down to smooth the covers over him that I had pulled away. I envied his ability to sleep through almost anything.

I went into the kitchen and took a beer from the refrigerator. Popping the top, I looked out the window over the sink. The moonlight bounced off the leaves that itched the glass. There are these things in my head I can't get rid of.

Like the night my father presented our future stepmother to us. He was all sideways glances and deferential to her. I guess the word for her would have been sumptuous - diametrically opposite from my mother, who in the presence of this lady would only have been merely interesting. She was lit up like Christmas - all sparkly from the diamonds my Dad had given her, which looped down from her ears and in a singlet over her wrist. She drove herself to the house to meet him and I was the one who caught the door as she opened it with her own key which, by the look of her face, she realized was probably not the right thing to do.

"Hi!" she said, "I'm sorry I should have let you open it. You're such a gentleman." She looked at me as if I should have responded, then went on. "You must be Nicholas." A pause. "I'm Lydia."

"I'll go get Dad." I said. I ran back into his bedroom. He was snapping a tie clip closed. His bedroom was dark, musty from his shower. "There's a lady at the front door. She let herself in."

"Her name is Lydia."

"She told me that already."

"Then use her name," he said, "and be nice to her." He turned around and stared me down.

I said, "Okay, but who is she."

"A friend of mine," Dad checked himself again in the mirror, "Go get Peter and come to the living room. I want both of you to meet her."

"I already did." I said.

"Nicholas, why do you have to do that?"

"Do what?"

"Just go get Peter." Dad went into the bathroom, checked his hair and turned the light off. I still stood there.

"I don't want to meet her," I said. "I just don't."

"Well, you're going to and that's that." There was a shout from Peter coming from the living room. He had just found her.

"Dad, there's someone here!"

"I know, Peter," he said calling, then to me "Thanks for getting him, you're a big help." He shot his eyes at me then went to his bureau and pulled a white handkerchief from one of the small drawers. He folded it neatly from corner to corner then flipped it over onto itself and smoothed out the small piece of fabric to create a crease. Then he smartly stuffed it in his pocket and fluffed out the ends poking out from the deep black. He looked once more into the mirror, smoothed a hand over a loose shock of hair. I followed him out to the living room. He flicked switches on as he went and the house lit up from one end to the other. Lydia stood next to Peter. I could see that she'd won him over already because Peter was beaming like an idiot as if he'd just happened on to something he could call his own.

Dad took her arm gently, covered her palm with his. They did look good together, like two people who belonged. She was truly beautiful and seemed nice, yet there was something wrong and when you're five you still believe that your own family as one is much better than parts put together.

The four of us stood there stiffly. From that moment on there was a feeling of intrusion, as if a piece of the puzzle was forced rather than placed perfectly.

Maybe it was just me, but I stood there watching them and Peter and I felt some sort of permanence, that no matter what I said or did, that this gathering of people would stick. I went up to her and took her other hand. Dad smiled.

"Well, I guess we better get going," he said.

"I wish we could stay now," Lydia said looking at me. "But we'll see you two tomorrow maybe. Okay?"

"Right on," Peter said.

Then they left for the night. Peter turned to me. "She's kind of nice."

"She's all right, but she's not mom, I said and left the room.

"Where are you?" Matt moved up behind me, his body warm, the hair on his chest scratched my back.

"What?" I said, "Oh, hi." I put my arms and hands over his where they wrapped around my waist.

"You shouldn't be up now," he said. "You've got to get some sleep."

"I don't know what I'm going to do, Matt." I picked up the beer and offered him some. He shook his head. "She has really messed me up."

"I hadn't noticed." He kissed my neck. "What are you going to do?"

"I used to think about her all the time at different parts of my life. Then it got to a point where I just put her out of my mind real easy. Then today she said something about my Dad that has kind of been bothering me."

"What's that."

"It had to do with Peter, too. She said that Peter betrayed her to my Dad. I know what that was now. Peter called my Dad to tell him what she was doing when we lived up here as kids."

"What do you think really happened?" Matt pulled tighter on me.

"I don't know yet." I turned in his arms. "Matt? What do you think about me?"

"What do you mean?" he asked, pulling away a little. I just looked at him and then he sighed. "Sometimes you're tough to get at. Especially in the last day or two and you haven't left anything in the book for a while.

When Matt moved in, he bought a book with blank pages in it. He'd written, "Thank you for letting me share your life, your house. Here's to our life together. I know it'll be hard sometimes to adjust, but I know we'll work through it. I just want you to know what it means for me to be with you. Love, Matt. He'd drawn a cartoon of a dog with big eyes, droopy ears and a thin tail sitting on its haunches.

When I got home I found the book and wrote on the following page how glad I was to have him here, how he'd centered my life finally, made me the object of his care. I tucked a newly cut house key into the binding.

The book became a touchstone for us. We'd leave messages as mundane as "I'll see you later" or what to get at the store. Sometimes we'd write what was bothering us about the other, but mostly, as we moved deeper into the relationship, we'd talk about the good things we saw in each other, how one night Matt had made a sandwich and left it for me after working late. Or how I'd found a picture of the Deschuttes River that he'd love so much as a kid growing up close by and tucked it into the book so that he'd find it.

After a couple of months of living together, Matt had gained some power over me, which I wasn't comfortable with. He was always trying to figure out where my head was. Sometimes it was okay because I wanted to have him try and understand me, but at other times I just wished he'd not try so hard and just wait and watch what happened.

Now was one of those times because I didn't understand what was going on and I was spending every waking moment trying to get at the history of my family. I wanted a little bit of my power back.

Matt sighed heavily. "I still question whether you really want me around." He dropped his arms and stood back now, then folded them across his chest. "I don't enter into these things lightly, you know, us getting together."

"I know that," I said. "I don't either. I just hope you'll stick through this with me."

"Oh, yeah, there was never any question about that." he said. "It's just that you get so wrapped up in yourself and I can't understand that. It's like you don't ever need anyone."

"Well, I haven't ever needed anyone before. But this thing with my mother... I don't quite know what to do. I don't know if I want the responsibility."

"I think you do," he said. "I think you really do. I think you need her to find out some things."

"Like what?"

"I don't know, but you've been your own person for longer than anyone I know and have built up your guards so well that I really don't think you want anyone to need you."

"I do, though." My eyes filled up as if I had just put a finger on what it was I wanted that had eluded me all these years. "I do now."

"You're just angry all the time, it seems. Like somebody owes you something."

"They do."

"Tell me what it is."

"I need to know that I'm worthwhile," I said. I slowly moved into Matt with my hands, face and legs. My whole body stiffened and strengthened. I cupped my hands under his butt and lifted him up against the refrigerator. I was outside of myself, remote, as if I was watching someone else, because I had lost control of my life and wanted to take it back. The only way I knew how was to take control of this relationship so I pressed into Matt. He could feel it so he pressed back. But, as he pressed back, I just let go. I was a mass of moving limbs. I pulled my sweatpants down over my thighs. Spit into my hand and grabbed hold of myself. For the first time I whispered in his ear, "I love you," then I shoved him back and up and shoved myself into him. He cried out, and I pushed up hard again. He shouted, "Nicholas, stop." But I slammed his body flat against the cold door and kept thrusting. I could see his face all flushed and frightened. The noise in the room increased as the insides of the refrigerator toppled over and crashed against its walls. Matt continued to resist. "Nick, don't do this," he said. He pushed back against my chest and reached back with his face and brought it close. I felt his breath and the wetness of his mouth against my ear. Quickly he said, "Nick, stop... now." Then as I pushed again I brought my head down to his chest, clenched my eyes shut and began shaking. My body lost its strength and I slipped out of him and down his legs. I held onto them as he stood there looking down at me. I began to cry hard. He turned around, his back against the refrigerator, shuddering, angry. I felt his hands on my shoulders and then on the back of my head.

"Nick, don't," he hissed, "don't cry." He pushed my head forward against the refrigerator door, held it there.

"I'm sorry," I said, "I'm so sorry."

He put his mouth against my ear and whispered, "What do you want me to do, Nick? What is it you want me to do? Do you want me to go? Is that it, because I will now."

"No." I grabbed at him to pull him closer. I was trying to catch my breath as I knelt on the floor facing him. "I'm sorry, Matt." I wrapped my arms around him.

"I thought you wanted me to take care of you. So I did. Are you mad at me? I'm not the one to be angry at here," he said.

"I know," I said. "I know you're not."

"Then what was that all about?"

"I don't know." To stop his questions I attempted to kiss him, but he pulled back.

"I don't want this," he said. "I don't." He started to get up but I held on to him. He got up off the floor and went back to the bedroom. I followed him. He went to the closet and took out his pants and a sweater. I came up to him and put my hand on his arm as he pulled the pants out. He started to put them on.

"Tell me how to feel, Matt."

"I can't do that," he said.

"I need you," I said.

"Is that what you call need? Is that it?" He turned around holding his pants over himself. Then he took a long look at me and said, "Well, I need you too, Nick, but I don't want this." Matt bent his head down and started to cry. It was then I realized that I'd frightened him deeply and I could tell that he felt weak and unfocused and now I wanted to make him strong again. I pulled him towards me. I took the pants from him and draped them over the edge of the bed. I laid him down on the bed and brought my face against his and pressed my lips to his.

"I'm sorry," I said.

In the morning there was a note from Matt on the kitchen table with a cut yellow iris from the garden. 'Didn't want to wake you. Thought you should sleep. Let's talk about last night. I love you. Matt!' I smiled and put the long-stemmed flower in a tall plastic cup. It was nine-o'clock and I knew I'd be late for work. I called the hospital. The nurse told me that my mother was asleep so I said I'd be in at the end of the day.

As I showered I thought about Matt and the night before. We had been fierce with each other after I pulled him into me. He began to feel strong again and when he went to enter me I gave myself up to him. After a number of hard thrusts he rested inside of me and we stayed like that for a long time.

"This is it," I said.

"What?"

"What I need." I pulled him deeper inside me. I didn't feel as if we had to accomplish anything, not needing to be in a hurry to push through it. "I need you over me and inside me like this, even when you're in class or at the market or just doing nothing. I need to know that you are thinking of me and that we can have this all the time because it's what I've missed my whole life.

Matt's anger subsided and we were raw and connected by more than just flesh and it felt good. Now he moved slowly and gently inside of me until he came. Afterwards, I held him hard in my arms.

"I like this," I said, "I like this very much." I smiled at him.

"Me, too," he said as I stroked his legs. He let out a long breath.

"Did I hurt you earlier?" I asked.

"No, I was just scared. That's never happened to me before," he said, "Nick?"

"What?"

"Have you ever loved anyone before?" he asked, "I mean, anyone at all?"

"No. This is very new to me."

"Is that the closest you're going to come to saying the words - I love you? Because I love you."

I tightened a little. Had I set myself a trap to tell him I love him out loud? I worked around it. "I never really knew what it meant. I mean, we assume that you're supposed to love certain people unconditionally, I guess like your parents or something, but I've never felt that." I pushed Matt over on his back and looked at him. "Why are you asking me this now?"

"Because I have your full attention," Matt said, laughing a little.

"You certainly do."

"I'm going to help you through this thing with your mother, but you've got to promise me you'll make an effort with her." He narrowed his eyes.

"I promise," I said. I wasn't used to negotiating like this, but I was learning to like it. In the space of twenty minutes I'd come to learn more about him than I had in the ten months we'd been together. He had an impressive resolve and I thought how wonderful it felt to be filled up and to feel love from someone for the first time - and how anguished I'd become at having never been loved by anyone until now.

10.
Marjorie

I stood in my shower letting the last two days run off me. The water streamed down my body slick as a glove. I moved slowly under the steady flow. I washed the ocean salt from my hair and ran my hand down over my smooth, dark skin. Afterwards, I dried myself off, packed some clothes in my backpack, pulled on an over shirt and jeans and then stepped out into the night which had turned cold and damp from fog.

I walked to Lincoln Boulevard, put my thumb out and picked up three rides that eventually let me out at the cliffs where Michael's accident occurred. I looked down to the beach and saw a large fire burning, the sparks heralding the sky, and a small group of people surrounding it.

I was pulled to that place - all that I'd known up until then were a few fleeting moments of pure freedom and tragedy, but it was necessary for me to have more information about Michael, more to hold on to. The day was finished and night had come without my having time to take notice. On the way out of my apartment I had simply grabbed at things and thrown clothes over myself that hid my body. Up until then my body was like some vessel - a car that is simply transportation without adornments or a sleekness that you'd be proud of.

Standing at the cliffs, with the soft wind darting up its sides, I became aware again as if I'd woken from a dream. In the light of the fire I crawled down the cliff.

Approaching the people on the beach, their faces glowing dark to light from the fire, I saw that they were sitting in a large circle. No one moved until I had reached them. Then the woman from the gas station, who'd leaned from the car and asked me to come rose up and stepped towards me.

"Come, sit over here," she said. I followed her to her place in the circle. People shifted over, raised their eyes to me and then went back to watching the fire. It was almost surreal and I wondered if I'd made a mistake.

"We are observing a silence for Michael," she whispered, "I'm Patsy."

"I'm Marjorie." I crossed my legs and took in the warmth from the fire. The wind had kicked up and the fire smoke began blowing sideways, which made some of the people stand up and move over behind others. The rest sat silently as I looked around the group. There was no real leader, or none that I could detect. They looked clear-eyed into the blaze never averting their gaze. The warm glow danced shadows across their faces. I didn't know whether they believed that I was the cause of Michael's fall or that it was what it was - an accident.

I was handed a joint and I took it. I drew the pot in deeply and held it there. I let out a long breath and watched as the smoke curled up in the air and blew quickly away.

I was tired and wanted to curl up there and go to sleep, but instead I concentrated on the fire and the heat of it. I thought of my father in the dark, in his driveway wondering to himself what he had done. I thought of him dancing around a similar campfire when we were young, me standing on the tops of his feet and both of us sending spirits and omens away in the breaths of the burning embers.

When I met your father, I was half out of myself and half asleep. My head was bowed and I'd closed my eyes. When I looked up, Eric was standing at the edge of the group taking in everything.

He was sturdy and small, barrel-chested with strong, knotted arms. His face was round, eyes large and burnished blue and topped by a crown of blond hair. There was a look of disapproval from him when he surveyed the group - though LSD and Mescaline had not fully been taken up by this group yet, it would have seemed to any stranger that we would have been the first to indulge.

One of the men came up to us and said, "This is Eric, a friend of Michael's."

Another woman, who was staring at him, invited him to sit by her and shifted over. I kept glancing at him, wanting him to notice me, but he walked around the group, his dog trailing behind him and chose a place across from me so that the fire, which only gave me a view of him when the wind shifted the flames, hid me.

Throughout the vigil, and as the fire dwindled, I began staring at him and wondered how much he knew about Michael - what kind of friend he was - maybe he was an old lover of his. When people started to speak and laugh again and bottles of wine and alcohol were passed, and as the night pressed on, I kept an eye on Eric. I could see him become loose and more comfortable.

Patsy began talking to me, but my concentration was on him. I nodded to her at the right places, but I could feel myself watching his every move - how he cocked his head when he spoke, used his thick fingers to make a point, kept his upper body rigid. I was attracted to him - aching a little so I shifted in the sand, but the ache was still there.

Then he saw me, smiled and turned back to the man who was talking to him. Elated and then crushed by the shortness of the smile, I fully engaged myself in Patsy's blathering in that shrill voice of hers.

We talked quietly together which brought looks from the others. I was wary of the group I felt I was getting myself into. I felt like I was beginning to fall into their way of life, which was new and interesting to me but not what I really wanted. The rigors of that life - the sleepless nights, the smoky air, the cold, the bad food, the drugs, took their toll on the people around the campfire. You could see it in their faces, on their bodies and in their conversation. This new man, Eric, was apart from all that and the only thing we had in common was knowing Michael, and I only for a short time.

"I knew Michael back East. We were in college together," Eric said.

"I only knew him a couple of days. I was with him when he fell." I didn't want to tell him the whole story - not just yet.

"It must have been awful," Eric said, pausing to take stock of me, "Mike sort of got lost up here. I lost contact with him until his parents were called, then they called me. I think they sort of blame me, but I couldn't tell him what to do."

"Did you know he was homosexual?" I asked.

"Sort of. He never really came out and said anything, but I knew." He looked past me down the beach. "We were friends, you know, but I think as he became more aware, he didn't think I wanted to be involved with someone who was like that. I guess I gave him enough signals to let him know that I didn't." He took a passed bottle of wine and brought it to his mouth. "He was always kind of quiet." Then he took a drink.

Now we had something between us. He gave me the bottle.

"I've got his van. His mom and dad told me to keep it, but I don't really want it. It's such a mess." He leaned forward, "Do you want to get out of here?"

"I'm tired," I said, "and I need to make my way back home somehow."

"I need someone to drive the van back to my parent's house. Can you drive?"

"Yeah, I can drive."

We walked down the beach towards the cliff. He spoke quietly the entire way. "I was driving through Arizona on the way out here. It was near the four corners just outside Mexican Hat where the four states join together. Anyway, I was driving down this highway and it was about as desolate as they come and I passed this Indian sitting by the side of the road. Not doing anything, just sitting there. So I stopped. I mean this was in the middle of nowhere. I couldn't believe someone was out there. He's wearing this red bandanna and his hair is streaked gray, but he's wearing these regular clothes too. He must have been seventy or so, but when he stood up he was taller than me. So I asked him if he needed a ride. I'm usually not one to do this, you know, but like I said we were miles... but then he stood up and he motioned to the car, then climbed in. So I got in and he points down the road. We drive about five miles and he motions for me to stop and back up and points at this dirt road. So I pulled my car into it and drove down. Now I'm getting a little worried. Like I would drive down there and no one would ever know what happened to me. So we come to this little house made out of scavenged plywood. There are old cars and pickups, mangy looking chickens and children running around the yard. I stopped in front of it, he got out and said, "thank you." Those were the first words he spoke to me. I'm sitting there dumbfounded because all the way there he hadn't so much as said a word. Then some guys came out of the house, they were big as him, but not so old, like maybe thirty or something, so I backed my car up, turned around and headed back down the dirt road. I looked in my rearview mirror and what do you think they're doing? They're waving."

"I don't get it," I said.

He stopped, turned, and looked at me. "Well, that's how I felt about Mike, I guess. I never really knew who he was, but I felt like I had to help him anyway."

"But that's not it, really," I said.

"No," he said, "no it isn't." Eric started to walk again, his head bent. "It's like that Indian, you see, I was willing to help him to a point, but I couldn't commit to the experience." His face sort of twisted then. "I couldn't let myself just go with it because I couldn't understand and when I don't understand something I immediately pull back."

"So then it was you who let Michael go away," I said.

"I suppose... but now this," Eric said, "is what had to happen."

His dog ambled behind us, wary of me, then he darted past us and headed off into the dark. We reached the cliff trail and ambled up. Eric followed me calling his dog after him. When we reached the top he handed me the keys to the van. "Follow me. We'll drop it off and I'll give you a ride to wherever you need to go."

"But it's late."

"Yeah, I know. I don't mind."

We took the van up winding roads to his parent's house. It was pitch black along the streets and very early in the morning before we got there. I couldn't see anything as we wound up a long drive. Eric got out and took the van to the side of a carport and parked it while I stood waiting for him slightly shivering from the cold.

When he came back he pulled a sweater from the trunk of his car and offered it to me.

"Here. Do you want me to take you home?

He didn't wait for my answer. Instead, another question came, only from him it was more a statement, but he leaned further into the car a little more insistent, "I can do that now if you want or you can hang at my house and I'll take you back tomorrow morning."

"Let me get a blanket." He said as he walked down the hall of his apartment. He only turned one light on and I could see the large windows looking out on the ocean. He went to the side leveler windows and closed them and turned to look at me. "Do you want a shower?"

I shook my head. He opened a cupboard and took out a blanket and held it up to me. "Here, follow me." I wrapped the blanket around my shoulders to stop my shivering which were now caused by nervousness rather than cold.

"I only have a bed and a small couch, so if you don't mind sharing..." He looked at me expectantly.

I answered him by going over to the bed and propping myself up against the pillows at the headboard. He stood looking at me and smiled. He was nervous too, but he turned and went to a closet, took down some clothes and went into the bathroom. I waited on the bed, my eyes wide trying to take in the bedroom, but the lights from outside were only enough to see where to go and not enough to see the details.

When Eric came back in the room he'd changed into sweatpants and a t-shirt, removed his glasses and came to the other side of the bed where he lay down on his side and angled himself towards me while he pulled a sheet over his legs. We talked for a while, but I started to drift off and fought to keep my eyes open. The warmth of the blanket had calmed me and Eric's voice became hard to hold onto. We slept until the afternoon of the following day when Eric's mother called to ask about the van and his plans for the evening.

The afternoon light filtered in through the curtains giving what looked to be a sterile environment somewhat of a warm, musty glow. His apartment was as tidy as a hospital room. There was nothing extra in it. Everything seemed functional and set at right angles to each other. Mrs. Welch, I suspected, (and suspected rightly), had a good deal to do with this, but I also felt that for some perverse reason, Eric kept it that way to keep himself uncluttered. I got up and went into the bathroom. It was spotless. The towels were folded neatly together, the mirror was clean and there wasn't a spot on the sink. I guess I remember this so well because the hospitals I was in were much the same; everything was so sterile that life seemed to be stripped away. Eric was still on the phone when I got back into bed. Even though the sun was out, the room was cold and the bathroom itself had chilled me.

When he got off the phone, Eric rolled over towards me.

"My mom invited us to dinner." His hair stood up on end and his eyes were puffy. "What do you think?"

"I don't know. I really need to get back and call home."

"You can call from here. I'll leave if you want me to." Eric propped himself up on an elbow and reached over and touched my arm. I looked at him. "You don't have to go if you don't want. I told my mom I'd think about it, but we still have to go and get the van. I was thinking that maybe you would want it."

"Really?" I asked.

"I don't have much use for it and really no place to put it. My mom, I know doesn't want it sitting outside her house." He chuckled at this and then said, "What would the neighbors think?" Then he laughed some more and I joined him. When the laughter subsided he stared at me, then looked away.

"You're very pretty." He touched my arm and moved closer.

"You're hung over. Wait until it wears off."

"You're very exotic looking."

"My father's Indian, my mother was white, Irish or Scottish I think."

"I'm so white it's scary," Eric pulled his shirt up and indeed his skin was as white as the sheets, but there were little freckles and larger moles over his belly. "I'm Scandinavian, British and Polish. Extremely WASPy. The captain of all whiteness."

"I've noticed it's pretty white over in this part of town."

"Extremely. I guess that's why I'm drawn to you. You're different."

"Probably too different for me to go to your parent's place for dinner."

I moved to get out of the bed, but he placed his hand gently on my back, which kept me there.

"That depends on my Mom's mood," he said, "sometimes she gets weird."

"How weird." I said, laughing a little, "Wait, don't tell me. I can pretty much tell by your apartment." He sat up with me, looked around. "You don't even have so much as an extra piece of paper lying around."

He burst out laughing and moved over me and kissed me putting his lips hard over mine and pulling my arms up over my head holding them together. My body tightened. I didn't know quite how to respond. The nervousness I'd felt last night returned, but instead of fatigue an excitement overwhelmed me and I pulled him into me to let him know that it was all right. Eric ran a hand down over my neck and said "Relax," but my arms and legs seemed to shorten and stiffen. He moved the T-shirt I borrowed from him up over my hips then slipped it over my head and arms fluidly, expertly. He kissed me down my body, each point where his lips landed exploded in soft eruptions. When he brought my legs up I whispered to him, "I haven't done this before," though, as if by instinct, I brought his head down and began to feel the warm tremors that sustained me throughout the afternoon. When we rested afterwards he talked to me while he stroked my body and held me firmly against his chest.

What I learned about him was this. He was just finishing medical school and feeling like he had done nothing but go to work, school and sleep. He'd been a shamble of emotions, locked like a box sealed tight. Eric lived his days and nights under fluorescence and bad air mingling with the dead, sick and dying. As I learned more, he told me of the women he'd been with that he'd met in bars or in the hallways of hospitals. They were all defiantly ambitious. Their conversations and sex hurried as if their time together was just another appointment to be filled and dispensed with. As he approached the end of his internship, the emptiness of life took hold of him like a sudden gust of cold air on an August afternoon.

He got out of bed and stood at the side, naked. "We should go get the van. You don't have to have dinner with them if you don't want, but my mom can be rather insistent."

I got up and sat right in front of him. My head came to his waist and he drew me against him.

"We'll see," I said.

I gave him a slight squeeze and stood up to follow him into the kitchen while pulling his shirt over my head. This time I got a good look at his place. There were very few photographs, no plants and very little furniture. It was a place that didn't look like it was lived in much and probably wasn't. He'd said he'd spent most of his time at the hospital, but I also began to think that the rest of it he spent at his parents or someone else's place.

"I don't have much in the fridge," he said. He pulled on his sweats. "We'll grab something on the way. There's a little deli in town." For some reason there was no awkwardness with him. He was genuinely pleased that I'd stayed, had slept with him. As we moved around his apartment to get ready, he'd smile at me and come over to kiss me. I accepted those kisses because I was more amused by them than needy of them, though that would come.

Dinner with the Welch's was indeed strange. She'd coaxed us to stay, or rather for Eric to stay and I could eat so long as I was there anyway. They lived in the Pacific Palisades, which were lush and tree-filled. The air seemed damp there for summer and the small, winding streets were wet. The houses being built up the hill were allowed the ocean view, which stretched out on either side of the palisades as if painted in by a wide brush.

Their house seemed a larger version of Eric's apartment. Spare, spindly, modern furniture in muted oranges and browns mingled perfectly with bold, impressionistic art. They seemed to play off each other in a color scheme that was jarring to the eye, but exactly right. There were dark, metal sculptures on end tables and pedestals lit by special lights shot from the ceiling or the floor. It was all reflected in large, glass picture windows to capture the views during the day. It was truly impressive, unlike my overstuffed and haphazardly filled apartment, but their home was particularly devoid of warmth that said, 'welcome.'

In some ways their attitudes were progressive for the times. When Eric told them the story of Michael and how he had figured out he was homosexual his parents just nodded, asked a few questions and then let the subject drop. Maybe it was his father's work as a doctor that had given him a larger perspective, or his mother's college education. Her diploma was proudly displayed on the wall in her own study that she'd lined with books and art, sculptures, glass and paintings. Eric took me around the house and I had never before seen so much elegance and evidence of money.

Before dinner, while we stood in the backyard by their pool, glasses of wine in each of our hands, I studied Mrs. Welch with her hair done in a soft swoop down the left side of her face, gold earrings looped from her ears. She was dressed in a finely knit pantsuit that seemed to match the interior colors of the house. But what I noticed most of all were her sharp eyes, fine-lined with mascara, clearly saying, "You, my dear, are a tad out of your element." I responded by silently resolving to torture her by my presence for as long as possible. At dinner I learned that she had been with her husband for almost thirty years and had learned how and when to exact revenge.

After our salads, Mrs. Welch leaned into the table with her glass held near her cheek and said; "I think we should all be thankful for the children we bring into this world. It's the little things that are so important." She stared down the table at her husband, who was as short as Eric was, and asked, "Isn't that right, Frank?"

"That's right, honey," he replied in a way as if he hadn't heard her. Then he waited a moment and added, "That's right, children are so important."

During the rest of the dinner, I was continually dumbfounded that he really did listen to her as he went about eating as if it was the last meal he'd have on earth.

She turned to Eric and asked, "Have you heard from your sister?"

Eric stopped eating for a second and considered what to say. It was the first time I'd heard of a sister and I looked up from my plate to catch Eric stop eating and put down his fork when Mrs. Welch had asked after her.

"Melissa called yesterday. We spoke, I mean, she talked, I listened." Eric laughed at his joke. Mrs. Welch averted her eyes from Eric for a moment then looked at her husband. I could see that she was hurt or maybe jealous.

"Eric, would you tell your father to slow down. You know it's not good for the system." his mother said, chiding her husband indirectly, and Eric too, because he had also eaten very quickly. Eric smiled at his Dad who smiled back expecting the next thing that he'd say, but Eric just simply said, "Dad."

By the time I was finished with my potatoes the others had cleaned their plates and sat looking at me so I just stopped eating and said that I wasn't very hungry. Sitting there with them had unnerved me.

When we left, Mrs. Welch took my hand and shook it quickly and said, "how nice it was to meet you and I hope the rest of your school year goes well," as if it was the last time she was going to see me. I thanked her for dinner and stepped out into the front courtyard and watched her come up to Eric and hug him and smooth down his chest as if she were fixing a lapel.

"You do what's right by Michael. Give me a call in the morning." Eric looked over at me and smiled. "Eric?" she said drawing his attention away again.

"Will do. Thanks for having us over. We've got to go."

"Drive safely." Then the door was closed and we were both left standing on the front landing. I started laughing a little and Eric joined in.

"I hope I don't have to do that again," I said, glad that the dinner was over and that we had escaped from their house unscathed.

"No, I believe she has been satisfied... well, for a little while anyway. She likes to keep me in the fold as best she can. It nearly killed her when I went back East."

We went to the side of the carport where the van was. Eric fished in his pocket for the keys and opened the car door for me. It was the first time that had ever happened. I got up in the van and sat there while he closed the door. I rolled down the window and said, "Well, thanks for everything. I better go." I'd been gone now since early the night before and I was tired and beginning to feel a little sad about Michael while I put the key in the ignition. Though I hardly knew him, he'd worried himself into me in an inexplicable way.

"I've got a place I want to show you before you go. Will you follow me?"

"I don't know, it's been a long...."

I turned the engine over. It caught on the third try. I felt like I might be getting involved in a family that had too many silences between them and didn't know each other except for the things that were unimportant. The matter of his sister nagged at me, how she too might feel at odds with her parents. I thought that even though my father and I were now separate, we were still together and he knew that I would always come around for him if he needed me. Despite my pulling away, we were still close in a way that was unbreakable.

Eric pushed against the door and rocked back on his heels as he cocked his head in a pleading sort of way. "Won't take long, I promise... it's not that far." I looked at him and he seemed as if it was important to him that I go, so I nodded my head and found the clutch on the floor and locked the car into gear.

I followed his car down to a small inlet that was sheltered by cliffs and thick undergrowth. I was surprised by the ease at which I clambered down the steep rocky slope. I wasn't thinking of danger.

When we reached the sand he ran down to the edge of the water where the sea collected, foamed and disappeared in a frenzy of popping bubbles. He pulled his shirt and shorts off and waited until I joined him. He was white as daylight and practically hairless.

He coaxed me to him by waving his outstretched arms. I stood there, still not understanding his desire for me. I was not attractive in the way I thought I should be for someone like him and I didn't want him to see my body like this, frail as a spider web. But he stood there and I undressed for him to let him see me fully as I was - a woman with the misfortune of having large limbs for my body and breasts that folded out from my chest as if they'd been attached as an afterthought. But Eric drew me in with his short, thick arms and pulled me out into the water where our sounds were blanketed by the rolling surf.

"Nothing remains of me," he said, holding on to me in the dark roiling water. "I've spent so long getting to where I am, I've had no time to find out who I am. Now with you..."

I reached my arms around him and pulled him into me. There wasn't anything I could think of to say except, "Come here," and I said it in the most awkward way.

That summer we slipped into a routine together that would have upset my father had he known. I stayed in Santa Monica under the pretense of summer school, but I rarely attended class to make up the sleep that I lost as a result of my nights with Eric.

I used the van to drive back and forth between our apartments. I spent the first weekend cleaning out Michael's gardening tools and supplies and planted the remaining flowers in pots on Eric's balcony. The Cosmos grew to be enormous and bright as if they were meant to be the most beautiful of Michael's plantings, and as if he were somewhere looking down in approval of Eric and me.

Eric inspected a particularly handsome flower and said, "This one's so tall Michael could bend down and pick it if he wanted to." He'd fall silent for a while. The next day, when he was gone, I cut that particular flower loose and put it in a vase on the kitchen table to pretend that Michael really had reached down from the sky and chosen it just for us.

11.
Nicholas

When I was young, my Grandma almost always appeared at our house with gifts. They were the latest, best toys we'd seen advertised on television. I couldn't imagine how she found out about them because whenever we were at her house, she kept us so busy with yard work or swimming in her pool that we never turned on the set.

I'd been growing up awkward. My brother called me 'Gumby,' said I walked and talked like him. Some called me Stretch too, because I got so tall in junior high all of a sudden and stayed that way until my second year in high school when everyone else caught up. I also lacked coordination. During the summers at Grandma's house, I'd slip off the diving board or finish dives flat on my back or stomach. I remember bruises and the constant throb of pain in my legs as I hit them on the sides of the pool and the outside furniture that littered the decks. From what I remembered of my mother, I assumed I got her genes exclusively and Peter was lucky to be a mix of both her and Dad.

At home I was given the responsibility for the animals we kept, to feed them morning and night and also take out the trash. We had a couple of dogs and a cat that had strayed in one day and stayed. In summer, I was given odd jobs every morning before Dad went to work and usually finished them just before he got home.

When we were at our house my brother hung out with his friends on the beach. At twelve, he became this hormonal thing, which set the entire house on edge. He was very impressed with himself in those days and prone to long stretches of silence. Where I, on the other hand, talked endlessly about nothing. I'd walk behind him when he was home chattering about anything that came to mind. Finally, he'd turn around and say 'bug off.' Lydia, our stepmother, just let him be most of the time. She didn't know what to do with him from the beginning when she was brought into the picture shortly after we moved back with our father. In any case, she had my half-sister, Catherine, to worry about as she began teetering around the house.

Peter and I still shared a room though Dad split us apart for a time when we moved back to his house because Peter kept threatening to toss me out the window so that I'd land, my neck broken, on the ground far below our stilt-supported house. It got ugly some nights. Dad said it was just a phase, but when he and Lydia had our half-sister Catherine, I was moved back in with him. He cautioned me that Peter needed his space now that he was twelve and to just let him do what he wants. So I let him lead his life and I led mine - which, at ten years old, really didn't amount to much anyway.

I had stopped asking questions about Mom years ago. She'd faded from memory and was never discussed. In fact, Grandma pretty much took over when we came back. She practically moved in. She'd be there early mornings when we woke up and was the last person we'd see before bed. She smelled powdery like biscuits, but she never cooked. Her dress was smart and streamlined, nothing billowy or loose like the clothes Mom wore. Her manner was pointed and direct, she would say almost anything, but it wasn't out of shock value, it was more because that's just the way she was. Direct. People who weren't like her suffered miserably and I was one of them because I got to things when I got to them and not a moment sooner. I meandered around tasks eventually getting them done, but in a fashion and especially in my own way. Grandma and I locked horns plenty. If there were two people who were any more different, you'd have to go to the ends of the earth to find them.

I never got over being wary of my father, which had some bearing on our relationship. Mom had instilled in me a natural mistrust and though the events of the night we left her became faded and unclear, there are certain things once done that can never be undone.

Dad never started things. He'd never get out the ball to play catch or shoot baskets in our front driveway. But I didn't necessarily invite him to play anything either. We spent many years circling around each other like the spinning wheels in gyroscopes creating a singular energy between us, but moving in opposite directions. His attentions lay elsewhere and I couldn't say I was jealous of them really, because I had my own agenda. But as I grew older, less sure of my place in the world, there was nothing grounding me to an existence that I could hold on to.

Lydia commanded all his attention when she first moved in with us. She was blonde and pretty, her features set firmly. She had this easy way with everything though. It was as if she was an expert the moment she was born. Nothing was too difficult. She knew how to fix things, was a whiz at dreaming up snacks for Peter and me after school and casually ingratiated herself into our lives by impressing our friends.

Soon after she moved in, she dressed up in a sleek evening gown of blue satin with these bright, white heels that matched the fine string of pearls she put around her neck. She pulled Dad's best tux out and dressed me in it from top to bottom folding in the sleeves so that it would fit neatly. She even hand-tied the velvet blue bowtie Dad bought to match her dress. We pretended we were going out for the evening though the afternoon sun shown brightly through the house. Peter was our escort and did all the things that were requested of him. He served us Ding-Dongs, cookies and milk that we pretended was the finest meal we ever had out on the balcony overlooking the ocean. When we were through we strolled all around the house, moving from one room to the next as if at an opening of a museum. She had decorated the house thoughtfully. She chose pictures that reflected the colors of the hills in spring, the purples of the Jacaranda trees, the pinks of the ice plants and the yellows of all the flowers she planted along the edges of the walks and driveways. When we were done, she took Dad's clothes and put them perfectly back in place so he wouldn't know.

She truly enchanted me and treated us with such care that eventually I forgot that she wasn't really ours, but lent to us by our Dad when he wasn't home.

Our family was made up of teams that on any given day changed to fit the need though these little factions usually didn't include me. There was Dad and Lydia, Dad and Peter, Lydia and Catherine and Dad and Grandma. Once in a while it would be Lydia and me, but the occasions got rare as I got older. Grandpa stayed out of the picture altogether. He'd taken up gardening and, 'of all things', as Grandma would say, lawn bowling.

"I get so tired of pressing and trying to keep those all-white clothes clean that sometimes I just take them to the cleaners and let them deal with it. Your Grandpa's a lot of work, always has been, and always will be." Grandma usually smiled at herself after making such pronouncements. She'd gotten so she was tolerable now. Three grandkids had made her loosen up a bit. But she still had a way of intruding on our lives by buying us clothes we didn't like and inviting herself over for even the smallest occasions; even Catherine, who, at seven, was still soft as fresh dough, found things to do when Grandma was over.

One night she showed up just in time for dinner with Grandpa in tow. Lydia had come to expect Fridays with them, but it was a Wednesday, which caught her off guard. She'd looked over at my father who just shrugged and led his parents out of the room so places could be set for them. After a few moments Grandma returned to the kitchen and moved into it as if it was her own. Lydia took this in stride, but I came to feel contempt for grandmother, as I grew older. She was devoid of humility and compassion. Ultimately, I came to view the people in the Palisades as an extension of them - players in a game of one-upmanship with our family centered squarely on the wrong side. But in those early years, it seemed that nothing came hard for us and we passed through our days easily without struggle.

As I got older, I came to see that we had indeed struggled. Struggled internally. We never got close to being on the winning side. Grandmother tried to keep the boat of our family from listing and used her opinions and actions as ballast. If one member quietly slipped to the wrong side of the ship, she'd balance it out by a remark or an insinuation that cut through the easy demeanor of our lives. As a consequence, as we sat around our large table at our Friday dinners, we were acutely aware of each other's presence without ever stepping over the lines drawn in our shifting patterns of family alliances.

Though we weren't old enough to live in memory, conversations at dinner were always centered on the day's events and plans. The parade of accusations was stored up in memory that might or might not lead to family stories when we got together for birthdays and celebrations in the future. For now my Dad and

Grandmother kept the people at dinner on edge with their own particular brands of talk that at times would lead to awkward silences or impassioned rebuttals from those involved.

On one of those occasions, during a spring that seemed to be announcing summer early, so that all of the windows in the house were left open for the ocean breezes, Grandma sat picking at her food. She struck up a private conversation with Dad, talking low and into her plate.

"Your father is beginning to lose his hearing," she said.

"What are you talking about?" My Dad said, still chewing his food, but looking up at Grandpa. In that moment I detected a fleeting glimpse of horror on his face. Did he finally feel the onslaught of age hit him? Was he beginning to calculate the years he had left with his father? When he was faced with the certainties of age and death was there a moment of pure detachment from the world, as if all that he knew vanished and the world would keep on churning without him?

"Well, I have to shout at him all the time," Grandma said, "I have to repeat myself to him. Just today I was standing there looking him in the eye talking to him. After I got done with what I was saying, he just looked at me blank-faced. I asked him 'Did you hear what I said?' All he could say was 'sort of.' I couldn't believe it. I wish you would take him in and get his hearing checked. He won't do it with me."

"Do we have to talk about this now?" Grandpa asked.

"I just thought Eric should know." She looked at my Dad. "You should spend more time with him," she added. Dad stabbed at his steak.

"I'll try."

"He's not getting any younger, in fact he's a lot older than I am. Maybe a hearing aid would help, but I doubt he'll wear them." She talked as if Grandpa wasn't even there.

"We'll go next week, right Dad?" Grandpa nodded weakly and rolled his eyes. Dad said, "Can we talk about this later?"

The wide palate of Grandpa's forehead was perspiring from the heated dish that lay so close to his face. He was a retired doctor who had spent his whole life surgically removing the excesses of rich people's lives, making them live just a little longer and giving them reason to hope that they'll be remembered and loved, making them feel useful again. That was it, I thought, and yet here was my grandfather who, himself, had become useless, frail and bewildered in the eyes of the one person to whom he had devoted his life.

"I've noticed that, too," Lydia said, "I wanted to mention it."

Grandma said, "Well, it's a family matter," then she stopped. Dad shot his eyes sideways, which she caught. "Meaning you can bring it up if you want." Lydia fell silent, feeling unsure of her place in our family. Peter spoke up, "Yeah, I've been noticing that too." He looked over to Lydia and then at my Dad. At every chance, Peter stepped in to make things right even when it seemed hopeless, especially when it came to Grandmother. He made it a point to contradict her, and he was the only one she allowed to do it, which baffled me. As he grew older, it became a constant battle of wills with Grandma and after a few years, dinner with her became less frequent.

What happened finally was this. Lydia told my Dad that she must call before coming over and if she wished to stay longer than say an hour, Lydia would leave and come back when she was gone. My only wish was that I had had that much clout. I aligned myself with Lydia and she came to understand my desire to escape the scurrilous blandishments of my Grandmother by taking me with her when she left.

On those trips we'd go up to the village for ice cream and meander through the sidewalk shops. We ate out at the tiny restaurants or drove all the way into town for a movie. We'd run across the parks as lunatics, swooping over the grass with our arms and hollering up into the sky brazened with the knowing that we'd escaped the torments of Grandma. Sometimes I thought she was as young as I was and now I wished that my own mother had been as strong as Lydia and had learned to fight her as Lydia had learned to escape.

These were the only things that we kept from my Dad. We never told him what we did on those nights and days that seemed to drive deeper the wedge that kept our circular lives apart. Lydia only brushed his questions off with a kiss and a promise that she'd tell him later because we both knew that he'd forget to ask. She was the only person I came close enough to love, but there was always a scratch of something, a fluttery feeling I got in the pit of my stomach that kept me from giving myself over to her completely. Later I came to understand that it was because she belonged to my father first.

12.
Marjorie

Your father and I had been commuting for most of the summer between my apartment and his. The summer was hot, so much so that I'd stay at his place most nights because it was closer to the ocean and the cool air filtered through his apartment better than in my one room that only had a window and the screen door.

On a long weekend, we decided to escape the heat and went up the coast along the ocean. We drove all day, windows down; the highway filled with hundreds of people our age hitchhiking here and there, all of them with knapsacks and bedrolls, clothes that hung loosely over them like curtains. They seemed to multiply as we traveled farther north. We barely stopped to eat or fill up the car until we reached Big Sur where we made an early camp. The trip there and the campgrounds reminded me of Topanga because of the young people milling around their tents and vans, the way they looked, their eyes glazed over and hazed from drugs, their skin (underneath sunburns) pallid and ashen. I remarked to Eric how they looked and he just shrugged and was amused. I felt out of place again because they were like Michael and his friends, those people around the campfire. How they talked slowly and deliberately, working their mouths around words they could barely form in their minds because of what they were on.

When we pulled into Riverside Campground in South Big Sur, just below Big Sur Center, we managed to find a place to park the van, away from the other groups of cars, in an area of people like us who simply sat in their lawn chairs watching wide-mouthed as some of the people splashed around in the river nude, washing themselves and their clothes and then draping them over the rocks in the sun.

Riverside was the first place where I really listened to the sound of water. I can't explain to you how its soft music finally came to me, but I was sitting with Eric on some rocks that reached out into the wide river. Everything became silent except for the water.

My mind eased and cleared of all the things that had happened to me since leaving home for college, and Eric seemed content to just sit there with me, letting the sound of the water wash his face of its tightness. Even the light gave rhythm to the river as it filtered through the stands of redwoods that angled up into the sky like bridges to the clouds. In the morning you could smell their sweet dampness and watch them steam dry in the sun.

We were right to head north. In the deep valleys of the mountains, which rose up from the ocean, it was cool. Eric and I hiked up along the riverbed, stopping to eat, make love and talk. It was at the end of the day that he asked me to marry him.

Eric came up behind me. I could feel him against my back, wet from the uphill hike.

He was out of breath, "Marry me, Marjorie."

I wasn't startled, but surprised and pleased. But still I hesitated, "Are you sure?" He turned me around. He was very serious. "Of course, I am."

I was caught up between where we were in the mountains, and how he was that weekend - all deferential, open and light - that I didn't think of his family and what they might say and do. It wasn't important at the time.

"Okay," I said. At the time, it was important that I thought someone loved me other than my father and that no one could change that or interfere with it. How wrong I was to believe that a blanket of love could protect me from others. I was wrong to think that I could be strong enough to withstand the pressure of marriage into a family I didn't understand and everything that I wasn't a part of. But, for a short time, we found solace in those dark glorious canyons, the snap of cool air, smells of liquid bark and loam. There was nothing like it. I knew I would return someday. What I didn't know was that Big Sur, its sweeping coastline of palisades and mountains; its carpets of golden grass and tangled masses of cypress would eventually become my refuge.

When we came home after the thrill of the weekend, trouble found us the moment we walked in the door. We drove straight to my house to pick up some of my clothes. I was looking through my drawers when the phone rang. "Get the phone, will you?" I didn't realize that Eric had gone outside because of the heat in my apartment. The phone continued ringing. I moved around my bed, dropping the things I'd picked out on the floor, but then Eric ran in and plucked the receiver from its cradle.

"Hello," Eric said into it as I stood there out of breath.

His look said 'beat you to it' since he was still in a good mood from the weekend, but a little tired. "Can I tell her who's calling?"

"A what?" His forehead crinkled up. "A Mrs. Jorgenson?" I put my hand out and mouthed to him: "Give me the receiver." Eric began to be condescending, "Are you Swedish? Wait, I can't understand..."

"Now," I said, then wrestled the receiver away from him.

"Mrs. Jorgenson?" She was crying. "Wait.... stop, Mrs. Jorgenson."

"Your father," She coughed, a loud smacking kind of a noise, "the car, the car was in the garage..." The room around me disappeared.

"Mrs. Jorgenson...please, go slow. What happened?"

"Did you see the news?" she asked.

"No, no I haven't. What is it?"

"Henry lost so many friends... so many... the accident must have been awful," again, the coughing and then a wheezing sound. "I guess that's why he did it," she said.

"Did what.... Mrs. Jorgenson, what?" I screamed into the phone.

"Henry killed himself....the garage....in the car. You know the windows were up and all." I stopped hearing her. Eric looked over at me laughing at something on the T.V. then he stopped, got up from the chair and came over towards me.

"Marjorie...Marjorie...look at me..." He took the phone from my hand. "Hello, Mrs. Jorgenson. What's wrong?"

I stood there still as frozen water and when I came back, Eric was hanging up the phone, picking the keys off the hook in the kitchen and pulling me out the door towards the van.

We drove around the corner and came up the street where the houses I'd known growing up were shuttered and closed, the neighbors having deserted the cul de sac. Mrs. Jorgenson, however, stood out in my father's driveway, her hands knotted together over her large white sweater. I didn't come home much during the summer, though I was only forty minutes away. I made a conscious effort to move away from that life, coming up with excuses for my father when he called.

I stepped out of the van and walked up the driveway staring at the Dodge sitting silently in the garage. Mrs. Jorgenson followed close behind, "They've taken him away, "she said, "they just left." Eric came up and held me around my waist. I moved away from him and he and Mrs. Jorgenson stood on the outside of the garage and watched me go in.

There was still a lingering stench of exhaust, heavy and delineated that burned my eyes. I ran my hand down the side of the Dodge, still slightly warm, and climbed in. My body sank into the seat and the familiar, dented in feel of my father's weight.

I thought about his life there in that house. How isolating it must have been for him after I'd left and Mrs. Martinez broke away from him when her son moved home. How, over the years, he'd tried to befriend the neighbors, but felt their mistrust because of his imposing size. Not once were we invited into their homes on holidays or during special occasions. My father had made an effort towards each of them when they moved into his neighborhood - he had been there the longest - and never was his kindness returned.

A rush of anger came over me and I scrambled out of the car smashing my arm against the door. I ran into the driveway shouting, "How could you do this? How could this happen? Get out here in the street! I want to see you!" I screamed at the neighbors' houses and their inhabitants for their secretive selves, for never once allowing us to enter into their worlds as we had offered ours up to them. I felt hot, my neck contracted tightly and my arms broke out in small beads of sweat. I ran around the cul-de-sac, my shouts echoing off the shuttered houses.

As I reached the last house I saw Mrs. Martinez come up the street, her fat shoulders exposed under her sundress. I started for her, my legs carrying someone I didn't know. She saw me and stopped. "You!" I shouted at her, "How could you! You fucked him for fourteen years and just turned him away! Just like that." I ran towards her. When I reached her I shook her. "How could you let him die?" I grabbed at the fleshy arms and she cried out. Eric came running from the driveway and yanked me back but I tore away from him and walked away towards another house bordering our street.

The woman shouted after me in her thick, accented voice, "I didn't know...I was at work...I just found out..." I spun around to go after her again, but she sank to the ground, curled herself up on her hands and knees and began wailing.

Her back heaved. I frightened her so badly she was sick on the pavement. I felt myself go slack. My own knees gave way to the hot asphalt. I doubled over gasping for breath and held on to the only person who shared tender memories of my father.

Mrs. Jorgenson lifted the woman to her feet from the pavement and took her inside the house.

"What the hell was that all about?" Eric said standing above me. "I don't know what got into you, but I think you'd better apologize to that lady." He threw a handkerchief on the ground in front of me, "Here, wipe your face," he said, and then walked past me into the house. I was left kneeling in the middle of the street, fighting for breath and smudging streaks of black dust from the street across my wet face.

Until that moment, I hadn't realized my contempt for other women. I'd no experience with them save for Mrs. Jorgenson, so they came to me as mysterious creatures unfocused as pebbled glass. I'd never shared their confidences so it was easy to dismiss them as meddlers in my life.

I stared at my reflection in the window of the kitchen I'd taken refuge in. It was now a face at odds with what I'd remembered of my mother. Her coming back to me was a surprise. I looked at her, the lines on her face, the way one eyelid sort of closed at half-mast; her lips centered perfectly and tightly under her small nose. I put my hand up to my face and her reflection disappeared to reveal mine. I wanted her there, but all I could feel was loss and a feeling of desolation, as if the house had finally given up its last occupant and breathed a sigh of relief. I knew I wanted to be rid of it as soon as possible.

Eric came up behind me, wrapped his arms under mine. "I'm sorry I was angry with you. Here's ice for that shoulder," he said.

Mrs. Jorgenson came into the room and held out a bag to me. "I'm going to stay with Mrs. Martinez," she said, moving the bag up to the hurt. "Here hold it like this." Then she went down the hallway to the restroom.

"What do you think we should do?" I asked.

"We can stay here, if you want."

"No."

"We have the rest of the day. I don't have anything I have to do." Eric reached up and pulled my hair back in a ponytail and stroked it. I could feel his fingers, the way they caught and moved through. I didn't know what I would say to Mrs. Martinez.

She came unsteadily out of the bathroom with Mrs. Jorgenson. I watched her come down the hall and turn into the living room. I could feel Eric tighten his fingers on me then let go. I went to where Mrs. Martinez sat on the couch. "There was the accident on the television," she said softly, "Five of them are dead. I saw it. They said Henry caused the accident. He was driving a tractor and split a water pipe and flooded a ditch where the men worked. "I left my shop to come see if he was all right."

"I should have been here," I said. "I should have stayed the summer."

"You didn't treat him well," Mrs. Martinez said, "he wanted to see you more. And this boy who comes with you he never met. Don't tell me about turning him away. We stayed here together sometimes after you left."

My voice flattened out. "Please go home now."

"There are some things I want of his," She said and stood up, her face inches from mine, "There is a necklace I gave him, and a shirt."

"Take whatever you want."

"And a photograph he had of me and him." She stared hard at me, unblinking. "You will want him some day and he won't be here anymore." Then she left down the hall to his bedroom. I turned to Eric and holding on to him said, "I need to go."

Mrs. Jorgenson dug a shaking hand into a pocket and pulled out a tissue, which she wiped at her eyes. I went to her and brought her sweater back over her shoulder and patted her there. She cupped her palm over my cheek and brought two fingers to my lips. There wasn't anyone to call, no relatives to speak of. Dad was the last. I looked around the room, took in what I needed to remember and walked out the front door.

I made arrangements for my father's funeral from Eric's apartment and through Mrs. Jorgenson. The other men who died had a large funeral, parts of which were on television. It was the worst accident in the water district's history and caused by negligence they said and blamed my father who'd worked for the district almost twenty-five years.

There were only a few people for his service at the cemetery. Mrs. Martinez stood stiffly by in a pleated dress that billowed in the wind. Her son had not been invited and I had a thought that she would take this love to her grave also. There was a representative from the water district, who didn't speak, but a few of the other employees showed up and the presiding priest kept the service short. I held a strand of beads we danced with around the fire on those camping trips we went on. I shook them a few times to hear the sound once more, then I laid them gently over his casket as they lowered him into the ground.

13.
Nicholas

I've never believed in four-leaf clovers, the lucky rub of a rabbit's foot or the star that hangs in the night sky to wish upon. Luck wasn't part of what I knew when I was twelve. Life was life. You either got bound by it or stuck wishing for things that seemed forever beyond reach. My stepmother, Lydia, called my attitude "horribalizing." She said I always expected the worst in things. I called it the study of reality, where things expected to happen, happened.

There wasn't much room for the extraordinary and wonder disappeared from my life just as surely as I put years under my feet. But every so often things came forward to restore my faith in the wish or the trepidation I feel when heading into something unknown, hoping that the outcome will lead me down unexpected paths. I felt like this when my older brother, Peter, and I decided to build a fort.

My father's house was situated on the bluffs overlooking the ocean. Next to it there was a flat patch of ground before the earth escaped into a ravine. There was a stand of eucalyptus trees that surrounded an oak the size of the sun. In the thick limbs we decided to fashion a fort from scraps of plywood we scavenged from underneath the stilts of our house and some neighbors who'd leaned discarded pieces against the walls by their homes. We promised the speedy return of saws, hammers, ladders and crowbars. We found two-inch nails and leftover pieces of two by four that we nailed into the side of the tree for steps. We pulled the larger rectangles of wood up with a rope over a limb. Peter, older than I was by two years, did the sawing and I held the wood in place. Soon the floor took shape.

We worked all day. The sun was hot and Peter went shirtless. He had begun to put on weight, his body thickening into adulthood. He'd started to slip into the bathroom quietly, wrapped in a robe. He took to running on the beach and when he came back, the sweat glistened off his changing body. For me, there were surprising moments of change in him. He became quieter and more deferential to the women who came by our house. It didn't matter whether they were just neighbors or friends of Lydia. He treated them all with a gentility that before was nonexistent. I sensed that the building of this fort was going to be his last childish effort before slipping away from me in his need for independence.

Dad came down in the evening to inspect the progress and offer suggestions. That first night he ended up nailing in the supports for the floor in his business suit, ripping the sleeve of his white shirt on a nail. I stood and watched as he and Peter worked. They were good together, not needing to talk, but knowing instinctively what each other wanted. I handed up more supplies as they were needed, but mostly listened to the rapping of the hammer on the wood going into the limbs. As it grew dark, Dad and Peter scrambled down. We stood there with our hands on our hips, Dad holding a hammer and Peter the nails as we looked up together into the tree and were satisfied.

"You've got yourselves a good hideaway there, boys. I feel a little better about it anyway."

"Can we sleep up there tonight?" I asked.

"You need to get the sides up first. Maybe tomorrow night. Let's go. Lydia's probably got dinner on for us."

Walking up the hill we were like three men coming back from a mission; self important, flush with accomplishment and full of the silent knowledge that we had achieved something great, something that we knew in our heart of hearts would keep the demons at bay.

I woke in the middle of the night, turned in my bed and looked out over the wooded ravine that was just beyond my window. The moon draped shadows over the ground like curtains until the fog moved in silently and took the view away. I fell into sleep, but when I woke up, Peter was dressed and at the kitchen table gulping down Cheerios and jellied toast.

"Slow down, slow down," Lydia said to him, "I don't want to have to turn you upside down when you choke." When I walked into the kitchen she turned and looked at me. "Hi, sleepyhead! I didn't have the heart to wake you."

"Where's Dad?" I said, as I pulled myself into a chair.

"Already gone. What do you want for breakfast?" She got up from the table.

I looked over at Peter. "Same as him."

In these few days, Lydia became just a step mom. She facilitated our work by bringing us sandwiches, cold drinks and in the afternoon, lemon pies and chocolate chip cookies. She knew the score. She brought our sister, Catherine, down to sit and watch us build the sides of the fort, cut in the trap door, then fasten in the rope so we could pull it up to secure our domain.

At the end of the day we'd finished it. We brought sleeping bags out from the house and laid them in, spreading them out over an old blanket Lydia gave us. She bought us a lantern that ran off a 9-volt battery, the largest battery we'd ever seen except for the ones in the cars. We took Dad's binoculars so we could watch the stars and keep a lookout for intruders. Lydia brought us down a thermos of milk, slices of cake and sandwiches, which we hid in a cubbyhole we'd built for secret things.

Night came. After television, dinner and showers we ran down the hill towards the fort. We climbed up the tree using the rope and pulled it up after us. We took off our sweatshirts. I climbed into my sleeping bag and sat up to look out over the edge. Peter got into his bag next to me and switched off the lantern. I lay down, grabbed the binoculars and brought them to my face. I picked out a star between the leaves and focused on it. The flickering light appeared and disappeared as the wind shook the leaves and the weight of the binoculars made it hard to hold them in place.

"Here, let me see." Peter said, as I gave up the binoculars to him. I sat up and placed my hand over the front of them. "I can't see anything," he said. I laughed when he found out I'd covered the glass and then he punched me.

"Hey, don't hit me."

"You're such a pain in the ass sometimes. Why do you have to be such a pain in the ass?"

"I am not," I said. Peter went back to the binoculars.

"I wonder what it would be like to be up there like astronauts," he said, "It must be pretty neat."

I lay back down and gazed up. "Yeah, it must be. Do you want some cake?"

"No, let's save it."

"Okay, but I'm going to have some milk." I took out the thermos from its bag and unscrewed the top. "You want some?"

"No," he said, still peering through the binoculars.

I took two swallows, put it back. "This is pretty great up here, isn't it?"

"Yeah, pretty cool." I stretched out in my bag again and fell silent listening to the outside noises.

After a while Peter put down the glasses, "Do you remember Mom very much?"

"No," I said, "Not really."

"Nothing?"

"Well, a little bit, maybe."

"What?" Peter got up and sat against the side of the fort.

"I don't know, the house up north, I guess."

"Do you remember the time Dad and I left after all those people came and talked to us?"

"Not really," I said. The days after we got back were a blur. I stayed with Grandma for a couple of weeks. I remembered Grandma taking Peter out to buy clothes though because they seemed so different. He came back with two suits and matching shoes.

"Nicholas?"

"Yeah?"

"We didn't go fishing," He sat and stared at me. I sat up too and looked back at him. "We drove up to see Mom..."

"You saw Mom after we left her?" I was surprised, but bright light slipped across the branches. Peter came over to my side and we both looked out across the ravine. We heard the low rumble of a car as it came to a stop against the far edge. The engine idled then stopped. The headlights shone directly on our tree then snapped off. The car doors opened and we heard voices, laughter. We couldn't make anything out, but we listened hard. The voices seemed to come toward us. Leaves rustled and branches broke; I could hear the people running down the hill. Peter looked at me and put a finger up to his mouth. I nodded. There were two distinct voices, one high and soft, the other low, deep. As their noise rushed toward us, we bent down so that just our eyes and foreheads poked out over the side.

When they ran under us, we ducked down farther, then swung over to the other side and watched them as they disappeared into the blackness. Peter pushed our bags to the side and opened the trap door.

"What are you doing?"

"Get our sweatshirts!"

I reached over and pulled them out of our knapsack. Peter threw the rope down and was halfway out of the fort before I turned back around. "Throw me the shirts." I tossed them down. "Now you go," he half whispered. I pushed myself out of the hole and slid down the rope and jumped the last couple of feet.

"Shh." Peter put his palm out to me. I stopped in my tracks. We listened. We heard a shriek echo up the ravine. We started down the trail towards the beach. The trees and overgrowth blocked out the moonlight, but our eyes adjusted and we made our way down easily. As we came close to the beach we kept low to the ground. When we crested a small hill we saw them out on the sand, which was blue against the dark, glassy reflection of the ocean.

They had moved into each other so it looked as if there was only one heavy person. The shape kept changing as they pressed together.

"What do you think they're doing?"

"They're just kissing," Peter said, "c'mon let's go."

"Now?" I was fascinated. I didn't want to move.

"Now." he said. So we scrambled up over the dirt hill and crawled against the cliff. Peter stopped halfway. "Stay put."

"Okay," I said, wide-eyed and hot from the sweatshirt.

Peter inched away from me and stood up against the wall of dirt. Then he slipped into the darkness to where I couldn't see him anymore. I turned my attention back to the two people. They split apart and walked towards the water and sat down. When she sat in front of him and he brought her in close between his legs they moved as one person again. Silence interrupted their laughter and talking. I thought I could make out his hand touching her face, how he lightly ran his fingers over her cheek and then bent his face into her. I saw how she moved her face into him and reach up to meet his kiss.

Peter let out a scream and yelled, "We see you!" Then he laughed loud and flashed by me. "C'mon, Nicholas, c'mon!" I saw one of the two jump up startled.

I got to my feet and ran after Peter over the hill and onto the trail leading back up the ravine. "Jesus, Peter, what'd you do that for!" I yelled after him. He was running just up ahead.

I heard the man shouting at us down on the beach. "Get out of here you little shits!"

I looked back. I could see his shape standing on the hill looking after us. I stopped and squinted my eyes hard at him trying to make him out. But he turned and disappeared back over the edge to the beach.

"Nicholas, let's go!"

I ran up the hill after Peter who was still laughing, choking down breaths of air between squeals.

"You didn't have to do that." I said.

"They weren't doing nothin'."

"So. What if they were going to?" My heart was beating a thousand times a minute.

"I've seen it before." Peter said.

"You liar."

"I'm not lying. You wouldn't know what it looked like anyway. Let's go back to the fort." I followed Peter and climbed up the rope first. I took my sweatshirt off and stuffed it in the knapsack and put it up to be a pillow. When Peter came through the hole in the floor he latched the trap door and climbed into his bag. I could hear him breathing, but he kept himself sitting up and looked out over the side of the fort towards the beach. He was very still, his broadening shoulder rested on the strong side of the fort.

I lay down and peered up through the branches of the oak tree. I wondered then what it would have been like to be her. How it would feel to be held by someone that tight, never letting go. I saw the stars and wished for one of them to grant me that feeling - something that was in my realm of possibility, a gift that I could feel lucky about, to find in the clover a four-leafed blade. Because, at that moment, that was all I wanted, to be held by someone just like that.

14.
Marjorie

When we were married, I refused to wear white - I insisted on wearing a pale yellow chiffon gown. It was a compromise between myself, and the feelings of the Welch's, who'd agreed to throw a small reception afterwards. I looked like one of The Supremes, all angular, skinny to a fault and curiously out of date. My only guest was Mrs. Jorgenson, who gave me away with a soft push towards the priest. I kept looking at her as my only link to the past, but she smiled constantly, unaware of my need for her that day.

Eric wore a black tuxedo with a white cummerbund though he matched my dress with a tiny yellow boutonniere and a satin button-snap bow tie. We looked more like silly prom-goers. He had a somewhat dazed look to him and his eyes were watery and distant. I asked him if anything was wrong, he said, "No."

Mrs. Welch flitted about like a fly deciding where to land. It was the only day I was going to let her fuss about me because I knew it was for her benefit more than mine. She'd relaxed into the fact that her only son was going to marry me and convinced herself that she would make the best of an awkward situation. I was not the kind of person she had in mind.

Mr. Welch watched casually from the corners and was pressured into dancing by his daughter who had flown in from the East. She seemed pre-occupied and loose-limbed when I saw her, her face all smirks one minute then deadly serious the next. I couldn't really figure her out.

I was trying on make-up at the Welch's a couple of days before the wedding when she arrived. She came in looking almost distracted and was overburdened by her luggage. It looked as if she was going to be staying for a while, but as it turned out she was gone shortly after the wedding because there was no one left for her to talk to when Eric and I left.

"Why you're so pretty," she said off-handedly, "I didn't expect you to be so pretty."

I said, "Oh? I'm not disappointing you, am I?" Maybe I was too glib. I suspected she got all her information from her mother.

"I'm sorry," she said, "that was a rotten thing to say. My name's Melissa, how do you like me so far?" She laughed in a fluttery sort of way. She seemed to not be connecting with herself. Her body did one thing, but her head caught up with her as if it had just remembered something. Her actions were vaguely familiar because they reminded me of the people we'd seen in Big Sur and up in Topanga. I thought that maybe she was on something.

"I think what I need is a glass of water." She threw her luggage in a heap on the ground. "It is always so hot out here. That's why I left. No seasons to speak of. Follow me." Even her brain tittered.

I gave her a couple of feet as I walked behind her. I stood clear from her in the kitchen as she shuffled through some cabinets looking for glasses.

"Mom always moves things around. Usually, you know, most mothers kind of leave things where they've been for thousands of years." She gestured to a cupboard, "Plates go here, then the good glasses, then the shitty glasses and the shitty plates. But no, every time I come home, everything's all turned around." She found a glass. "Would you like one?"

"Sure," I said.

"So, Eric tells me your father just died a few months ago."

"Yes."

"That must have been awful. I don't know what I'd do if Dad died. As it is I hardly ever see him now." She paused for a moment considering this. "Wow, you must have had a busy summer."

"I had a lot of stuff to get rid of. I sold the house. Got rid of most everything. There's some of it in storage." Mrs. Jorgenson took some of the furniture over to her cousins. The Dodge I put in the newspaper and sold over a weekend to a couple of kids looking to restore old cars. I closed the house up and left it for a real-estate agent to handle. In retrospect I should have done it myself. There was very little left over after the commissions and the bank loan. That area where we lived hadn't appreciated considerably and my father only put a small down payment against the loan. Financial dealings were something I wasn't prepared to understand. Eric was too busy with finishing up his residency.

Melissa filled the glasses from the tap. "I already miss New York. This place is so boring." She picked at her skirt, a paisley frilly thing that shook at the slightest movement so that the designs blurred and dazzled the eye. I wanted to clamp my hands on her to make her stay still, but since she came into the house she was a whirligig of movement. The women of that house flustered me so.

We went back to the make-up table, which was covered with colored vials of lipstick and nail polish and all the paraphernalia Mrs. Welch had for what she called "putting on my face."

"You would look so pretty in this!" Melissa said. She picked out a loud, reddish-orange color. "Here, let me try it on you." She applied it in two swipes then carefully followed the line of my lips. "There." She stepped back. "Hmmm. No, I was wrong. Lean forward." She took a tissue and, taking my lips with her, wiped it off. "You definitely need something modern, though."

"I'll find something," I said.

"Oh, this is the fun part. We've only just begun." By the time Mrs. Welch came out to discover that her daughter had come home, my lips were sore after trying every color there was.

"Honestly, Melissa, why didn't you tell me you were home." She studied my face as she talked.

"I just got so involved here, I forgot." She said, never looking up from what she was doing. "Well, I just don't know what color will work. Maybe we'll go out shopping later." She sat back in her chair, exasperated, and looked at her mother.

"You really need some more modern colors, Mom."

"I just got some of those last week. The saleswoman was very insistent that they were the latest." She picked up one of the vials and held it out to her. "Especially this one if I recall."

"You were snowballed."

"Then you two should go out." Mrs. Welch turned and walked out the sliding glass door to the backyard.

"I think I offended her," Melissa shook her head, "I better go make up." Then she got up and left me with cleaning up the mess we made and the same plain face I had before she arrived.

After we got back from shopping, Eric came over to his parents early from work to see his sister. I watched them. They were very close and I suspected they needed to be growing up. They called each other across country several times a week and Eric would lie about laughing and interjecting every so often and I would listen to the conversation, what little there was of it on my end. Every time I asked Eric what they talked about he would say, "Oh, just stuff."

We stood together in the living room. "So you met Marjorie?" Eric said.

"Yes, we've had a fine time, haven't we?" Melissa said. I wouldn't have said that, but I nodded my head. Melissa continued, "We went shopping and found the best lipstick and nail polish." She smiled at me. I smiled back. "She's going to be stunning so you better buck up." She grabbed Eric's arm and guided him outside leaving me standing there with a dumb smile and nothing to do.

Eric was deferential to her. She stood over him by a couple of inches, and the way she did her hair doubled that - which was part of it, but she sucked up the air around him so that he didn't have any choice. I imagined she fit in very well back East.

Through the summer, Eric was very talkative. After seeing the way his mother and sister were, it was no surprise. He'd stored up mountains of things to say, and the past three months had been an avalanche of information. The curious thing was, however, hardly any of it had to do with his family. It was as if he'd had enough of them.

But I listened to him intently, and as I listened, I became more necessary to him. He needed to be filled up. It didn't matter what it was he said. My father had died and there was no one else to listen to. I escaped into his world and eventually left school shortly after the fall quarter had started. At the time, we fed on each other and I grew to need him.

Robert Kennedy was shot a month after you were born. It was a time of assassinations. You came out brownish and wrinkled as crumpled grocery sacks. We thought that you had a rough go of it in the womb the way your body curved into itself. Your hands, too, were boxed over your ears as if to protect yourself from the shouting that began to occur in our house. The doctor lifted you up and stretched your arms and legs out, shaped your head, then cut you from me.

Eight years had passed since your father and I married. Mr. Welch gave his practice over to Eric in the fourth year and Mrs. Welch had asserted herself into our family even more. Eric was spending an enormous amount of time at the office and left me to deal with her. When he opened the door to the delivery room, I felt a rush of cold from the overly air-conditioned hospital corridor. He came just in time from his own surgery in another wing to look in on us and see you come brightly into the world.

When Peter was born, he was a wondrous, but petulant little thing with large blue eyes like his father's. Mrs. Welch had slipped her genes in me because the child was clearly a combination of both her and Eric. He had merely passed through me. Peter learned early to hold onto things and to keep them hidden. He had a way of hooking his thumb up under his chin so that his fingers wrapped tightly around his ear like he was on the phone. Because he was the first, and because it was becoming clear that he was all I had, I forgave him everything.

You were born in the last days of August. Light from a hazy sun bounced in from the white outside walls of the hospital. The air in the room was moist and warm from my struggle. Your birth had been hard and yet I'd been told several times the second was supposed to be easier than the first. Maybe it was because I didn't remember, or maybe the pain got lost in the excitement of first time experiences, but you caused my body to shudder without rest or time to breathe. My screams shattered the air from the pain and I believe the walls were soundproofed because no one came in to see what all the fuss was about. I swore to myself that your birth would be the last.

When it was over, the Welch's came bouncing in as they had the first time, all toothy smiles and perfectly wrapped gifts.

"Oh, Eric, another perfect little boy. I wish Melissa could see this. Next time you'll have a little girl, O.K.?" Mrs. Welch said, giving the nurse the flowers with her best 'please take care of this' look. She was a marvel of unspoken language and had a way of wearing people down so that they'd automatically do what they thought she wanted. Now though, I thought I was taking part in the shared knowledge of women who've given birth, that bond that is always there, but never talked about. I believed I could get to her because of that, but I was wrong. She only wanted to see that I'd done my job properly without complaint, much like a broodmare who is only there to breed and bear. I was stunned the first time around, but when you came, I was prepared and was silent whenever she came in the room.

Mr. Welch stood back beaming against the wall after shaking hands with his son as if Eric had done all the work.

"Good job, Eric, good job indeed."

I laid there, legs still wide open, my body melted into the soaked sheets, feeling a bit like a spectator, but dazed and half crazy from the emptiness watching everyone around me. I also felt as if I had just performed for them. That the fluids and sounds emanating from my wasted self had very little to do with emotion and suffering, because I had suffered, but more because it was expected of me and that my performance had allowed me the luxury of living among the Welch clan with a certain degree of elegance.

15.
Nicholas

I was surprised to find Peter waiting for me in my room. He was a sophomore in high school and I was in the eighth grade. Peter was still thin, yet finely muscled from surfing and sometimes fighting. His brown hair was streaked blond and his body had a tan even in winter. He belonged to some sort of surfing gang that guarded its turf like hoodlums. But he had also discovered girls while I was still coolly detached. Peter wanted to borrow money.

"C'mon, ten bucks," he said, "I'll pay you back when we get our allowance."

"But that'll take two weeks," I said. "Maybe even until your birthday."

"No it won't, I promise."

"What are you gonna do for the next two weeks?" I tried to reason, "My ten dollars will be good as gone."

"Thanks, anyway," he said. He walked to my door. He was being unbelievably nice and I think that's what got me. "Why don't you ask Lydia?"

"Are you kidding? She'll want to know what it's for."

"What is it for?" If it was going to be me lending the money, I should have a right to know. Peter just looked at me stony-faced.

"Nothing, forget it." He turned to walk out the room.

"O.K.," I said, "I'll lend you the money, but you've got to promise..."

"I promise. I promise."

"O.K. Don't turn around," I said, moving secretly to my bottom drawer. I stashed my money in a worn, yellow cigar box. I pulled out two weeks worth of allowance I'd saved up, closed the drawer and then handed him the money. I lent it to him because I was surprised that he'd asked me. Dad really would have given him the money if he'd kept on him a little. He probably would have been too pre-occupied to ask what it was for. So it must have been really important that nobody knew. It was also a Friday when we got our allowance anyway so the additional five dollars we both got would have given Peter fifteen dollars. It gave me a fact-finding mission.

That same night, Aunt Melissa moved back to Los Angeles from New York and lived with us because she couldn't stomach the thought of living in that 'god-awful shrine to modern-living' she called my grandmother's house. We kept expecting her everyday for a week and just about seven in the evening we'd get a call saying she'd be there the following day. My father said that she was perpetually late even when they were growing up. I didn't mind her miscalculations because it was my room I was giving up.

When she finally did arrive, dressed head to toe in sheer, dark blue wool, the house seemed to balance itself out for the first time because all of our attentions moved towards her. She was exotic: a mix of high society and a cavalier world-weariness. I wondered how she escaped the Palisades and developed such an odd bent on life. From the moment she stepped through our doorway that evening, the walls echoed with high-pitched shrills of laughter.

She brought gifts for everyone, fancy wrapped presents with bows so big they sometimes overtook the presents themselves. "I haven't seen you all in so long, I just couldn't wait 'til Christmas Day." She rustled us into the living room where she passed her gifts around to each of us. To Dad she gave an umbrella, "It's from Saks...." My Dad dumbly looked at her, "Saks Fifth Avenue, silly. You can't get them like this out here."

"That's because we don't need them, but thanks anyway." Dad said.

"When did you become so ungrateful, Eric?" She slapped him across the leg lightly. Dad just shrugged. Aunt Melissa continued, "You're just like Mom. I couldn't figure out what to get you. I should have just given you the cash." She took the umbrella from him, opened it and twirled the colors this way and that, "Well, you never know when you're going to need it for travel."

"I don't travel much," he said. Aunt Melissa just glared at him, then turned her attention to Lydia.

She gave her some translucent pink bath oil beads. "Now these are from a little shop down in the East Village. I know you can't get these anywhere else. They bring them in from Vermont from some lady who makes them out of her house. A friend of mine owns the shop. They make you feel all tingly on the outside."

'They smell pretty,' Lydia said, glancing at my Dad, "I'll try to figure out a time to use them."

"Don't you and Eric take baths?" Aunt Melissa looked at her and winked.

"Mostly showers," Lydia laughed, "Baths are too much trouble."

"Why they're no trouble at all. God, if I couldn't take a bath at the end of the day I don't know what I'd do. It's the only thing that relaxes me. Well, that and men sometimes..." My aunt's laughter descended upon us again as my Dad looked at both Peter and me and then at his sister.

She brought me a rectangular gift that revealed a book bound by burnished red cloth when I opened it. It was old and battered and the gold marking had flaked off, but you could see the picture of what it was, a silhouette of a dog with a halo above its head like an angel. The side panel said, "Dog Stories."

"Since you can't have any dogs here on account of your stepmother's allergies, I thought that you should at least read up on them." She sat down next to me. "See, there are lots of pictures. The book may be a little young for you, but you should at least read the stories anyway." She turned to my brother, "Last, but certainly not least, " She handed him a long object, "for you, Peter."

Peter pulled off the paper that covered an old golf club made out of wood and iron. "Thanks, Aunt Melissa, but I don't know how to play golf," he said.

"That's just my point, " my aunt said, "it's time to learn." She took the club from Peter. "Everyone who is anyone in New York plays golf." She stood up and pretended she was going to putt. "This is supposed to inspire you. The lady at the antique shop looked me straight in the face and said that this club belonged to Rockefeller; that he used it to make a hole in one during one of those big tournaments he liked so much. I just had to buy it for you."

"Thanks, I guess," Peter said, trying not to laugh.

"Don't thank me now because you'll want to thank me later and you will have already used it up. Same goes for all of you." She said, looking around at us as we sat there staring at her. "We have to be forward thinkers. It's time that we got off to a proper start." She handed the club back to Peter grip forward. She looked at me with her hands on her hips as if she'd finished her job and smiled. I felt I'd found my comrade in arms.

She presented herself strong as an ox, but the real reason my aunt came to live with us became apparent after only a couple of days.

The following night she disappeared down to the beach. It was cold. The wind struck me full when I went out onto the deck we'd built up from the cliffs overlooking the ocean. I called out to her, but there was no answer. Lydia came outside from the kitchen and shouted after her and turned on the searchlights mounted on the roof.

"Go down and look for her, Nicholas. I'll finish up here. Find Peter too. Dinner's almost ready." I went to my bedroom, got my coat and turned around to find the contents of Aunt Melissa's handbag dumped out over my bed as if she was in a hurry. I could see small bottles of pills, like the ones Dad brought home with him from work sometimes for Lydia. There were at least fifteen of them strewn among lipsticks and compacts, wadded up pieces of paper and tissue, single keys, vials and pens - all kinds of pens with different markings on them. I started reading their sides: The Plaza Hotel, The Waldorf Astoria, The Regency, and The Mayflower.... There were at least twenty different pens from twenty different places, all worn on the outside as sea glass from being in her purse for so long. I took all of her things and scooped them back into the black bag and smoothed out the bedspread then took off down the hall in a dead run and out the door. I had to hurry.

As I raced down the steps leading down to the beach, the wind hit me, damp and icy. I gripped the railings heading down for balance and called out to my Aunt. In the floodlights from our house, I saw my Aunt in the water, her dress whipped around her body by the waves. She was laughing and bouncing foot to foot. I called out to her again. "Aunt Melissa!" She was holding her arms out, testing the rising and retreating water and slapping at it as if trying to shoo it away, willing it away from her body as she stepped deeper and deeper into the dark.

I ran into the waves shouting, "Aunt Melissa, Aunt Melissa, what are you doing?" I stopped.

She turned towards me as if she was taking a dip on a hot afternoon, "Oh, hi, Nicholas," she said, "I was just going for a swim."

"It's night, Aunt Melissa, it's winter."

"I know that, don't you think I know that?" She smiled at me. "You've come to rescue me haven't you?"

"Lydia sent me down. It's dinner.... I'll help you out." I started to shiver in the water as I reached for her, but she stepped farther away from me. The waves came stronger and I jumped to avoid the cold, my arms wanted to push the water away and Aunt Melissa too. The noise of the waves made me shout at her, but I really didn't want to because the louder I raised my voice, the deeper she went.

She swung her body towards me and said, "We should go up then, shouldn't we?" Aunt Melissa turned back to the waves, "but first, I think, a couple of more splashes." She stepped farther into the water and jumped up and down, flailing her arms.

"There's a drop-off, don't go out there." I shook now as the water soaked its way up my shirt. She seemed to consider what to do before she would have moved into the darkness.

"Perhaps not. Let's go to dinner." She twisted her body towards me and began walking out of the water. "Are you coming?" she asked. I stared at her.

"Yeah," was all I could say as I stood waist high in the water watching.

When we got up to the house, me following her, bent over into myself for warmth, Dad came running out through the back door. My Aunt fell into him, grabbed the front of his coat, and looked up into his face saying, "Hold me Eric, I'm sorry."

She kept repeating it as Dad moved her down the hall and motioned for me to go into his room. I watched them a moment. Then I opened the door to the bedroom and went inside. Dad came in as I was getting out of my clothes.

"Are you all right?" he reached out for my pants. "Here, let me have those." He took them as I nodded my head. My neck and shoulders involuntarily convulsed from the cold.

"I'll get the shower going. You stay in there as long as you need to." Then he looked at me, his eyes distant, "You did a brave thing," he said. "Thank you for that." I could see him losing himself, the lines around his eyes twitched as he blinked continuously. I went into the shower and stayed there through dinner and came out after Peter and Dad had left the table. Lydia heated up my plate again and made me a cup of hot chocolate. I ate there alone and listened to the quiet of the house. The laughter had vanished and the only thing left now was to deal with what was coming.

In the days that followed, Dad and Aunt Melissa talked endlessly. I watched him lead her outside to the porch, wrap her in a blanket and sit her down on one of the chaise-lounges. I could see her throw her head back and then let it slide to the side of her. She would be in a daze sometimes and it gave me a clear picture of my mother long ago. Grandma came by to see her and talked quietly to her just beyond the glass doors. Then she'd leave, her face streaked with black, and not talk to anyone as she walked out the front door.

Aunt Melissa and I made it through "Dog Stories" together. We spent long hours in the sun reading through each page like it was the last. We'd split the lines up for each character and she'd speak in a cartoon voice. I'd shake with laughter as I lay with her in the sun. To this day, I remember one of the stories about a hunter's dog, a bay retriever, it's coat gleaming from lake water who ran up to his master shaking and wagging his tail. The man was sitting down, resting, dozing in the hot sun when his dog shook out the water from its back, swinging his tail madly and accidentally knocked his master's gun down, making it fire. The man fell over to the ground and the dog sniffed around him never realizing that the blast had killed him. The dog stayed all day at his master's side wailing until someone came and found them. We'd just barely made it through the story when Aunt Melissa bent over in a fit of crying. I got up and looked down at her. She just sat there, her hands coming up to her face.

I went in and got Lydia, who came outside and led my aunt into my bedroom, poured out a cup of water and gave her a pill. I watched from the doorway and asked Lydia what happened. "She's just a little sad today, that's all."

"What's she so sad about?" I followed my stepmother into the kitchen where she picked up the phone.

"She's had a rough go of it, lately," she said dialing. "She'll be okay." Lydia looked at me. "I have to talk to your Dad by myself now, okay?"

"Sure." I said and went back outside. I picked up the book and reread the final page and found nothing that would have made me cry.

Aunt Melissa stayed through the winter and I saw a change in my Dad that was quite extraordinary. He stayed home now as much as he could. Instead of going out with Peter surfing in the early evenings, he'd sit with his sister or help Lydia with Catherine. He was more physical with us, often wrapping himself around his sister, Peter and me and standing with us for long moments. There was a gradual change in my Aunt as she became more consistent in her emotions. The five of us began to venture out for dinner. I could tell that this relieved Lydia, who would never let on that my Aunt's extended stay bothered her, but going out made her a little less on edge and everyone else.

We'd decided on an Italian restaurant in the village a couple of miles from home. We'd been served our meals. I sat and watched my Aunt move the spaghetti strands around her plate, then she stabbed at the lone meatball covered with the bright red sauce and just started talking, letting the words spill over each other. "I think what we have to realize is this," she said, "that the low pressure of life begins not in the first urgings of puberty, but when you are given carte blanche to act upon them. Everything is downhill from there because we place so many expectations on each other to fill our needs. That the best we can be is with another person. I, frankly, don't believe that. I have been quite alone for, let's see, eighteen years now and I've had nothing but trouble with the men I meet. Nothing but. Some people have asked me, 'well, have you ever thought it might be you?' I ask them, do you think it's me? Do you? They look back like I just slapped them in the face." She finished chewing her roll and went on, "I mean if you have a perspective on this, say of trying to do meaningful things in your life, and you keep getting stomped on, you're bound to say, 'Whoa, wait a minute. What's going on here?' Then you give yourself a few moments to catch your breath, and then you step back into the ring for some more one-on-one action with yourself. It's insane. I don't know. I'm tired of it, really. I'm really tired of it."

I looked at Dad because I couldn't figure out what she was trying to say. His eyes were watery and then he looked down into his plate. "Melissa, eat the rest of your food," Dad said to her quietly. "C'mon, let's just eat, okay?"

Melissa looked at him, then around the room. She twisted her fork through her fingers. Then she dropped it sharply to her plate. It clanged down and made me flinch. The dead ringing sound hung in the air. My father flinched too. He put down his fork and brought his napkin out of his lap and wiped up the splattered spaghetti sauce.

"How did you get so angry with yourself, Melissa?" He was upset now. "How did it happen?" He'd spent hours with her over the last three months and had watched his sister, someone whom he'd adored, disintegrate. It seemed to alter him and pull himself in. "I don't know what to do for you. I want to help you, but the disruption you've caused in our lives has got to stop. You've got to understand that we can only help you so far, so much, but now you have to get a grip on what's gotten to you. Mom doesn't know what to do with you and I certainly don't either." He put his hand over the back of her delicate fingers. He clenched down on them and brought her palm up to his lips and kissed it.

Melissa reached over to him and drew him in, "I'm not perfect like her, Eric. I try to be, I've always tried to be, but I've gotten lost trying." Then she reached out and gave my Dad a hard hug. Lydia sat through the whole thing quiet like a startled deer, all eyes and moving mouth, chewing on what she had left over from her last bite. Peter just sat back in his chair and watched what happened somewhat amazed.

"Who ever said you had to be like her? You know what she's done to my life, my kids, but we're hanging on I think. I can't understand why you came back after all these years. I really can't."

"What do you think my life was like back there? I was isolated, lonely, and all I could think of is how I'd failed at what I was supposed to be."

"What was that?" My Dad asked her.

"I was supposed to have a family. Look at your kids...Lydia. That's all I ever wanted."

Lydia, whose quiet disgust could be felt, but not heard, finally spoke up. "Yes, but look at what you've done."

"What?"

"You've been successful in business."

"Oh, bullshit," Aunt Melissa said loudly. "I slept with anyone who was higher up than me."

Lydia sat back, put her hands in her lap.

"Melissa," my Dad said, avoiding the eyes of the table next to us, "Melissa, stop."

"You have no idea what it's really like." she said, "You just have no idea."

"You always seemed as if you were doing great." Lydia hissed, "Eric always thought you were very successful. He told me so."

"Eric didn't know the half of it." Aunt Melissa pulled her body away from my Dad and tightened herself up.

"Then how could you come back here after all this time pretending your life was such a thrill and dump on our family like this. Not to mention the lies and stories you must have been telling Eric the past several years."

"Come on, you two. Stop this." Dad put his hands on the table. His face was white with anger.

"Do you want to talk about lies?" Melissa pulled her chair up next to the table. "You want to talk about stories? Have you ever asked my mother," - she gestured to my Dad - "our mother, how he ended up with the boys?"

"I know enough," Lydia said and moved into the table, too, so that by now the grown-ups crowded the table and Peter and I just looked at each other blankly expecting the worst when I looked at my Dad wondering what my Aunt had meant. There were things I remembered: my broken arm from my parents fighting between me and that long drive South from Big Sur, but I never was clear of the reasons my Mom and Dad had split up. My aunt had brought up something that had to be answered, but I knew that now wasn't the time to pursue it.

"Stop!" My Dad hissed. "Stop! We're leaving." He looked around for the waiter.

Just as the tempest had quickly grown, it disappeared and melted away. For the short time that my aunt had focused, became clear of her thoughts, I saw her as my mother, the scared rush of memory, the helpless pull of family dependency and the need to hold on to what was hers and only hers because that was all she had left. Her despondency rose up again like steam and crept across her face.

"I've made a mess of things again didn't I Eric?" She folded her hands up in her lap. "I've really done it this time."

"Almost, Melissa. I'm really disappointed in you, you too, Lydia, and I don't want this brought up ever again in front of the boys. Do you understand?" Finally the stress of the past few months forced itself out of my Dad. He really was helpless in deciding what to do, whether to break down or get up and leave the table. The confusion in his face was disarming, but in those few moments I saw him differently. I saw the chance for his own personal reconciliation and I felt an explosion of warmth and feeling towards my father that brought me back to him in a peculiar way, because I knew then that there might be a chance that we could meet halfway, that the return of his sister and her frightening condition had wounded him far deeper than he ever could have expected.

The following morning I came into the kitchen where Lydia and my Dad were. Lydia was standing at the kitchen sink looking out the window. My Dad was on the phone to my Grandmother. Aunt Melissa had left early that morning. Her things were gone and she left a simple note for my Dad. It said only, "Thank you."

We wouldn't hear from her for many years. But she did leave behind a changed man in my father. Lydia and he finally came together. They began taking off for the weekend together and seemed happier now. My Grandmother, on the other hand, almost never came over anymore and we rarely went to see her after my father had gone to talk with her about my sister.

I went down to the beach that morning to find my brother and tell him about Aunt Melissa. I also wanted to ask what Aunt Melissa had meant about our parents, but he was sitting there with a girl, his arm wrapped around her watching the surf. They were in blue jeans and colored t-shirts. Around her neck was a gold chain that sparkled new with a small heart medallion hanging from it. My brother looked at me and smiled. He introduced her. "This is Sandra, she likes to be called Sandy." He squeezed her and she gazed at me with bright green eyes. "This is my little brother, Nicholas." I extended my hand to her as I bent towards them.

"Nice to meet you," I said. She nodded and giggled a little in a tight, girlish way and moved in closer to Peter. I looked at him and he smiled at me. I decided not to tell him about Aunt Melissa's leaving just then. Instead, I looked back at Sandy, admired the necklace shining bright against her dark shirt and said to them simply, "I'll see you later," and walked away.

"See you back at the house, Nick," my brother called out after me in such a grown-up way that I was startled. He called me Nick, as if, I too, had been brought up out of the chasm of childhood into the world. As I walked alone back to the house, I looked down on them sitting on the sand. I brought my hands up over my head and stretched my body upwards. I wanted to touch what was just out of reach: that shocking blue sky that hung so heavily above me.

PART TWO

16.
Nicholas

My mother has been in the hospital five days now. She has been kept longer than anticipated because of some bruised ribs, internal swelling and a sprained ankle. I find myself growing numb to the blank, white walls wishing that some sort of color would splash across them overnight. I'm growing tired, too, of the drive to and from there, the stops and starts from the signs and the slow turns around the complex to the parking lot.

Matt is showing his frustration with me. I've become disinterested in sex. I don't have an appetite for it, which discourages him. I want to believe that he'll wait for me. I want to pull him into me again to make up for attacking him the night after my mother went into the hospital, but I can't. I can't summon the strength to reach for him across the bed, nor run my fingers along his face. When he runs his hand around to touch me, I pull it away up to my chest and urge him to just hold me. Our bed has become too small, the sheets pull and twist and the heavy covers barely keep me warm. I lie awake late at night.

I realize that my days are running together. The fog has come in permanently and doesn't lift above the pines. In the morning, I'm forced to run the wiper blades on the car it's so damp and thick. I drive to work, to the hospital at lunch, then work, back to the hospital, and then back home climbing into bed exhausted and worn as an old man.

I find myself sitting again listening to my mother's breathing: inhale, exhale, inhale, exhale... the sound she makes seems wintry and distant, like a far off plane passing through thick clouds. I'd gotten things to eat and brought them up, not wanting to sit among the families of other patients who murmur to each other and doctors who read their papers. The county hospital is grungy and unkempt, the walls old and curved. Patients with their IVs walk from one end of the hall to the other, bored and listless.

I called Peter, left a message; his voice comes at me thin and scratchy before the long beep. I feel that he's screening his calls now since he hasn't answered any of mine and never seems to be home. I decide to swing by his place later just to catch him in.

My mother stirs and moves her head to the side. Her eyes open and she looks at me. "You're here," she says, "You shouldn't stay so much."

"I had some time."

"You should go home to get some rest." She stares at me. Her face has lost a little color overnight.

"What's wrong?" she asks.

"Oh, nothing. We should comb your hair."

"That can wait." She sits up. I help her prop her pillow behind her back. She runs her fingers through her hair and adjusts it like she would a wig, sort of pushes it over from one side to the other.

"Last night there were these sounds like scraping metal, tinny and hard. It reminded me of the mental hospital they put me in. I heard them down the hall and

I had a picture of fat Louisa pushing that metal bucket around the wide day room. Mop, mop, scrape and then a loud clang."

"Don't think about that Mom. You're getting out of here in a couple of days..." I sit back down in my chair. There are things I want to know.

"That's where they put me, you know. Under lock and key in these white rooms like the inside of powder. Almost like you could float. And the people there, " she chuckles and bites her lip, "Well the people were a trip, way out there, and here I was just a little off, I guess. Here I was sitting there like I am now watching these people float by like angels in clouds."

Outside the room there is talking so low it sounds like thrumming. A deep hum takes me away from my mother's voice. I want to know what is being said. I feel like I'm becoming like her, paranoid and nervous, that any small thing could happen and she would be gone again. But my mother stops and I turn back to her. She reaches over to the water bottle, her hands stab inches from it, but her body is unwilling to make the extra effort.

"Could you reach that for me? They should always help you with this sort of thing, you know, when they put them so far away from the bed." I hand her a cup and pour the water from the pitcher into it. She takes a sip and the water slips down from the corner of her mouth. She doesn't try to wipe it up so I lean over and use the edge of my shirt-cuff to clean it away, but she jerks her head away and grimaces.

"There is just a little water," I say.

"If I'd wanted it gone, I'd have done it myself."

"I'm sorry." I fix my shirt again over my wrist and sit down. I wait a minute and try to change her mood, "So tell me what I was like."

"What?"

"How I was when I was little."

She considered me a while, then said, "Oh, you were quiet, kept to yourself mostly. I used to make these little buzzing sounds with my lips and zoom spoonfuls of food into your mouth. Even when I felt you should have been old enough to do it yourself." She looked at me, the lines around her eyes loosened, became wider. "Peter was very jealous of you. He hated it when I kicked him out of his high chair for you. But you'd sit and stare at me and accept anything that I'd fly in the air towards you. It didn't matter what it was or how much. You took such pleasure in eating that it scared me a little. You grew so fast. Then you got awkward and always fell down or caused accidents. I'd bandage you up and you were good as new."

I lean into her as her voice becomes flat and quiet. I'm concentrating on her words, her tone, but the life has disappeared from her memory.

"Both of you were always presenting me with gifts. You were still young enough where you gave me these wonderful little things like flower petals, every one of your stuffed animals and books, all kinds of books. Even the ones you had to drag down from the coffee table. But Peter had grown bolder and brought me dirt clods, the hair at the bottom of our showers and bugs and lizards from the back yard. I caught him peeing against the fence bordering the neighbor's yard; his little shorts were pulled down around his knees. I never had that kind of trouble with you. Never. But one day you brought me something that your father had..." She stops and looks away. Her eyes shut. I touch her for the first time because I want to. I reach out and place my fingers over hers and look at them. There is no movement from her, but I leave my hand there feeling the rough texture of the skin on her knuckles.

"I was in the kitchen fixing something for dinner. I remember this because it was something I never finished.... you came in, little hands in your pockets. You were making me guess which hand.... making a game of it. So I guessed and you held out your hand to me and showed me a tiny box. You said, 'I got this from Daddy's room.'

"What was it?" I asked, propelling her forward. I wanted to delve into my past and fill in the blanks, but she stops and motions for the water again. I go to the table and pour out the water, only this time I know she really doesn't want it. I can see her thoughts forming as I hand her the glass which she swipes at and sends it crashing to the floor.

"I will not take it." she says, "I will not take it again." Then she pulls the pillow from her back and sinks down into the bed like a sack of flour falling from a stack. "It is time for you to go," she says, "It's time."

"You can't do this, Mom," I bend down and wipe up the water. "You can't do this and expect to leave here in a couple of days." She doesn't answer. She pulls the covers over her head, as if to disappear into darkness. "I won't let you leave here like this." I take the towel and fold it neatly. I put it back in the drawer by her nightstand to avoid questioning by the nurse. I imagine her wanting to know everything that goes on with her patient. Why I wanted to hide the fact that I'd just cleaned up the result of my mother's irrational act I can't say, except this hospital was besting her and me, too.

I don't go by Peter's on the way home, instead straight to my house which is dark and empty as a black box. It doesn't retain heat these days and the air bristles and snaps with cold. I turn the thermostat up past eighty and strip out of my clothes, take my underwear off and climb under the covers much as my mother had when she didn't want to talk anymore. Thankfully, I fall instantly to sleep. It's only six in the evening.

Matt climbing into bed awakens me. He pulls the covers back and stretches his body out next to mine. I feel his legs and the hair on his chest and again he swings his arm over me and pulls me in. I don't know what to do, but I'm hard and turn to him and we make love. He pulls my legs up and enters me. I love him for this though it is an expression that is lost now. I keep it inside like a secret because I'm not ready to give into him. I want to, but not yet.

When we're finished, he gets up and goes into the bathroom. I hear the water in the shower running as he cleans up. It's so mechanical that I hate myself for it. There are so many things I want to be doing with him now, pulling his hair back with my fingers, stroking his shoulders, him... I feel all of this, but I can't force myself to move from the bed. I lay fully awake and as he turns off the water, I dread his shape in the doorway, his reappearance in bed and the smell of him that will be lovely as damp earth.

"I thought we'd never do that again," Matt says, rubbing the towel against him as he comes up next to me. "Did you know the heater was on full blast when I came home?"

"Yeah, I turned it up."

"Oh. I guess you don't care much about the heat bill."

"No I don't. Not right now anyway." I bury myself in the sheets.

"How's your mother?"

"She's getting there. Still a little out there. I never know what she wants. I try pulling information from her, but just as she gets going, she does something stupid." I'm wide-awake now - no more of the languorous, post-sex feeling is left and there is no going back to sleep.

"We need to talk," Matt says. I was waiting for this.

"Maybe I moved in too quick. Maybe you would rather be by yourself now." He sits on the edge of the bed right next to me, towel wrapped around his middle. I can smell him now and it strikes me deeply.

"Do you want to move out?" I ask and turn away.

"What I want is for you to be here right now and not look away. I need to know how you feel."

"I don't know how I feel," I say, turning back, "If I did, you would know. What I do want, though, is for you not to leave." I said it. I put it out there like a giant balloon, the heat taking it up away from me before I can reach out and pop it.

Matt just sat there and looked at me, his face a blank sheet. I couldn't tell whether he was considering it or dumbstruck as I was by my sudden need for him.

So I gave him an out. "If you don't want to deal with what I'm going through right now, I'll understand if you want to leave. I don't want you here if it is going to tear us apart. It's more than I want to deal with right now."

"Is this thing so terrible with your mom that you can't deal with me? Is it? I was here before she came back into the picture."

"I know."

"Suddenly she appears and you're gone. Just like that. I'm thinking that maybe we aren't strong enough together to make it through this. I'm thinking this and I just wanted you to know." Matt gets up from the bed and takes the towel from his waist and starts to dress. I watch him. There is a line that runs horizontally across his upper pelvis. I have studied it, touched it, and followed the length of it with my fingers and tongue. That scar, a blemish on his body from surgery didn't matter to me. In one of those small acts of acceptance of one another, I paid special attention to it, which made him smile when we began sleeping with each other.

He reached for his pants. "I'm going to my sister's. We talked earlier and she said I could stay with her for a little while."

"What do you want me to do, Matt? Beg you to stay?" I got up and went to him. "I'm not going to do that because it's really up to you."

"Is it? Tonight is the first night we've made love in a week, not counting the time you hurt me. You don't call me at work. I never know where you are and you come home and act as if your whole life has been blown apart." He looked at me hard. "I've got my own problems to deal with too, you know, it's a hard time for me. I've got school, classes to teach, my sister's put out by me not being there and I've never lived with another guy."

I reach out to him and put my hands in the waistband of his pants. "Decide in the morning. Don't go anywhere now." We stand in the blue light from the shade less window and the sliver of incandescence from the cracked door leading into the bathroom. Maybe it's because of the darkness or maybe it's the uncertainty of what lies ahead of him, but Matt allows me to remove his pants again and bring him back to bed.

I wake up again during the night. Matt sleeps across the bed from me. He's untangled himself from my arms. I look at the clock on the nightstand. It's two in the morning. I get out of bed and dress, put my overcoat on and find my keys in the pants worn yesterday. The house is hot now, the air heavy and dry. I turn down the thermostat, go through the kitchen door, and out to my car.

On the way to Peter's up the coast, my headlights snake through the fog and illuminate the glistening rocky cliffs. I listen to the radio and stop along the roadside in a pullout that allows cars to pass, and in the daylight a view that I know stretches out past Point Lobos. I just sit there in the car, turn the radio off and drink the coffee from the all-night store.

Matt gave in to me again. I can't figure it out. I would have left. I know that. In the year we've known each other he's grown attached to me and I to him, but in very different ways. It isn't sexual attraction or his love towards me, it is something that I can't pin down - a missing page stuck to another that provides the clue to the rest of the story. Maybe it's my need to just stop searching or desiring the unknown; each man coming at me with his own different set of particulars and going through the motions with each one just for sex. In some ways I'm a lot like Aunt Melissa I guess, throwing caution to the wind and eventually destroying myself because of it. There is a familiarity to Matt that attracts me. I'm settling in and liking the fact that I know what I'm getting, and when I wake in the morning he is there, unchanged, like the pines and cypress trees that have been in this town for thousands of years barely changing; you know they are growing and spreading out, but you can't see it, you can't grab onto it and know for a fact that that branch or needle was not there yesterday. Instead, you trust that they will be there tomorrow barring destruction by fire or lightning and go on about your way.

It's early morning and I'm sitting here in my old car along an old piece of road thinking this and I can't help myself. I love him and I am scared by it. Nothing this close to love has happened to me before. I want to turn and go back to the warmth of him, but I need to know if I love my mother, whether I will glean something from her that will bring me back to myself and to her. I also need to know if it's too late, whether I should just let it go and get on with Matt the way he wants me to. But I know we'll never make it without me trying.

I put my coffee in the cup holder and start the car. It grudgingly chugs back to life and lurches forward before I remember to depress the clutch. The coffee spills, the car dies and sputters, but I press on and turn the engine over again, only this time I do it right.

17.
Marjorie

How do I get myself clear again? The anchor of my father had been lost, our home sold and there was no other place to go other than the home that Eric and I had bought and called our own. Before Peter, before even Nicholas, we'd moved from the apartment into this house that sat on the bluffs of the Pacific Palisades. Eric had worked hard on the sellers - they wanted to sell fast - and his father had put up all of the down payment to get us in. We couldn't afford the house yet, but with the promise of Eric's practice growing and eventually absorbing his father's clients, the house itself would be a minor thing to worry about financially in the years to come.

It was so grand. I found myself walking through the rooms, each one opening into the other and each one with a view to either the ocean or the ravines on either side. There were things to fix, to change and replace, but I'd never before lived in such a place. There were four bedrooms and a large living room that connected to the dining room. The kitchen was expansive, long and light with counters that extended beyond anyone's needs. Our bedroom had two levels: one where the bed was and a lower level where we eventually put chairs around a built-in fireplace. There was a separate tub and shower, closets that when my clothes were added, still held room for four more families. It was here where our lives began to separate. We'd thrown our clothes together at his apartment and I wore many of them everyday - t-shirts, sweats, shorts - anything that the two of us could share we shared, but when we moved into the house we separated our clothes among the various closets and built-in drawers. His along the left wall, mine on the right. After that, he began to comment if a shirt was gone or notice if I'd been looking for something in particular to wear. I was soon conditioned not to go into his drawers unless I was putting away the clothes I'd cleaned for him.

There was no neighborhood to speak of. The house sat at the end of a drive that began in a cul-de-sac. The closest house was through a stand of eucalyptus trees, hidden from view. We'd occasionally see our neighbors down on the beach in the summer or leaving our drives. When we first moved in, the neighbors threw a welcome party for us and though Eric was welcomed instantly, I was spoken to cautiously and left to stand and watch the same view we had from our house, that of the sun making it's heavy way over the ocean's horizon.

Eric bought me a new car, a Country Squire station wagon, which took some getting used to. It was long and white with brown panels and lots of windows. It ran quietly compared to the van and I sat lower in it than I was used to. He said we'd need it when we started having children and he was right. We both didn't want to get rid of the van, though, so we had a carport built for it on the side of the garage and parked it. I took it out once a week to let it run - always on Saturday mornings. I'd drive it around the square in the Pacific

Palisades where it stuck out among the gleaming new cars.

I longed for the small apartment we had there. Our lives were far simpler. Eric would come home and because there wasn't that much to do, we'd lie around and make love, watch the television, talk. He'd hold me and tell me all kinds of things, recount the day, tell me he loved me.

I can't pinpoint at which time his mother began pushing her way between us. I can only say that the purchase of that house had a lot to do with it. Since I didn't have the talent or the mind or the experience of keeping up such a place, she'd hired us a maid, began to find furniture and art, even small appliances like toasters and one of the first-ever microwave ovens that I was scared to even use. At that time there were all kinds of warnings on the T.V. and radio about nuclear this and nuclear that. I wasn't about to bring it into my own home and after one of our first arguments, Eric took it out to the garage where it sat unplugged and safe.

"Why when you have the opportunity of modern technology don't you want to use it?" Mrs. Welch said to me.

"People have gotten along without it for thousands of years," I'd say back to her and we'd lock eyes for a moment before one of us - and it was always me - would look away. So our house began to look like her house and Eric and I began to hold each other less, but he still professed love to me and I to him and then Peter came along, which became my one addition to the house.

Every morning I took him out of his bed - Eric would already be at the office - and put him down on the shag in front of the big sliding glass doors that opened out onto the balcony, which overlooked the ocean. I'd roll him over three times to make him smile and laugh. Most mornings the sun came streaming in and warmed both of us and he was the one thing that I shielded from Mrs. Welch, which in the end finished what little civility we had between us.

One night, I'd taken down some pictures that had been hung while Peter and I were out. Their colors and shapes you'd call modern art, but it was as if they were tossed into a blender and spit out onto the canvas which created a whirlwind of ugliness that only Eric's mother could have found beautiful. I'd had enough, so I took the pictures from the walls and put them out with the microwave in the garage.

Eric came home and stood at the landing at the front door. "What happened to the pictures?"

"What pictures?" I asked.

"You know what pictures I'm talking about. I came all the way home at lunch to help hang them with mother."

That made me angrier. "Why didn't you ask me if I wanted them in the house first?" Isn't this our home?

"You were out."

"Then you should have waited." I walked out of the living room and into the kitchen. Eric followed. "You haven't asked me once whether I liked any of this stuff." I picked up a saucepan full of peas, carrots and onions and put it on a burner.

"I assumed you didn't care one way or the other." Eric put his briefcase down on the kitchen table and draped his jacket over a chair. Peter was in a high chair staring at us. He'd never heard us raise our voices at each other. "You never said anything."

"Why do I have to?" I asked. It didn't occur to me that I should have to have a say in what was put in our house. I just assumed that it would all appear like at my father's. I never thought that I'd have to fill a house with things, let alone all those bedrooms and living areas. I'd gone from a fully furnished house, which held the things I'd known since birth, to a tiny studio that required only a bed and desk to a home that was impossible to understand in size when compared with everything I'd been accustomed to.

"You don't have to," he said, "but I thought you would."

"I hate all this stuff," I said. "All of it except the stuff from the old apartment."

"Then we'll get new 'stuff'," he said, smiling, "we'll get all brand new 'stuff.'" Then he came up behind me, turned the fire off under the vegetables and lifted me up onto the edge of the counter. For those fleeting moments he became mine again while we made another baby. We never did get anything new, but he took those pictures to his office and hung them. I never saw them again because I never wanted to go there.

It takes two to ruin a marriage, but only one to destroy it. I could place all the blame on him and his mother, but I began to edge out of my existence there. I could feel myself letting go, reverting back to what I was before I met Eric. But now I had two babies, Peter and you, and I was ill equipped to deal with both. I was torn between them and me so I took to spiritual guidance.

During the days I'd watch television while you boys napped. On talk shows celebrities spoke of spiritual guides, transcendental meditation, yoga. It seemed as if everyone was searching for something, me included. I began my roaming again, first into bookstores where I leafed through the current spiritual guides then into stores that specialized in scents, candles and macramé festooned with colored beads, pearlescent and cobalt blues. On a bulletin board by the door were posters, some promising enlightenment, some beckoning one to spend an hour or two with Rama this or a man named Rashneesh. As I traveled over the maze of flyers, my eyes lit on one that advertised the visit of a Shaman - a medicine man. The word Shaman intrigued me because it suggested Indian ways and I was looking for a way to get back and into the good graces of my father whom I assumed was watching me from wherever he was.

Two weeks later I arrived at a home in Venice, which had a large sun porch that gave light to several spider plants and thousands of hanging offshoots. A spirit catcher hung on the wall and a collection of lanterns, paper, kerosene or otherwise hung from nails and hooks and were all lit like beacons drawing us in. When I arrived, a woman dressed in blue jeans and a long, silky maroon shirt, patterned with darker flowers and blue petals, led me into a room where seven others were sitting and waiting among pillows, candles and burning incense. All of the lights in the room were off. The men and women had been gathered around a small altar by our guest, who had seated us without a word as each of us arrived. On the altar was one candle, a spray of sage bundled tightly together by a beautiful length of ribbon, a large rattle, a bowl of sand with a burning stick of incense and propped against it was a large, flat drum covered in rawhide.

Some of the people looked around nervously, wondering if they'd come to the right place. They had their hands folded in their laps or were bending the paper handouts back and forth, reading over and over the description of the man we'd come to see. I sat staring at the alter, excited to find out what the purpose of each of the items were.

A woman came in to the room and closed the door. She bowed and walked around the perimeter of the group slowly blowing each candle out as she went, leaving only the one on the altar burning. From somewhere, I couldn't tell because of the light, a slight man came into the room. The air thickened and warmed it seemed and the candlelight caught the delicacy of the clothes he was wearing, which were loose, heavily wrinkled and were swaying as he walked between us. The woman came to the altar, picked up the drum and went back to sit down. She began drumming. Her hard temporal hits resonated so that I could feel it in my chest and down through my body. The slight man didn't say a word, but simply put his hands at his sides and bowed his head. His eyes closed as he lowered his body to the floor and lay there for several minutes before his eyelids began to flutter.

Because I remembered what my father had told me about Shamans - and because I wanted to take the journey with him - I closed my eyes. I imagined him going down into the Lower world, entering through a hot spring and following it to its source, the heat creating a bed of mist on which to float and navigate through the spirits. I imagined him coming out of the cave onto a high flat plateau that was first desert then green with wild mustard shot through it. I saw blue, but it wasn't sky or water, but a wide canvas through which I broke and on the other side were cliffs that rose up and up set adrift on shrouds of mist that when I, no he, went through. He stopped and stood at their edges and looked down into the void. The drumming changed tempos and there were four strong hits, then a long series of hits and four more like the first and then silence.

I opened my eyes. My body was chilled and I shook. My forehead was cold and wet. Others in the group began to shift. I could hear them sighing and begin to breathe in long, deep inhales and exhales. I didn't understand what had happened and waited for the Shaman to stir. When he opened his eyes and lay still for a moment, I smiled. When he turned his head he saw me and I began to weep quietly. The images I had of my father came back to me, dancing by the fire, fixing dinner, being loved.

The Shaman gave a talk afterwards about what he had seen and journeys that others had taken. He gave us exercises to practice and we bought his tapes, his books, some of the woman's sage bundles and incense. I bought a drum.

I stayed afterwards and spoke to the woman, Nancy, who'd been practicing the Shaman rituals for a couple of years and was working to become one herself by studying under the Shaman who'd led us that night. He had disappeared very quickly after he spoke. Nancy went around the room again and relit the candles and turned on an overhead light. I asked her what happened to him as people filed past her and into the living room to make their purchases. She just smiled and shrugged her shoulders; either she didn't really know or was keeping it secret.

"You're making your living room into some sort of an ashram." Mrs. Welch was shaking her head, hands on her hips when she came to get the boys who were propped up in the new pillows. I had found Indian blankets through Nancy and draped them over the backs of the couches. Eric didn't have much to say about the changes, but he'd mentioned them to his mother whose disapproval could be felt.

She'd arrived to pick up the boys. Nicholas was crawling around Peter who was trying to avoid him and pushed a dump truck through a bridge he'd made out of the pillows. I was hosting a workshop led again by the same Shaman who'd led the group the first time at Nancy's. She had turned into my first friend though there was something of a competition between us for the attentions of Shaman Martin. We'd attended many of his workshops together after which I'd stay at her house and she'd drum for me while I practiced journeying. Then I'd drum for her. She was far more experienced than I and would travel much longer and more deeply, after which she'd recount her journey as we sipped tea.

I had found something in journeying that awakened me, gave sense to my father's history and mine. I believe it made me a better mother. After having Nicholas, I felt lost and unfulfilled. Women that I'd spoken to had said how validating having a child was to them, but I didn't feel that. I didn't think that having a child gave me value, but rather it diminished me because all of my attentions went towards them. I began to think that I was selfish and the boys were just an extension, rather than an integral part of who I was. But when I began the workshops I changed. I valued my time with them, began to show them things of the natural world that I found when I came out of the tunnel and into the worlds that I'd discovered as the drum rhythmically beat under Nancy's strong hand.

After the boys left with their grandmother, I set out a number of candles and lit them. They made the living room beautiful. For the first time, I felt that this house had finally become home to me.

Shaman Martin arrived before the others and I showed him to our bedroom. He looked around and in his small voice he said, "Can I use another room?"

I stared at him a moment, wondering if I'd left something out or he'd seen something that made him uncomfortable, but I quickly scanned the room and found nothing. "Are you sure?"

"A smaller room would do fine." I led him down the hall to an unused bedroom. When I opened the door he sighed, smiled and said, "The energy is better here. Thank you." The doorbell chimed. I left him, but my mind kept working on wondering why he'd wanted to change rooms.

Nancy came in with three others. They'd met and carpooled. Gasoline was being rationed over even and odd days. We were in the second month of it and people were stealing license plates, filling buckets and bottles. Fights were breaking out at the stations.

By now, we knew each other enough and were chatty as we gathered and people took their seats. A few newcomers were always at the workshops and sat, wide-eyed as I did the first time. Nancy and I put out the things we'd sell afterwards in the kitchen while one of the men that came with her led the arriving people to their seats.

When I blew out the candles, I sat down and began drumming as Shaman Martin came in. Those with experience leaned against the pillows, put their head backs and let their bodies go limp and joined him in journeying.

I'd practiced with the drum and held the rhythm to fifteen beats per minute. I counted three. On four I struck the drum hard. We were twenty minutes into the session, the drumming echoed through the dark house, the one candle burned, people were strewn about like fallen trees, propped up against the couch and pillows or flat on the carpet. A woman screamed. I couldn't see if she was new or if it was one of the regulars, but her voice broke the spell. Everyone one sat straight up and started shaking and talking, yelling at each other. In the confusion, Peter burst through the front door and then Mrs. Welch carrying Nicholas. Eric entered and stopped short of the living room.

"What the hell is going on here?" Eric yelled. His mother came and stood next to him. Nicholas tried to wrestle out of her arms, but she held him firm against her.

Shaman Martin was the last to sit up. He turned and looked at Eric and then at me. It was then that I knew why he didn't want to be in our bedroom. He'd felt something wrong - in the future? Now? I wanted to ask him, but I knew he'd divulged everything he would, as he didn't interfere in the lives of his students.

When the confusion died down, the people left quickly, as if they'd been caught at something. I tried to get them to sit, but they were too rattled and nervous to settle in again. Nancy went into the kitchen to gather her things and was out the door with her group as quickly as the others. Mrs. Welch stood at the top of the living room with Eric and watched the group dissipate. She'd let Nicholas go finally and he'd scrambled across the floor towards the altar I'd set up, grabbed at the candle, which blew itself out as it fell to the shag and spilled wax that dried quickly in a clump. There was nothing I could do but stand there and watch everyone gather themselves and leave. Shaman Martin went to retrieve his case and exited out the front door like a thief. I ran after him and shouted across the doorway to him. He stopped at his car, opened the front door, looked at me for a moment and quickly got inside and drove away.

When I went back into the house, Eric had grabbed Nicholas and was holding him on the couch. "I thought this was some sort of lecture, not a séance or something, Marjorie."

"You're allowing this to happen in this house?" Mrs. Welch chimed in. I was still too confused to answer them, so I began taking apart the altar, picking the wax from the strands of carpet, trying to overcome my embarrassment. I began to cry.

"What do you think the neighbors might think if they knew what you were doing?" Mrs. Welch came up and stood behind the couch where Eric was sitting. "And the drugs, it smells like you were doing drugs."

"Mother," Eric said.

"Isn't it enough that we've taken you into our family..."

Eric jumped up from the couch and turned to her, "Don't say another word."

If I were someone else I might have gone to her and taken her by the neck and pushed her out the front door or stood up to her and shouted back into her face. If I'd been hard like her, I'd have taken her down, broken her with all of the words she'd broken me with. If I'd have been strong, I would have gathered the boys, my things and walked out the door then because the Shaman had felt something and had translated it back to me. Instead, I continued kneeling on the floor letting my children witness my humiliation, my weakness in the face of their grandmother.

"I think you better leave, Mom." Eric came around the couch and went up close to her. His mother balked, shook her head, but didn't speak. "I'll call you tomorrow."

"Watch the children carefully, Eric. See that she doesn't harm them."

"That's all." Eric said angrily, opening the door. Mrs. Welch went out and Eric turned to me, shook his head. "I don't know what you were doing, Marjorie, but if it involved drugs of any kind." He went over to Nicholas and picked him up. "I could lose my license, you know." He took Nicholas down the hall and to his bedroom. When he came back he didn't say anything. I'd gone into the kitchen, wiped at my eyes with a towel. Peter had followed me and was asking for milk or juice. Eric crossed behind me and went to the refrigerator.

"I don't know what's gotten into you, Marge. Help me understand because I go to work and come home and the house is changed. There are candles all over the place - which is dangerous for the boys, I might add. You're dressing differently again. What changed?"

"I was like this when you met me." I said, still staring out the kitchen window looking at the lights from the neighbors.

"But I thought you'd change. You have everything here. What is it that you want?" Eric handed Peter a small cup. "What is it? Goddamn it, look at me."

"I don't know." I said and looked at him, but then I turned away.

18.
Nicholas

The way to Peter's is steep and winds its way through twisted pines that have broken at the top from wind. The asphalt disappears in a riot of gravel; the sharp pings under the wheel wells keep me alert. I drive slowly across the small wooden bridge over a stream that comes out of the canyon. It has been destroyed several times, the water rising every so often and carrying the planks of wood off down the mountain like careening missiles. The air is colder here. It is sharp and threatened by the presence of frost, though the wet washes it away.

Peter lives up here for a purpose. It is hard to find and equally hard to get to. He has retreated into the backwoods so that his days and nights blend together, his cabin only receiving small shafts of light that float and bend depending on the weight of the fog and the denseness of the forest.

His wife, Linda, still small and mousey after ten years, tends to hide her fine shape under baggy, knitted sweaters and heavy jackets. She pulls her hair back in a ponytail and it lays flat over her skull like wet moss. You might say she was a carry over from the Beat Generation, all Jack Kerouac and Neal Cassady, but she's not. She's her own self and you can see that. She is nice and has stabilized my brother in a good way that had not seemed possible; his recklessness has been tamed by her calm.

In the daylight you can see the winding paths of bark that Peter has circled around the house and surroundings because the mud can get deep in places. He also didn't want Linda tracking it across the front porch he'd built up over the boulders bordering the front of their house. The cabin was sort of a rambling mess. The additions to it were made haphazardly without care of matching woods and styles reminding me of the fort we'd built that summer. The inside was uniform and you can move about from room to room and always find your way back to where you started. It is an odd sensation after seeing the house from the outside first.

Peter, who has heard my car coming up the lane, probably because it is so foreign it jolts him awake, meets me at the door. He is wearing sweatpants and a red jacket that is torn in front. A gaping hole exposes the inside where the lining is frayed and cut. He is barefoot and under his jacket he is wearing nothing.

"Jesus Christ, Nick, it's two-thirty."

"I figured you'd be home." I come up the wooden steps to the landing and stand there. He doesn't offer for me to come inside.

"Of course I am. Linda's asleep."

"You haven't answered any of my calls...." I see the look in his eyes. He runs his hand along the doorjamb, picks at the lock.

"I haven't been home."

"Don't use that bullshit line on me." I walk past him out of the cold and into his house. There is light bleeding in from the hall. I sit in an armchair after I scoop out the papers and magazines.

I look at my brother standing away from me, his back against the stairs leading up to the bedroom. Though he is not much older than I am, his face is like cracked earth. Intersecting lines furrow across his forehead and disappear into his cheeks. He has spent long hours in the sun and wind. He is a rigger on an oil derrick and heading into the weather and living in the channel off the coast every ten days has taken its toll. His fingers are thick and cut also: too many scrubbings with solvents have made his skin break and peel.

"What is it you want?" he asks.

"I want to know why you haven't answered my calls and refused to go down to the station when Roy called you in the first place."

"That's none of your business. Anyway, I don't have the time." He moves over to the kitchen doorway.

"Where are you going?"

"To get a cigarette. Want one?"

"You know I don't smoke." There was something he was holding back. I felt it because he was baiting me.

"I thought all fags smoked." He says this wearily, as if the weight of it has pressed him down for a long time. Everything in my head goes sharp like an ice pick to a block of ice. He looks at me as though I were small and broken.

"So you found out."

"It's a small town. You forget that." He goes into the kitchen. I get up out of the chair and follow him. I feel reckless.

"Don't come near me. I don't even know you."

"I didn't come here to talk about what I do in bed."

"Jesus, Nick, all these years and you couldn't even tell me. Have you told Mom yet?"

"It's none of her business. It's none of yours, either, if you want to know the truth."

"It becomes my business when one of my friends sees you messing around with some guy down on the beach. I wouldn't call that such a private thing." Peter shakes out a cigarette from the bent pack and lights it. The long curving tendrils of smoke obscure his face. "What is it you want, Nick? It's late."

"I'm sorry you had to find out about it that way."

"Yeah, well, fuck you. What do you want?" Peter has grown hard over the years. I know this and have resisted telling him because of it mostly because I didn't want to trust him with the information.

"I want you to tell me something about Mom." His head moves slightly registering a thought. "I want you to continue with something you were going to tell me a long time ago." Peter holds his cigarette up and considers it for a moment. He flicks the match into the kitchen sink.

"Well I don't much want to talk about her." Then I remember that he never brought her up except that one time at the fort in the ravine. He never mentioned her at all. It was he more than I who didn't take part in family functions He was always falling silent or going off someplace soon after he'd made his appearance.

"You have to," I say, "I need to know a few things." My brother goes to the cupboard, pulls down a glass and fills it with ice from the freezer. Then, as if remembering me, he asks, "You want some?" I shake my head, but change my mind.

"I'll take a little."

"You should have told me, Nick." He pours vodka tall in the glass. "You should have at least told me. God, George was so smug I wanted to hit him."

"George McRae is the one who told you?"

"Yeah. He was down at the water on some rocks when he saw you and that guy." He handed me the glass. I take a sip and I work the syrup around my mouth before swallowing it. My eyes water.

"His name is Matt."

"Do I know him?" I follow Peter into the living room. He switches on a floor lamp, sits in a chair and pulls a blanket over his legs and bare feet.

"I don't think so. He's pretty new up here. Works down at the University in Santa Cruz."

"One of those free-form Liberal Ed guys. Figures," Peter laughs. Then he gets serious again. "So what about Mom?"

"What about her?" I ask.

"Is she okay?" He stares at his glass and twirls the vodka and ice around with his finger.

"She'll be okay, but I don't think her mind is all there. I still don't know what I'm going to do."

"What is it you want to know, Nick, I don't remember much. It was a long time ago." Peter shifts uncomfortably in the lazy-boy. He knows a lot I think. I know I'll have to pull it from him slowly and deliberately. But he begins, as if a chest is finally opened and its contents spill out over the floor. I can see his face loosen and his fingers barely grip his drink. Now I'm afraid of him for the first time since childhood - an irrational, prickly scare that will either bring us together or finally tear our tenuous bond irrevocably apart.

"You remember I told you Dad and I went up to see Mom after that night in the cabin." He stares at me. "You remember that night, don't you?"

"Of course I do."

"Do you remember the drive home?"

"No, not really, except I remember Dad thanking you for calling home. My arm was broken. I was in a lot of pain."

Yeah, you cried a whole lot. I'll never forget that 'cause Dad wouldn't stop driving home. He'd made sure he had enough gas to get us there. Three hours of the drive home you did nothing but cry until you passed out from the pain." Peter took a swallow from his drink. "I'll never forgive him for that, Nick. Never."

"For some reason I don't remember much about the drive home. I just remember waking up in a doctor's office getting a cast put on my arm."

"That wasn't the worst of it, Nick. Not by a long shot." Nick takes another swallow, grimaces, takes another and throws his head back.

"What do you mean?" I feel bad for Peter. I watch his arms, the way they tense and shift against the chair and his body.

"It's... you know, it's hard Nick. Sometimes I wanted to tell you, but I couldn't." Peter fell silent. It was a long time before he spoke again. "How did we get to this, Nick? All my life I've wanted to just tell you. Let it go because it really wasn't me. It really wasn't my fault, but I guess time makes it my fault. Even I don't have control over that. I mean time. Well, I don't know, Nick. It's not that. I always wanted to protect you after that night in the cabin, but I didn't know how. I just let it be."

"You didn't have to protect me, Peter. I didn't know what to do in that house either. But you have to tell me what you did now. There is a lot more at stake."

He sits a while longer. Me eyes are intent on him, but a shiver courses up my spine and worries its way through my body.

"Well, a week later, before we came back to Big Sur, Grandmother bought me all kinds of new clothes, a couple of new suits, a jacket."

"I remember the clothes."

"She got them for me because we had to go to court."

"You what?" I am beginning to wish that he'd stop, but I can see the effects of the vodka gripping him, making his voice low and hoarse.

"We went to court. Mom was there and she was sitting at one table and Dad was at another. The room was small. There were only a few people there: a couple of lawyers - one was hers, and one was Dad's. A judge and a stenographer were there and a lady from a state agency... a specialist of some sort. The first day we were there was kind of short. We had this meeting with Dad's lawyer. They wanted me there so Grandmother came into my motel room after we had lunch and made me wear one of those suits." Peter empties his glass and swallows the remaining ice cube. He gets up and goes into the kitchen. The light flicks on. I hear the vodka being poured, a match light and a long, troubled intake off his cigarette. I am as still as a rock. Peter walks back in. He has zipped up his jacket and brought the half-empty bottle of Stoli with him. He pours some more of the thick liquid into my glass.

"What I'm going to tell you, Nick, is something you're not going to understand maybe. I didn't understand it then and I still think about it, though I've been pretty successful at putting it out of my mind."

"What was it?" I'd gone this far. The room seems to be closing in around me.

"They told me what to say." Peter is far off now. His eyes begin to fill up. There is a slight trembling in his cheek.

"Who told you to say what, Peter? Was it Dad?"

"Dad, Grandmother, the lawyer...."

"What did they ask you to say, Peter.... c'mon." Peter looked at me then as if the night sky had opened up to reveal clarity beyond anything imaginable. He began to cry.

"They told me she needed help and the only way she could get it was if I told them she was doing drugs that made her crazy and that it was her that broke your arm...." Then he looks at me. His face is going through a myriad of changes and then he is alone, so terribly alone and all I can do is sit there on the couch and watch him. He cocks his head to the side, I can see the vodka and pain combining to make him look drowsy and spent. I can see him now at our Dad's house, standing at the railing on the deck looking over the ocean. I remember him moving away from Dad, as he got older after coming to realize what he'd done, knowing that our family then was a fake. I can see Dad's feeble attempts at reconciling with him, with us.... the fort, surfing with Peter after work... I can see all of that and now all I feel is shame for Peter. I can't let that go.

A long moment of silence goes by. His breathing calms and he wipes his eyes with the edge of the blanket. He drinks the remainder of the vodka in his glass and leans back in the chair.

"You know I've hated him all these years, him, Lydia and Grandmother. I couldn't wait to get out of that house. I didn't move all the way to Humboldt or here because I wanted to. I moved far enough away so the temptation of going home would be tempered by distance. I didn't want to go home and I didn't want them to come see me. I had no idea Mom was still here. I lost track of her just as we all did. No one paid attention and that's the crime isn't it? And it's come to this."

"Don't talk, Peter. Don't say another word. Not just yet." I get up off the couch and slam my hand against the wall. I don't know why I'm angry.

"Goddamn it, Nick. Linda's asleep."

"So fucking what." I go over and stand in front of him. "There are worse things than that." Linda comes down the stairs. She is putting her head through a sweatshirt and bringing it down over her body. I see the edges of her panties. I see her shape and Peter's wildness growing up registers. The fights at the beach, the drinking and cars he wrecked. Dad never said anything.

"So you used that over Dad all those years."

"I what?"

Linda steps up next to me, sees the bottle of vodka and turns to Peter, "What's going on?"

"You acted like an asshole and Dad just turned away from it. He never said anything about your drinking. Not a word. Or coming home when you damn well pleased."

"What's that got to do with anything?"

"Nick, what's happening here?" Linda touches my arm.

"Shut up, Linda." Peter says as he tries to get up from the chair, but his head spins and knocks him down again. "Oh, shit," he says.

"What the hell is going on with you two?"

Then Peter bores into me, a last quick stab at lucidity. "Nick here is a fag."

My hand comes out and I hit him hard across the forehead because my body is too high to hit him in the mouth. His head snaps back against the back of the chair as his legs fly up. I jump on him and we both topple over the chair. Both of our bodies hit the wall and crumple against it. The lamp topples over and crashes throwing the room into black. Linda screams. Peter does a surprising thing and wraps his arms tightly around me I can't breathe. I can feel Linda pulling at my jacket, yelling at me to get off of Peter. But it is Peter's arms that have me confused. They feel like large strands of rope being pulled from opposite ends tighter and tighter. Peter is whispering in my ear. "Don't, Nicholas, don't." He calmly repeats it over and over and then kisses my neck and cheek. He is crying and I am crying with him. Linda releases my jacket and just stands back against the wall looking down at the both of us on the floor. Peter brings his face down into my chest and says softly, "I don't ever want you to hurt again." Then he pulls away and kneels next to me. His face bends down to his stomach and his arms wrap tightly around himself.

I pull myself up and sit. I stare at him. I reach over and put my hand on his arm. "Peter," I say slowly, deliberately, "Peter, I have always loved you. I've always thought that you'd do right by me." He brings his head up and our eyes finally meet, our drunkenness worn out, forgotten. I can see him in the faint glow of early morning just as I saw him when I got there. He knew what I'd come for and it frightened him.

I can feel Linda remaining motionless against the wall, not understanding.

"I didn't mean to lie," he says. "I didn't mean to."

"I know that," I say, "We'll figure it out."

Linda moves across the room and turns on another light. I can see Peter clearly now. There is a large bump and a bruise forming on his forehead. I move over next to him. "Linda, could you get me some ice please?" Linda goes into the kitchen without a word. I wait and put my hands up to his face and bring it up. "I need some help with Mom, Peter. I really do because I don't know what to do."

"I'll try," he says, "That's all I can do."

When I leave their house the sun is a barely seen round disc through the fog. Though the day is just as the one preceding it, dark and gray, the world seems changed, unspecific still, but newer. It is as if the actions of my family are becoming clear to me: the subtle glances and alliances, the not-so-subtle machinations of my father trying to assuage his guilt.

I work my way down to the paved road leading out to the highway from Peter's. I left he and Linda to sort things out, the messed up living room, the broken light bulb glass and their own problems. Linda kissed me as I left, her lips firm and pinched. I believe her eyes were closed when her lips touched my cheek, hoping that I had brought Peter out from a place she couldn't reach.

I make my way home along the Coast Highway. I roll the window down and withstand the cold for as long as I can. It feels good and keeps me awake, but my body quickly turns my mind away as I fight off sleep.

19.
Marjorie

When your father pulled you from my arms, Nicholas, I knew I wouldn't see you for many years. There are things of yours that I've kept: the jacket you were going to wear, a few of your stuffed animals and a pair of shoes I'd bought for you when we moved to Big Sur. Peter's things I took and put in a bag. I gave them to the woman from the State who gave them back to Peter. I had no desire to hold on to the memory of him, though now I regret those thoughts and wonder if I have been made to suffer because of them. I don't know. It happened for very specific reasons, which after that night in the cabin was beyond my control.

For two days I stayed in that cabin and drank myself blind. I stayed in your bedroom for the first day. The silence was unbearable. I screamed against it as dogs do to sirens. I hurt myself. I pounded my head against the wall until my forehead bled leaving blotches of blood on the white in little sponge-like patterns. I scraped the insides of my arms till they, too, bled. The funny thing is that I never felt any of it. I ask myself now why I never felt the pain. I believe it was the numbing effects of the alcohol and my own heart. Nothing I could have done to myself would have hurt more.

The policemen found me shrunk up in the corner of my bedroom, the shades drawn and me sucking the air out of that room like fire to timber. They had to sedate me to pull me out. I remember this because of the policeman's hands, like my father's: big, lined on the palms like a map, but reaching out for me to hold my arm steady. From then on I knew the consequences of the constant prick of needles, the value of being afraid. You are treated more tenderly if you act as if you're afraid, but you should know that for most of my life, I have never been afraid.

No, that's a lie. I'm sorry. I have been afraid since the day you left. For many years, my life was guided and coerced by people in uniforms: black, white and blue. Each one of them led me down hallways and into rooms that were foreign to me: all of them different, uninviting, and even hostile. I'd wait for hours in those rooms and as I waited and sometimes drowsed, I'd replay those final moments you were with me and see the terror and confusion on your face, the anger in your father's.

I won't make excuses for my drinking during that short time, but despair had collared me and I couldn't force myself out of it just as you couldn't understand. I did what I thought was best for you. I brought you North because that summer was hotter than I ever remember our summers being. When I found out about your father, I gathered our things and came to Big Sur with the money from our bank account.

It was September. The leaves were becoming brittle and long shadows bent across the front slope of the cabin in the late afternoons. The water in the creek bed running along the south wall had slowed to a trickle. I rented that cabin for cheap expecting to be there through the fall and winter. The woman from the realty office asked no questions.

Do you remember hiking down to the palisades overlooking the beaches? Remember how the seabirds swooped and hollered next to us? You jumped and shouted at them and ran along side them as they caught the drafts. Peter just stood and watched. He was silent and reticent, angry for pulling him away from the beach he loved. But you! You acted as if we were on vacation. You rolled and skittered about on the lawn in front of the cabin, your small arms tackled the ground or waved in the air, disappearing and reappearing around trees. You played across the wide lawn imitating crabs or starfish. I watched you from the window, but I couldn't join you.

You and Peter built seaweed piles out on the beach and when we went to the tide pools, both of you hunkered down and sat for hours, arms around your knees, watching the animals do their daily work in the captured water. I sat on my perch high on a rock and watched your shapes against the crashing waves. When you came up to me to complain about Peter, I shrugged it off because I knew that you two only had each other and I wanted you to learn to work out your differences. It wasn't out of a lack of love or my inability to care. It was because I cared too much. I wanted you to succeed. You had to learn how to reach out to each other because I knew that you'd be taken from me. I felt it coming. You did not. Peter would be wanting his father soon enough because he was older. He'd begun making forays into your father's territory, digging in deep against me when I asked him to do things, refusing unconsciously to come to me to comfort scratches and bumps. My usefulness to him ran its course.

I was still useful to you, though, as flowers to fruit trees, as tides to the moon. I knew that if we were to be together you would have been mine forever; that your father's love would always be secondary.

I was terrified of our future because I knew that our lives could not continue as they had those days after I left your father. Your grandmother would not have allowed it.

Your father was weak. He showed this to me gradually as I became aware of the hold his mother had on him. It was like a vine creeping over a building. Year after year your grandmother worked her way into him until there was nothing left. When he married me it was an act of defiance against her, but she grew stronger and after a few years he became silent, the nights we had together were vacant and lonely for me. When I showed him the ring you gave me I could see your grandmother manipulating him, making it all right for him to take a lover that would have gained her approval finally. For me, that particular night, that long disenchanted black, retains the mystery of my life; what I'd become after my father died. It was the long insolent silence that I became accustomed to and the unbearable daily task of living with a man who was a coward. I showed him that ring, displayed it accusingly in the palm of my hand from which he tried to pluck it away. But I closed my fingers around it and held it hard.

"That isn't yours," he said. He had turned toward the wall.

"It is now. I'm going to keep it."

"You can't. It doesn't belong to you."

"Who does it belong to?" I asked.

"My mother."

"But your mother already has a ring. I saw it on her today. Besides, it's much nicer than this one." I looked at the ring, turned it in the light and watched the shine move around the band.

"I need it back."

"You will have to find that bitch of yours another one." Because our marriage lacked confrontation, I went out of our bedroom and into the kitchen. I threw the dinner I'd started down the drain. Peas, potato casserole and the salad I had begun while the other parts of the meal were heating up. I washed each dish methodically and placed them in the dish drainer. I wiped the counter clean, wrung out the sponge and placed it up next to the spigot. By the time I had finished he'd left the house. I went into your bedrooms and packed your things. You boys had not come up from the beach yet and he had forgotten about you.

I packed my things in boxes and bags, loaded them into Michael's van, which sat on the side of the house and filled two thermoses up with milk and water. I packed his books, the ones that I would read over and over again. I took the blankets and pillows from your beds. I did all of this perfunctorily, as if getting the family ready for a car trip, but I knew I would never be back in that house so I took other things: pictures of my father, a few of the old baskets I'd collected in college and the blanket Michael had left for me on the beach. I can't really say why I kept it over the years, but there it was, frayed, the colors blending together where water and beer and sweat had been spilled and it's smell of dust from years of lying over the couches of our various living rooms. You may have that also.

You two came up from the beach after I had packed the last box of things into the van. I made two spaces for you to sleep because I knew we would drive through the night.

"Where are we going?" Peter asked.

"I don't know," I said, "I really don't know. I think we'll just drive, okay?

"Are we going on a trip?" you asked. I came over to you and took the t-shirt you carried and pulled it over your head.

"Yes we are." I looked at you straight away as I said again, "Yes we are. For a very long time."

"What about Dad?" Peter asked.

"He can't come," I said. Up until then, I'd done everything I needed to do to put our lives back in some kind of order, but I realized that there was no order from that moment on. "Get in the car, Peter. You too, Nicholas. Hop in." I swung the van door sideways to open it.

"But what about Dad?" Peter stopped short of the wide mouth of the van. "Does he know we're leaving?"

"He knows."

"But you never told us about this."

"Peter, you have to get in the van now."

"What about my baseball game tomorrow?" Peter stepped away from the van. "I have to be there."

"We'll talk about it later, Peter. Get in the van, now." I wasn't shouting at him. My voice came in a whisper, my throat breaking each word. "Please, just do it."

I can recall when the pain started, the rolling force of it. Both of you had fallen asleep. It was late. We kept to the coast all the way up through Santa Barbara then inland through San Luis Obispo and back to the coast at Morro Bay. I stopped just above there along the road. There was a hard cut of cold in the air as I pulled in the freshness of it and filled my lungs and realized what I'd done. I'd stolen you boys from your home. Though Peter would feel the full weight of that, you Nicholas, gave up everything that you had grown accustomed to save for me. It startled me to think that your coming detachment from things familiar would become a burden more intense than leaving your father. How would I make your lives simple again? From the moment I put you two in the van, your lives changed forever. That was more than I could bear at that moment so I left you and Peter sleeping in the van and walked down through the dunes to the water's edge.

The ocean, the deep forbidding ocean, would become my safe haven for the coming years. Each time I went to it I was gathered up in the pitch and roll, the elegance of the light upon the water and the mysteries of the deep. I imagined myself jumping into it and never coming up for air again, but swimming deeper into the dark. Into the caverns and tunnels being caressed by the kelp, by the undulating beds of seaweed and coming to rest on the sandy bottom where I would float free and never again need to seek warmth from people or experience the pain they bring. As I sat on the sand, looking out at nothing, I imagined these things as I came close to leaving you for good.

That would have been my second cruel act and as such, I was unprepared to inflict more pain on you. Did I not know at the time that pulling you away would be just the start? Was I too selfish or naive to understand the consequences of what I'd done? I didn't think of it, Nicholas. I was flying blind and the anger towards your father hadn't settled into the space we hold for such things. It was still outside of me, just in front. My grasping at it was futile so that is why I came back to you, to finish what I had started. Had I known what would happen in the two weeks after and in the coming years, I would have pitched myself into the sea then and there.

20.
Nicholas

When I get home, Matt's car is gone. I look at my watch. It is past seven-thirty, and he would still be in bed even now. I go to the kitchen door and enter and I can feel the emptiness already. It began in the car because I knew that he'd had enough and had probably made the decision to move out.

There is a note on our bed. It is in a plain white envelope. Before I read it I look around the room. It is horribly clean. None of his clothes are strewn about the floor or hanging from the corners of cupboards and closet doors. I look at the note. On the envelope there is a simple, Nick, written quickly it seems because it is not his usual labored handwriting. I tear it open, read it and place it back in the envelope. There is nothing left for me to think about in the shape I'm in. I switch off the light by the bed and lay over the covers fully dressed and fall asleep.

When I wake up it is a bit past one in the afternoon. Light stretches in lines across the far wall from the blinds. My clothes are warm and sticky and my shirt is loose and wet at the collar. I reach under it and feel my chest and run my fingers down to my stomach. There is a light film of perspiration over me. I kick my shoes off and pull my shirt over my head. I vaguely remember the phone ringing a couple of times in the morning, but I let the answering machine pick the messages up. It is warm in the house. I get up and go into the bathroom. I have a slight, dulling headache. My eyes are rimmed with a fine line of red. I turn the shower on and remove the rest of my clothes and throw them against the corner where they slump to the floor. Everything is happening in slow motion.

Before I get in the shower, I go to the living room and turn the stereo on loud. I think by drowning out my thoughts I'll be able to relax again and let the steam and music blend together. But it is a simple device that doesn't work. I ache. In that ache I reach out and turn the cold water down by half, step back away from the spray and squat down in the shower. My head feels as if I could rub it and massage my temples all day and still the pain wouldn’t go away. The only thing that happens is that the stall fills with steam, the hot water burns the bottoms and toes of my feet and the air becomes impossible to breathe.

I turn the knob on the answering machine and it clicks to life. The tape whirs back to the beginning. I have not dressed yet and during the time it takes for the tape to rewind I run back to the bedroom, grab a sweatshirt and throw it over my head. Matt's voice greets me when I return. It is quiet and hushed. There is a background set of voices I can hear over the speaker. "I can't talk now, but the least you could have done was let me know where you were going. I left some things there and I'll be by to pick them up later. Please don't be there." The tape clicks, the computer voice announces the time of the call and then my boss' strong, sharp voice comes, "Nick, I need to talk to you. You're missing deadlines and now my butt's in a sling. Get back to me as soon as you get the message."

Click. The house goes silent again but for the scratching of my hand over my belly and the rustle of the sweatshirt. I pick up the phone and dial work. Patty's voice comes on the line.

"Patty."

"Nick, where the hell are you?"

"I'm at home."

"Home? Why the hell for?

"It's where I live." There is silence on the other end of the line. "Sorry 'bout that," I add. There is another stretch of silence.

"Look, Nick, um, I need some help here. The newsletter has to be done by tomorrow."

"Okay, we'll work on it. I'll be there in a half hour.

"Nick?" Patty's voice is tentative.

"Yeah?

"What's going on with you? I've never seen you like this."

"Matt's gone. He left this morning."

"No."

"I'll explain when I get there. Bye." I hang up the phone and stand there a moment. I call the hospital and go through the usual number of switchboards. A voice comes on the line. "Station six, may I help you?" I recognize the voice; there is an automatic sweetness to it that is pleasant and hopeful.

"I'm calling for Marjorie Welch."

"Oh, hello, Nick."

"Hi."

"She's just gone down for a nap. Do you want me to wake her?"

"No, no. Just checking on her." I feel somewhat relieved.

"She's doing fine, just fine, but I have to tell you we're a bit glad she's asleep." The woman laughs a bit.

"I'll be down later this evening."

"Okay. Bye now."

When I set the receiver down I lean back in the chair next to it and close my eyes. I think of Matt, his dark hair - how it lays flat on his head and over his eyes, how I like to push his bangs up to see his full face.

Matt had come to me quite unexpectedly. A few months after we met he'd taken me down to Pfeiffer Beach, which is larger than most of the beaches nearby. I kept watching Matt run up and down, waving his arms and laughing, trying to bring me out of myself with the sharp cackle and throaty guffaw of his voice. He'd run up to me and pretend to tackle me and then run off again down the beach. He'd begun taking care of me, making meals, washing my clothes with his, cleaning after me. It was an adjustment because I'd spent so long taking care of myself and had come to accept that I'd probably be alone for quite some time. I linger for a moment more in the chair and then get up and go into the bathroom and ready myself for work.

I walk into the office. Patty is sitting at her desk, mountains of papers precariously stacked at all corners. She has her back to me and I come up behind her. "I'm here," I say, but know that I'm not.

Patty is hunched forward over her computer, but she turns around in her swivel chair, which she uses blatantly and obscenely like some power broker. "Nicholas!"

"I'm here to help." I say gallantly.

"Well, glory be." She studies me a moment. "You look like shit."

"Thanks, Patty."

The office in its entirety is one room. There are two desks, hers and mine. In between are computer equipment, magazines, books and an array of fast food boxes and bags. Patty is addicted to hamburgers, tacos and anything else that is deep-fried or fattening, which makes me hate her all the more because she never gains a pound. She has become a good friend from all of the hours we've spent together. She's a ball of energy with a pageboy haircut, which she chomps on continually when she works.

She stares at me. I look back at her. I know what she wants to know.

"I'm all ears!" she says. Then she pulls my chair up right in front of hers. "Do you know what time it is Nicholas?"

"I know where this is going and I'm not...."

"It's time for you to spill your guts to Aunt Patty." Our last long talk was disastrous. Patty had just signed her divorce papers and was teetering off into long silences. That was over a year ago. She'd bounced back admirably after our talk.

"C'mon, Patty, not today."

"Here, sit." Her eyes look at me mournfully. She enjoys mothering me as if her life wasn't in disarray also. She has a kid who shuffles between Big Sur and Santa Cruz. A father she lives with that has found no purpose in carrying on after her mother died, but instead sits in front of the TV all day or ties flies for fishing trips he never takes. She also has a barn full of animals, each having one disorder after another. Through it all she manages a sunny resiliency, which makes me wonder about her but makes me love her also.

"What do you think of Matt?" I ask. Patty is the kind of woman who will give away her thoughts if she feels she needs to.

"What do I think of him?" She leans back in her chair, "I think he's really nice and, if I may be so bold, perfect for you." She smiles. "Before the mother thing happened anyway."

"He left this morning." In the swell of the room silence falls. I feel warm like a fever had moved through my body and taken hold of me. I work around the edges of my thoughts about Matt. How easy it had been for him to fall in love with me and how hard was it for me to understand what that was. He had begun caring for me and he had turned me from always thinking about myself into thinking of him first. All of my bad habits of speaking out of turn, propping myself up in the eyes of others, making sure people knew I was there had begun to leave me. I was growing content in leaving room for Matt to take center stage, make the decisions, pull me up between his legs and wrap himself around me much like a sea anemone that closes in around anything that touches it.

Under the glare of the fluorescence, Patty is studying me. She gets up and moves to the small refrigerator we keep, pulls out a bottle of apple juice.

"Want some?" She takes a Styrofoam cup out of its tubular wrapper.

"No."

"Nick, I think you should call Matt. Your Aunt Patty will be here with you. You just call him up and say you're sorry you're such a fuck."

"Jesus, Patty, I don't think that'll make him come running back."

"Probably not, but you should tell him something." She comes back to the chair and sits down gingerly. She has over-filled her cup. "You should at least make an effort. How hard could that be?"

I stop. I lean back in my chair and let out a big sigh. My body needs to stretch so I spread my arms out and tighten the muscles in my legs. Patty watches me in mock horror. "I've been wanting to do this," I say.

"What is your problem?"

"My problem is, is that my whole life is breaking up in my face and I don't know what to do. My brother's a mess, I'm a mess and now Matt's a mess and he's living at his sister's." I let out a long sigh.

"Well?"

"Well, what?"

"Well... I don't know what to say."

"There's nothing to say, Patty. I just need to work this out. If it's all right, I'd like to take a few days off."

"We have all this work. The newsletter for the Gas Company is due tomorrow and there's still a lot of layout to do."

"I'll help with the newsletter and get that done. But I really need the time..."

"Do you think it'll help? I mean really help?" Patty looks at me as if she's already made up her mind. I nod. "Good then, we'll jam through the work and then I don't want to see your face until you get yourself together."

"Thanks, Patty."

"Don't thank me, 'cause I'm going to make you bleed when you come back." Then she laughs that slow-pitched laugh of hers that barrels through the room. She claps me on the thigh. It stings and winds away from me as though the pain was the least of what I had to think about. I turn to the computer and pull up the file. It gives me a chance to turn away from Patty's bemused smile and wonder what I am going to do next.

After a while, she comes up behind me and peers over my shoulder at the computer screen. She whispers in my ear and says, "You know you love him."

"I know," I say. It's the hardest thing I've said all day. Those two words of revelation, of terror and unforgiving sadness at what I'd gained and lost. As singular as a strand of hair, a blade of grass looked at closely. Now I am so tired my eyes can't focus on the screen. I put my glasses on and that barely helps. My head feels weightless and I can't seem to concentrate on the work before me. I push my chair away and get up to go outside. "I'll be back in a minute," I say.

"I'll be here."

I go outside. The air smells like fried butter from the cafe. There are people in coats pulled up at the neck. I am only in a long sleeve shirt hoping that the cold will break through. It does. It breaks through so deeply that I bring my arms up and hold myself close. Then it comes to me, a prevailing need to see my Dad, to get help for Mom because I can't see clear to relying on help from Peter. Dealing with Matt will have to wait, my expectations of us together put aside to find my past. I'll call him, sure, let him know I'm leaving, give him the space to see if he wants us to continue, which I hope he does. Rain begins to fall as it does here, first in a light drizzle then hard as the clouds back up against the mountains to release their full weight of the gathered ocean. I go back inside.

I call my brother from the office. This time he picks up the phone. "Hi, Peter. You okay?"

"Yeah. I'm fine. My heads banging away though." He laughs a little. "You owe me a light bulb."

"Sorry about all that last night... I..."

"It's okay. I knew it was coming at some point and I just put it off too long."

"I've got a favor to ask. You're not going to like it, but you have to do it for me." There is silence at the other end as if Peter was waiting for another shoe to drop. "I'm heading down to Dad's."

"What for?" There is surprise in his voice and it rises up a couple of notches.

"We need his help."

"No we don't, Nick." Anger rises in his voice and shifts into urgency. "You stay here, he's not going to help."

I stay calm, sure of myself. "In my mind he doesn't have a choice. Besides, you and I can't afford to put Mom up somewhere."

"We'll manage. I'll try to figure something out." I know Peter won't pursue it; his track record on such things has always been poor.

"There are other things," I say, "I need to talk to him and I don't want to do it over the phone. It'll be easier if I see him. But I need you to look in on Mom while I'm gone. It'll only be for a day or two. I'm driving down and right back up."

"Only for a couple of days?" Peter's voice now is unsteady.

"That's right, Peter. C'mon, it's not much.

"He's not going to help," he says with resignation in his voice.

"Well, we need to take that chance. We need help fast. An agency will put her in the wrong place again and this time, I won't let that happen." I wait for his answer. Outside the cars move silently, their taillights reflecting in the window dappled by raindrops hitting the glass. I need Peter now more than my mother does.

"I'll go in and see her," he says quietly. "I'll do it."

"Good. I'm going to call the hospital and let them know you're going to be looking in on her." Then a thought catches me. "Peter? I'm really sorry about last night and everything..."

"It's okay, Nick. Just don't leave me out of things. Don't just disappear like you have the last couple of years. I was wondering why you didn't come around much."

"I won't. It was just something I needed to work through."

"I know now why you did it. Call me when you get back."

"I will. Bye." I hang up the phone and sit back down in my chair. I stretch my legs out feeling tired, yet restless. Possibility is the word that comes to mind and the disposable way I've used it in the last few years. I've squandered it away like gift money. Then Patty looks at me and I look away.

"Jesus, you're a mess," she says and takes a long look at me.

"Thanks Patty. I needed to hear that." I get up and take my jacket from the back of the chair. "I really needed to hear that right now."

"I'm sorry... I didn't mean to...." She puts her hands on her knees, squeezes them like melons. "Are you going to call Matt?"

"I don't know." I stare at her. "It's really not high on my list." I say it to shut her down which I know is unfair. "Look, I need to figure that one out too, but I can't right now."

"By all means, take your time. Just don't be a dick." Then she turns back to her computer. "See you when you get back."

"Patty?" She lifts her head slightly. I know she is listening. "Don't pull away from me, too. I know you like Matt. It's the best I can do."

"Yeah," is all she says and she goes back to her typing at a feverish pace, her fingers pressing harder on the keys than usual. I shoulder my jacket and leave the office and head down the stairs to a rush of air. It is not quite dusk, but you really can't tell because of the rain. It lays thick over me as I get in the car, but I've learned to keep my head low.

I get home to my rented house and go inside. I wander around slowly and go from room to room. Nothing seems to be mine. Not my stereo, my books, my pans or even my clothes. Someone else has been living here. My artificial life is over. I am different. Matt has made me that, finally. I can go home now.

I pack a small bag - one change of clothes, blue jeans, a shirt and sweater. There isn't much I need to take, but I hope to be bringing back something: for my mother, for Peter and for me. I can say this without feeling selfish. It has been a long time since I haven't felt that.

21.
Marjorie

When the police took me to the station after taking me from the cabin there seemed only two things to do: give myself in to the demands of authority or fight like hell to retain something of myself. Had I been in a state of mind to do the latter, I surely would have fought. My mind was disoriented and I was pushed along into things I couldn't comprehend, the assignment of state lawyers, a battery of tests and processing me into government run agencies. Things began to happen so fast that I couldn't order them in my head.

Three days after I was taken from the cabin and was locked in a small cell by myself and looked at by psychologists and made to answer countless questions, I was led down a hallway to meet with the lawyer who'd been assigned to me and had shown up only an hour before. He was young and had a nervous manner. His fingers were white and smooth with freckles covering them. His red hair was dark to light at the top of his head. He managed a smile as he handed me a dress.

"You should wear this," he said, bringing a heavy blue dress out from a paper bag, "We have a meeting before the judge."

I looked at him. "For what?"

He bowed his head and stared at the floor. "To see if you should be given over to the state."

"The state?"

"You kidnapped your children. There are charges against you."

"That can't be. I only took them away for a while."

"It's not how it's being viewed by the other party."

"Who is that?" I wadded the dress up in my hands. The taste of sugar filled my mouth, sweet and sick like honeyed tea.

"Your husband."

"How could he do this? How? I need to talk to him."

"It isn't possible," the lawyer said. His hand came up to my shoulder and I backed off.

"What do you mean it isn't possible?"

"There are rules we have to follow."

"Bullshit. What rules?"

"Just rules that need to be followed before we see the judge."

"This can't be." Fear filled me and I clutched his arm. "This can't be. What's going to happen?"

"I can't honestly say. We have a number of things to talk about." He led me into a small room where we spent the hour. I told him what happened, but I jumbled it all up so that by the end he was hopelessly confused. We went in to see the judge who glanced at me and then looked me up and down. I felt unfit in his stare and smoothed out my dress, brought the bangs of my hair away from my face and ran my bracelet around and around my wrist. The lawyer tried to make his case, but I could tell he was struggling with the facts, looking down at his notes, constantly shuffling his feet. In the end, there was silence as the judge took both of us in. He paused and made a sigh. Another lawyer sideways to us asked to talk with the judge a moment. He went up to the bench, spoke a few sentences and the judge nodded.

He looked at me again. I felt a sense of dread and my body went numb and my head cleared of all thought and I shouted at the judge. "What is it?" The lawyer next to me grabbed my arm, pulled it down close to him, but I yanked it away. "Where are my boys?"

"Control your client, counselor," then he turned to me, "Apparently, your boys are fine. They're with their father."

"Their father? Eric?" I was sobbing, "Do you know what he did?"

The other lawyer spoke, "Your honor?"

"I know, counselor."

Then to my lawyer, he said, "Counselor, she is to remain in custody at the state hospital for observation and, may I suggest, you do your homework."

"Yes sir." Then my lawyer pulled me to the side of the table after a loud clap of the gavel. He took my elbow, which I again pulled away from him. He said, "You didn't help matters much."

"You don't know what you're doing," I hissed at him and turned. "Where are they going to take me? What did they do with my stuff, my van? Where am I going?" I pleaded with him as if that was the only thing left to do.

"I don't know," he said. "They usually impound cars and stuff like that, but you'll get your things in boxes and they'll be stored... the things you don't want anyway."

"I want everything," I said, "I want everything that's mine. Do you hear me?" I grabbed at him and he motioned for the guard. "I want everything that's mine. Everything, goddamit."

"I'll see what I can do." He shrugged himself away from me. The guard pulled me away and down another corridor. I started to pull my dress away from my body. It ripped at the shoulders and the top of it fell away. The guard took the material and brought it up over my shoulders and led me away under the bright light of the hallway. I screamed hard until my throat cracked and the door slammed behind me.

Two weeks later the same thing happened, the lawyer showed up with another bag of clothes. I talked with him for a short period of time. He led me down the same hall towards the courtroom. I'd become more panicked and frightened as each day passed. I was alone with strangers for those two weeks and questions were put to me quickly and perfunctorily. I was given drugs that fed my haziness and kept me numb. My body became slack, and heavy, filled with nothing.

I had a conversation with another woman there. She had white hair, was almost ancient I thought, like me now I guess. I said to her, "I've got two boys and they were all mine for a little while."

"That's nice," she said, "had me two children myself."

"Oh?"

"Don't know where they went off to. It's like they just up and disappeared. No thought of their mother."

"What about your husband?" I asked, my voice low.

"Dead," she said, just like that. No emotion. "He was killed. Can't get it out of my mind, really. Guess that's why I'm here." The woman, clear-eyed, stared out into the courtyard from the window where we were. She went a long time between blinks.

"I killed him, yep, that's what I did." Then she took her wrist and held it in her hand. "He fell in the bathroom while shaving, he was older than me, almost seventy. Lost his grip is what he did and he couldn't get up, so I grabbed his wrist like this, see, and I took his razor and cut clear to the bone. Clear to the bone. Can you imagine what that must have felt like? It felt good to me. I can tell you that much. Felt real good. It was that hand, you see, that hand struck me all those years."

Then I noticed a healed wound on her wrist too, saw the scar cover the length of it.

"I cut myself too," she looked at me, "for the children. Didn't want them to think it was me who killed him." She moved off into the room clutching her wrist and holding it against her stomach.

I felt like I wanted to do that too. I felt that way for two weeks. Two weeks! I kept seeing that lady's eyes, just looking all the time and couldn't imagine that she slept. I kept away from the other patients after that. I demanded my things, my books. I didn't read so much though. My head never got clear and every time I struck out against whoever was bothering me, they took my things away or put me in a dark room, told me to think about what it was I'd done. The worst thing about those hospitals is how they talk down to you like you were a child. They think it soothes you and helps you along with the least problems. I knew what they were doing. I knew they'd just as soon take you out back and let you go along your merry way. Put you out and make your own way in the world. Especially the worst cases, the ones where there just wasn't any way the patient was going to get better and return to the world. They'd just as soon turn them loose and let them rot upon the earth.

Some days, the way I acted, I'm sure they were close to just opening the doors and letting me walk out of there. Don't think I wouldn't have. I'd have moved so fast that no one would have seen which way I'd gone. No one. I'd pass into legend. Instead, on most days, I just lay on my bed staring at the wall, my forehead pressed hard against it, spit running down the side of my mouth and tried to think of my father, my two boys – and tried to make them disappear from my memory so that my head wouldn't hurt any more.

22.
Nicholas

I drive down to my father's house in the dark, but I can smell the fields, the ocean and see the signs that mark my progress. I've driven this road countless times since I was four, but this time seems strangely odd. I can see myself small, young, peering over the backseat, see the dashboard lights reflecting around the rim of my father's glasses, off the sides of his face. I can hear the slapping of the wheels, my brother telling me to quiet down. "C'mon, Nicky, c'mon. Only a little ways to go." I can see him looking at my father who keeps his eyes forward on the road. I can see my brother's eyes filled with tears as I wail in pain down the coast road in blackness.

My eyes become blurry and sore, but I keep on. I lose myself in time; venture into the past then quickly into the present as the car swerves into the down-slope of the shoulder. I bring the car to a stop after pulling over in the dirt. There's quiet as I put my head in the corner between the back of the seat and the curving lip of the door where the painted steel gives way to glass. I fall asleep.

When I wake up, the cabin of my car is stifling hot. So hot that I can't breathe it seems, and I yank open the car door and fall out onto the gravel bed running along side of the highway. I am away from the coast. There is no fog so the sun beats down hot like it's reflecting off metal. I bend my neck and my face takes in all of the heat and it feels good. I stand there for a long time; cars speed past every so often. They are mostly farm trucks and trailers carrying immigrants to the fields. There are two crows circling in the sky and their calls come drifting in like shrill cackling. I'm reminded of brakes screeching, in need of repair. I pull my shirt off and wad it up to wipe my brow. It's momentary shade over my eyes brings me back into night and the long trip down and what I thought it would be like if I never saw the sun again. Driving, driving down. I play those three words over in my head faster and faster, then slow like I feel. Driving, driving down. Driving...driving...down. Driving..... driving....... down.

I walk away from the car into the field. The dew on the grass soaks my jeans as I head out towards an oak tree. I bend towards it and run my fingers along the rough bark and follow the lines it makes. I sit for a while. Big Sur is far behind and I'm in no hurry to see my Dad. I lean back against the trunk, watch the cars go past, their windows blinking at me as they go by. I sleep again.

I haven't had any dreams for years except the one about my mother. There is nothing that comes from my subconscious when I sleep anymore. Now, my memories reach me in abstract moments: pulling a towel down from its rack after a shower, a glance at a bench on the side of a road, waiting for the telephone to ring. When I wake, there is another moment. I see in my drowsiness the back of a road sign. The sun has shifted so that its reflection hits me squarely across the face. It is warm. My grandmother is standing above Peter and me. We are in her pool and the sun is behind her and I am squinting my eyes to see, but I can only see the black outline of her body. I was eight. Peter and I had been swimming most of the afternoon. She called us over to the edge.

"Nicholas," she said, "your father has just called. It seems your mother wants to talk to you. Get out of the pool and come to the phone. He gave her my number for God's sake. Peter, you get out too." It had been several weeks since I'd heard her mentioned so I hesitated.

"Nicholas, she is on the phone now. Hurry up." I pulled myself out and Peter stayed in the pool. Grandmother wrapped me in a towel, rubbed my body free of the sudden cold. I ran in towards the kitchen where the handset sat on the counter, the yellow cord dangling over the avocado green Formica. When I picked it up I listened to the other end and couldn't hear anything. There was no breathing and I looked at my Grandmother and said in the phone, "Mom?" No answer. "Mom?" I said again and listened to the silence.

"It's just like your mother," Grandmother said, "irresponsible to a fault." She took the phone from me and hung it back up, grabbed my hand and brought me back to the pool. "Peter," she said, "swim with your brother." I stood on the lip of the shallow end, the water shimmering, the waves blinding my eyes, and I dove head first into the water and swam the length of the pool without a breath for the first time.

23.
Marjorie

There was a nurse at that first hospital I was put in. She knew I didn't sleep at night and wandered in every so often to look after me. I could see her shadow sweep across the hall and could see her coming. When she entered she had a way with her eyes that took in the entire room at once. I believe it's a nurse's special privilege to be able to do that. Enter, immediately seize the room, take mental notes and still be able to have that look of caring, but the woman came every day and her routine never altered.

She'd come to the bed, look at my chart, scratch a note on it, come to my side and look me straight in the eyes. It was as if she was taking the temperature of my mental state. She'd take my arm and without ever mentioning it, drawing my attention away from what she was doing with small talk, and took my pulse. She'd gently put my arm down again, smile, run her hand over my forehead and give it a little pat as you would the head of a dog. She'd look over at the window and ask me about the weather as if I'd know, "So how's the weather today, Marjorie?" Before you knew it, the blinds would be drawn up, the window opened and fresh air came streaming in.

She made my life bearable there by taking a special interest in me. When the trial started she cut down my medication to half so I'd be more lucid and see to it that I looked fresh. She spoke to the new attorney assigned to me, told him what had happened - as much as she knew anyway. She provided a private room where the attorney and I talked.

He was young and dressed sharply. His eyes were dark and button-like, but I could see that he would be no match to anyone my mother-in-law had probably hired. On the first day of court, my suspicions were confirmed as we were brought in and I had my first look at them.

Two lawyers to my one were sitting at the table among papers and reports, which I had assumed contained the results of the many tests they'd subjected me to. They were dressed in matching, dark blue double-breasted suits. Only their ties gave any hint to their personalities. I remembered one of them who accompanied several of the specialists they'd hired to find out every detail of my life. Four of them came to ask me questions about my childhood and chart my answers on graphs that made no sense to me. Most of them just sat back and looked at me as I smiled at them, unwilling to give them the satisfaction of thinking they had bested me. I made up answers and they had complained to the judge that I was unwilling to cooperate in their interrogations.

My lawyer gave feeble objections, but I harbored no resentment towards him. He was outmatched and he knew it too. The hearing lasted two days, the first was all medical histories and findings presented by the specialists with meager cross-examinations by my lawyer.

The second day sticks in my mind. I awoke early. The late fall had finally given way to winter. There was cold rain coming and the air snapped like apples. The heat from the furnaces kicked in down the halls, but I'd kept my window open because I wanted the cold. I wanted it to keep me alert. When the nurse came in as she always did, I was standing at my window looking toward the trees going up the sides of the mountains, though they looked like ghosts now in the descending clouds. She looked at me oddly because I had broken her routine by already being up, dressed and ready to go. I'd been off drinking for several weeks, gone through a period so hard my palms had bruises from clenching my fists so tight and had sweated down my clothes and lost weight.

She smiled at me, took a brush from the nightstand and combed back my hair into a long rope down over the nape of my neck. She fashioned a ponytail out of it, worked the loose strands over the crown of my head. I remembered Mrs. Jorgenson, how she'd fix me up in the afternoons after school and step back to take a look, be dissatisfied and start all over again. Why were the women in my life so concerned with the way I looked? I guess they knew that I didn't care one way or the other how I presented myself and took it upon them to fix that.

When she was finished she went to the window and reached up to close it. For a moment she stopped and just looked out and said, "I see so many women come and go here never getting a fair shot." She held her hand out through the bars expecting a raindrop, "and I don't know why I care so much because almost all of them don't. I hope you'll be one of the few." I went up to the window next to her and looked out. Her hand was wet now; the rain began hitting the window. "I don't expect I'll be one of those." She said, "I expect not." We stood there for several more minutes. I thought that even she might have wanted to escape from that hospital.

When my lawyer and I walked into the courtroom there was an air of finality as if they all knew and expected the outcome. As we made our way toward the table where we sat the day before, I looked out to see the people who came. I expected Eric, his mother and Melissa, who'd flown out from New York to see this, but what I didn't expect was to find Peter sitting between them in a new suit, hair neat and face scrubbed. When I looked at him, he looked at me and then down into his lap. My body got hot and weak all of a sudden, but my lawyer was holding on to me and his hand squeezed my arm harder as he sat me down behind our table.

The light in the room was different that day. Where before the light had come in hard from the tall windows, that day it only added haze to the harsh overheads. When the judge came in we all rose and me, feeling like the world had been taken away, only stood for a moment before slumping back into the chair.

The lawyers quickly finished with the remaining specialists. It seemed like a whole new hearing had started. Eric's lawyer got up with a flourish and asked that Mrs. Welch take the stand. When she passed, she looked over at me and I at her because I had refused to look back at the people sitting behind me. I studied her as she took the stand. She wore a severe suit, white blouse that bloomed out of her jacket sleeves like carnations. She'd cut her hair short since the last time I'd seen her and she wore a simple gold chain around her neck with even simpler gold studs in her ears. I decided that she'd dressed down. Her attorney welcomed her to the court, made her relax a moment by standing at his desk and walked slowly up to her like he was strolling in a park.

"Mrs. Welch, how long have you known the woman who sits in front of you?"

"Several years, I imagine."

"Could you be more specific?" The lawyer looked at her and at to the side windows like he was simply passing time.

"Let's see. Peter is now seven and he was born within the year they got married.... I'd say almost eight years."

"Eight years. That's a long time to get to know a person."

"Why yes," she said.

"Would you say that you had a cordial relationship with the defendant?" The lawyer put a hand in his pocket and walked toward me and smiled.

"Yes, at first it was very cordial." I looked at her and rolled my eyes, which the judge caught. I leaned over to my lawyer and said, "She's lying."

"When did your relationship begin to deteriorate?" Now the lawyer moved back to Mrs. Welch.

"A couple of years after Nicholas was born," she said and then added, "If I recall correctly."

"Why did it deteriorate?" the lawyer asked.

"Well, my son, he..."

"Let me rephrase that." The lawyer stopped her from going on and carefully considered his next question.

"Did you find that she was not properly caring for the children?"

"Objection, leading the witness." My lawyer said casually.

"Sustained."

"Let's look at this another way." The lawyer began circling the space between our table and the witness stand.

"Can you tell me why your relationship with the defendant began to deteriorate?"

"She stopped bringing the boys over and they'd be left to fend for themselves at home without supervision. I mean she began to neglect them until finally..."

"Objection, irrelevant."

"Over-ruled. Please continue."

"One day I finally had to go over there myself. With what my son, Eric, told me, I just had to go over and see for myself. She nearly attacked me." Mrs. Welch fidgeted in her seat.

"Let's back up." The lawyer approached her.

"What did your son tell you to prompt you to go over to the house?"

She looked at Eric who was scratching at his pad and concentrating on the lines he made. I wanted to bring him up there, make both of them testify at the same time.

They wouldn't have time to consider what to say, which might have made them tell the truth of things.

"There were these strange goings on. Séances, drums, and maybe drugs."

"Drugs?" the lawyer came toward me.

"Peter said that there were strange smells in the house."

I could go on with Mrs. Welch's testimony, how she believed I was hurtful to the children, spent hours at other peoples home doing "God knows what," not being a good wife to her son, Eric, whom she built up like he was wronged by me. I'll skip to the real hurt, the one that sent me reeling away from all that I knew, the one when Peter walked past me and into the box where he sat down and fixed his gaze on a spot behind me. He was asked several of the same questions as Mrs. Welch, but he began talking about the cottage and what had happened, and how he'd been taken there against his will.

I shouted at him, "But I am your Mother. I can take you where ever I want!"

The judge shot a look to my lawyer. "That's the last time. One more and I will ask that she be taken out of the courtroom.

"Understood," my lawyer said as he held my arm under the table.

Then the lies continued as Peter recounted the time at the cottage. I went slack, disbelieving that my own son would tell the court that I trapped him there, that I told him I would send him farther away if I tried to contact his father and the final, most hurtful lie: that it was I who broke his little brother's arm in a fit of anger to get back at his father. There was a murmur when he said that and then quiet. Not once did Peter look at me, but tears formed in his eyes and by the time he was finished a stream of them soaked his collar.

My lawyer, who was still gripping my arm, causing red marks that turned to bruises the following day, wouldn't look at me as if something that Peter had said brought up memories of his own. When he was asked if he had any questions he shook his head and Peter was released back into the benches where the Welch's, perched like vultures, folded their arms around him and pulled him in.

"So, how'd it go?" the Nurse asked. I didn't answer her. "That good. Well, I was hoping it would be different for you." She smoothed her hand over my bangs and swept my hair down so that it rested on the pillow. She patted my arm and left to tend to her other patients.

There is a place in Big Sur - a bridge that spans a river. The gorge itself empties out into Pfeiffer beach and the river tumbles down out of the mountains, through the deep ravines and works its way to the ocean. I've swam many times in the pools during the summer and looked up to see the iron of the bridgework gleaming in the sun. It is a long fall if one were to use the bridge to jump. Many have – some out of hurt, some out of despair, many out of both. I was thinking of that bridge when I was facing the window of my hospital room having laid there most of the day staring out at the roof and all of the hardware that heats or cools the hospital and the sky that matched the gray of all that sheet metal. Had it not been for the bars, I would have plunged my way through the window and put my fate, twisted and burned, in the hands of anyone who might have taken me up.

Instead, I began drumming. I thrummed my fingers on the sides of the bed. I took whatever I could find and began hitting the rails that held me in place. I wanted to fall into journeying, which I hoped would take me away. It brought the nurses and doctors in and I could hear their muffled conversations beyond the door trying to figure out what to do. I drummed through the day and all night. They tied my hands to the rail. I drummed with my feet. They tied them together so I drummed as if I were a mermaid – slapping both my feet down on the end of the bed. They tied them down, so I drummed with the back of my head until they restrained that. I drummed with my elbows and created such a racket, made the metal crib arms ping so loudly through the corridors that the others, all of them in various stages of mental disorder, began to scream and hit their beds in unison. When my entire body was tied, I began chanting, which finally brought a needle prick in my side and sent me off where I wanted to go in the first place, down into a hole that I wouldn't come out of for a very long time.

24.
Nicholas

When I get to my father's house it is late afternoon. There aren't any cars in the driveway, which relieves me and gives me time to relax after the long drive. I still have a key so I let myself in and have a look around. Not much has changed, a new chair here, a few new pieces of glass statuary and sculpture on the chests and tables. Lydia considers herself a collector, but only of Baccarat and Stueben and maybe a Waterford decanter or some holder of liquid or candy. I notice a wall of mirrors that lengthens the room and doubles everything. Overwhelmed, I go into the kitchen where it is hot because the sun hits it at a perfect angle this time of day. I walk down the hallway to my old bedroom where the door is closed. When I open it, it smells a little musty, like the room has been closed up for quite some time. On the small desk sit some of the things from my childhood: soccer pictures, a baseball cap, a beaded necklace made by a girl from high school with whom I'd dated and let go after a time. I drop my bag on the floor by my bed and lie down for a bit on the twin bed. My feet hang over the end. I bring the pillow up under my head and before I know it I'm asleep.

When I wake there is the smell of coffee and the day has grown dark. I keep still for a few moments and wonder who might be home, but I hear Lydia and my half-sister's voices who I haven't seen in over two years. I pull myself out of bed and go to the door of the bedroom and look down the hall to see where they are. Catherine moves across my view a couple of times. I'm surprised at how tall she's grown. She's now a senior in high school. I wish I knew her better, but our growing up had been separated by too many years.

I go into the bathroom next to my room and look in the mirror, smooth down my hair and splash water on my face. It occurs to me that I don't think I've ever looked this bad. My skin has developed creases and folds around my neck and my cheeks have doubled in size. My eyes have lost their clarity, the blue dulled to an opaque gray and my lids hang loosely over them. To add to the overall slackness of my appearance, I haven't shaved in over two days even though shaving wasn't much of an exercise due to a lack of being able to produce a beard. Errant stubble grew in patches around my cheeks and temples. In short, I looked like a mess. I went back into my bedroom and pulled my shaving kit out to take into the bathroom. On my way out, Catherine must have heard me and was standing in the hallway with a curious expression on her face and a sort of smirk that only girls of seventeen can give.

"God, you look like shit," she offered.

"You're the second person to say that in the last couple of days." I continued into the bathroom and looked back through the mirror at Catherine who'd come to the doorway and leaned against one side.

"Where's Dad?" I asked.

"He doesn't come home 'til seven thirty or eight so you still have some time to hang out. What's happened to you?"

"Nothing."

"Yeah, right." She turns and heads back down the hall and I can hear her shouting to Lydia that I'm finally awake.

Lydia is at the kitchen table gluing a small wooden chair together. When she sees me she comes to hug me with a bottle of glue in one hand and a chair leg in another. "Haven't heard from you in a while." she says and backs off to attend to the chair before the glue dries. I stare at the chair.

"It's a baby gift for a friend. I'm making it from a kit I saw at the craft shop in town. If I'd known it was going to be such a bother, I would have just bought the one they already had done."

I don't say anything, but I go to the cupboard and pull down a mug and pour myself a cup of coffee. "Why'd you come home, Nick?"

"I didn't come home, I came to see my Dad."

"Why didn't you call first?" Lydia sets the leg in the hole and turns to me while she lets the glue dry.

"I didn't want some lame excuse as to why he couldn't see me. This way I have the element of surprise on my side. Jesus, why can't I just come back for a night?"

"He hasn't heard from you in over two years.... you or Peter. It's like you two just disappeared off the face of the earth. You were always the one who held things together around here."

"I got tired of doing that."

"Obviously, but why didn't you just say something. He had such high hopes for you, for college...." Catherine came into the kitchen. Lydia continues, "... and you just left."

"What are you guys talking about?" I ignore her and take cream from the fridge and stir it in my coffee.

"Catherine, can you leave us alone for a few minutes?" Lydia looks at her daughter and lets go of the chair leg, which begins to fall forward. "Shit." she adds as she grabs hold of the leg and puts it back in the hole.

"Now?" Catherine looks at me and I just stare back at her. It's interesting how I have no regard for her. None. She is a product of my father and Lydia and I can't seem to get up the energy to feel anything for her.

"Please," Lydia says and watches Catherine as she leaves the kitchen. "You know, she misses having you around or even talking to her."

"She's thinks too much of me then," I say and I see that Lydia doesn't understand this, but it angers her. She gets tense, so I just drop it.

"Why'd you come back?" she asks and then lets go of the leg, lets it fall, sort of slams the rest of the chair down on the table. She goes to the sink to wash her hands. As she's washing, she turns to me and raises her eyebrows expecting an answer and so I just tell her.

"I found my Mom." She shuts the water down, turns; her hands drip water to the floor. I tell her what has happened and I follow her out to the porch with the chaise-lounges and the view and the night air, which is still warm from the afternoon. We sit down. She is silent through all of it and then she gets up and leaves me outside.

Dad comes home and asks whose car is in the driveway because he's never seen this particular car. I hear Lydia say from the kitchen, "Go see for yourself, he's out on the deck," in a frosty, sharp sort of way and I get butterflies in my stomach and my arms get so like their going to tingle off. I hear his footsteps hit the hardwood floor coming through the living room. They stop and I can hear him set something down which I imagine is a briefcase, a few more steps to the sliding glass doors and then, "Hello, Nick," as he steps out onto the deck.

I look at him a while before I say, "Hi." I'm not sure how to begin so he starts for us.

"What brings you down here?" He goes to the railing and leans against it and stares at me. He hasn't offered his hand and I haven't offered mine so I continue sitting there like I'm in supplication to him, which bothers me.

"We need to talk." I stand up and go to the railing and look out over the sloping hillside of sage and ice plant to the Santa Monica bay. By now there is very little light left, but I can see lights out on the water.

"Are you staying for dinner?" he asks.

"I haven't been invited," I say, which kind of upsets him.

"Since when did you have to be invited?"

"I'm not going to feel comfortable sitting there after what I've come down here for..." I look at him and see that he's started to have moles removed because I can see the little pockmarks the surgery makes.

"So I'll ask you again, why are you here?" I still don't know how to take this question - as an accusation or just a simple question for information. Because I hesitate he says, "Nick?"

"I'm hungry."

"Christ," he says and walks back into the living room and shouts after Catherine to set another place for dinner. Then he comes back and stands at the opening of the glass doors, "Don't tell me your sick, Nick, because I don't have much sympathy for you guys who go off and have that kind of sex." This statement pisses me off and I glare at him and say, "Oh no, Dad, it's much worse than that," and I storm past him and into my bedroom where I shake with anger.

When I come out, he's in talking with Lydia and I can hear her say, "It's not up to me to get involved. You ask him what it is, not me." But she says it like she is involved and angry and hurt, which I didn't mean for her to be.

Catherine comes back through. "God, what is going on around here?" She stops in front of me, says, "I've got a boyfriend, how about you?" I burst out laughing and she laughs too and I say, "I don't quite know yet, I did anyway."

"Got a picture?" she asks.

"No."

"Follow me," she says, so I march behind her to her bedroom where she picks up a picture frame and there is a kid who's quite handsome in a dumb sort of way. "Cute?" she asks.

"Yeah," I say and because it's the nineties, and because she wants to break the ice, she says, "We're sleeping together." Again, I laugh because this sort of shocks me. My visit here is beginning to get a little surreal which was unexpected.

Now I'm older and wiser, but I'm dumb to these young kids and say, "I hope you're being careful," which comes out hopelessly patronizing.

"Man, you're messed up. When'd you become such a Dad?" This throws me and I look at her. She's about as tall as I am with curves and breasts, long hair and clear skin. She's right. When did I become such a Dad? I think about it for a moment and realize that I've always been one, to Peter, to her and now to Mom and I realize that that is why I need Matt so much - I don't have to take care of him.

I go into dinner. Lydia has expertly made four servings out of Chinese take-out for three. I wait until everyone has sat because I can't remember the order of things. We eat in virtual silence, each taking glances at each other. Lydia knows what I have to say and Dad's upset with her because she knows and Catherine's mad because she's been left out of everything. I, having the trump card, keep my mouth shut between forkfuls of beef and broccoli. But I want to relinquish this power I hold over dinner and say, "What have you guys been doing over the last couple of years?" Lydia looks at Dad and he at her. He goes back to eating.

"We've done a bit of traveling, showing Catherine some schools we thought she'd like. Your father's been working his usual hours."

"I'm going to Stanford next year." Catherine chimes in.

"You are?" I say, "Good, then you'll be close by." Dinner falls into silence again. Forks clang, arms reach for meager seconds, I nod the chow mien around the table to see if anyone wants some more and everyone shakes their head.

Dad finally drops his fork to the plate. "Okay, I give up Nick," he says, "Why are you back all of a sudden? There must be a reason." He stares straight at me so I decide to tell him.

"My mother got beaten up, the police got a hold of me and now I'm taking care of her." Dad just sort of sits there stunned. "You asked," I say. Catherine gets up from the table to get some more water.

"I'm beginning to figure things out, Dad," and I emphasize Dad in a mean sort of way, "I'm putting it all together and maybe you can help me out with some of the remaining details." As I say this I lean into him. I begin to feel hot and my anger rises.

Catherine comes back to the table and Lydia looks at me and then at her and she knows to leave the kitchen and not contest it. She gets up with her water and as she's leaving Lydia says, "Thank you, Cathy." I've always known Lydia to be gracious and loving and I know she'll make this up to her.

"How is it that you were such a weak person? Why didn't you stand up to your mother when it counted? You ruined a life. No, make that three lives... you made Peter and me suffer... I can't see how you live with yourself." I shocked myself with this sudden outburst. It was as if the gates of hell had opened up and all the souls of the wronged came through me. The force with which I said this made my Dad sit back in his chair. Lydia watched him carefully, but she was as still as mirrored water.

Dad got up out of his chair and went to the sink and stood looking out the window. "We had one good time between us, didn't we? Building that fort. It's still there, but a lot of the boards are gone. It's the only thing I've ever built. Did you know that? It obviously wasn't built that well, but it was something, wasn't it?" He turned the water on. I kept my eyes on Lydia, who stared straight across the room, focused on nothing. "I thought that it would be all that it would take to bring you boys back to me. Peter and I hung out together, that's sure, but I always felt I was just tagging along. God, I made him do things" He bows his head, the spray of water stops, and silence circles in around us like wolves. After a moment he turns to me and I shift my eyes to him. "I've always loved your mother." When he says this, it hangs in the air like it's resting on so much heat. Lydia gets up out of her seat and leaves the kitchen because that one puzzle piece that has been missing for years has been found, though she always knew where it was. My dad doesn't do or say anything; doesn't make a move toward her, but he stares straight at me until finally I have to turn away. "What is it you want, Nicholas?"

"I can't afford to take care of her, but I won't put her in another institution."

"How much?"

"How much what?"

Dad's voice is slow, deliberate, "How much is it going to take to take to care of her?"

"I don't know." I say, which is true. I hadn't really thought about the cost, but before I could start adding things up in my head, Dad leaves the room. I hear the click of his briefcase opening in the dining room, then silence. In a moment, he comes back in and hands me a check. It is made out to me for a hundred thousand dollars. I stare at the check for a long time until he says, "split it up among the three of you if you wish, or give it all to your mother." He leaves the kitchen and me sitting there holding more money in my hand than I'd ever seen. I put it on the counter and back away from it and stand against the wall. I'm breathing hard, a bit shaken. I take the check up, fold it neatly and put it in my wallet. To calm myself, I clear the table of the take-out boxes and wrappers, Lydia and Catherine's dinner plates and take a dishrag from the edge of the sink and wipe the table clean.

When I leave the kitchen, Dad is out on the porch with a drink in his hand. Lydia is in talking with Catherine. When I go down the hall, she comes out of Catherine's room with a small, overnight bag and her purse. She is clear-eyed and looks like she knows what she's doing though I suspect it's just her own mechanism guiding her way until she gets out of the house. Catherine comes to the door crying after her mother. Lydia stops in front of me and looks up. I feel like she's going to slap me, but instead her eyes are vacant, her body rigid. I don't know what to say and I want to reach out and hold her for all the things she's done for me, but I just stare back at her, which in some ways is enough. Catherine's wails get louder as her mother moves past me down the hall and out the front door. I move back against the wall from the sheer violence of the wails and down the hallway again to the living room.

Most of the lights are turned off and Dad is silhouetted in the moonlight. He lifts his glass to his mouth and dangles it between two fingers over the railing. Catherine has gone back in her room and closed her door. Lydia's car starts in the driveway; the sound of the engine moves off into the night.

I'm wondering what it is I've done, but I know really. The money is meaningless; it will give my mother some freedom, maybe happiness after all this. It's like that line I've heard, "I stand at the corner of cross, don't cross." Should I go or should I cross the living room and go out on the porch. I come to the conclusion that there is nothing I want from him. I got what I came for, but with an unexpected outcome. I could go and comfort him, but I suspect there is nothing I could say to assuage his guilt, which I hope will consume him.

I had planned to stay the night, rest and leave in the morning, but I go collect my bag. I take a last look around my old bedroom and shut out the light. In the hallway I almost knock on Catherine's door. Instead, I stand there and listen to her sobs with my hand flat on the wall and my head leaning against her doorjamb. I take a few moments, continue down the hallway through the living room and then I'm safely out the front door of my father's house.

25.
Marjorie

During the first several years following the trial there was little I would do. Every day blurred into the next. I lay in bed not thinking about anything, working my fingers through themselves. As I grew more and more tired - weaker - I'd just lay there, my body melting into the sheets. I became worthless – not a wife, mother or daughter or a friend to anyone. I was sure that down South the neighbors had quietly talked among themselves over coffee or drinks about what had happened. Maybe the boys were shielded from their children's questions. Most likely not because children often repeat what their parents say in fits of spitefulness or anger.

When my depression deepened, I began losing Peter's and Nicholas' faces, their voices, how they looked when they walked. The terrible thing was that it didn't seem to matter to me and soon they were completely lost with the rest of my memories. My only concerns were to get to the toilet on time before I soiled myself, eat enough to sustain my heartbeat, listen for the unlocking of the gates to go out into the courtyard so I could sit in the sun and feel it beat down on the tops of my feet, on my hair and over my chest.

I can't pinpoint when everyone and everything in my life fell away. Little by little, my mind turned away from thoughts of my father even and I became alone in the world.

It is odd to feel that there is nothing around you. The people that were inside the ward with me I wasn't even aware of. We'd sit in groups during therapy. I could hear voices, but had no idea what they were saying. I couldn't feel their presence, the heaviness and heat of their bodies next to me. I think they keep these places white and sterile to make you forget - so that nothing jogs the memory of the bad things that happened.

After our activities I'd be led out of the room and back to my bed where I'd fall into it, as if I'd been forced to be awake for days and was finally given the luxury of sleep. Sleep was my one salvation and I clung to the emptiness of it as if it was the only thing that would save me.

My way back began ten years after the trial. I felt a nudge on the shoulder from the nurse who had cared for me during it. She was untying me from the bed. The straps loosened around my ankles, my wrists. I felt her hand on my cheek. I opened my eyes to see her dressed in everyday clothes, her hair down over her shoulders and a slight blush in her face from working to free me.

"It took me a little bit to find you." The nurse stroked my cheek. "But here you are. Remember me?" She worked her hand over my shoulder and arm. "I'm Ann."

I continued to stare at her and kept still.

"It's very early so we have to be quiet." She pulled me up and expertly slipped a sweater over my shoulders and put my arms through.

"Look at your hair. Hmmmm." She took a brush out of the table beside my bed and started to comb it. "We're escaping," she said, "not really. They know I'm taking you, but let's pretend we are so we have to be very still." She swung my feet to the edge of the bed and put my shoes on and made me stand still. I wobbled some, but she held me firmly and led me down past the other beds, past the night guard to whom she nodded and past the front doors into the early morning dark.

"We have to hurry before the sun comes up." She said as she started the car. I sat dumbly still - letting her be my captain - and waited for everything that came next.

We drove for a long time in the dark, but I could gradually smell the ocean, its heavy salt, that reached me in fits and starts. I sat up in the car and became aware of the rest of my body. The nurse was talking, telling me how she'd just been divorced and how I had haunted her all these years and now that she had nothing to do, but work and go home to an empty house, she had wondered about my fate. She'd asked her friends how to find me and searched the records for my name, remembering only that my first name was Marjorie. She'd been transferred from the first hospital years ago and had gone back and scoured the records to find me.

"It was easy, really. It's not such a large place, but I was worried that maybe they took you back down South to where you had some sort of family." She pulled the car off the road onto dirt. The headlights fell on rocks and low shrubs and fell off into blackness a few feet beyond the car.

I spoke for the first time. "My drum. I need my drum." The words tumbled out of me, slow like syrup. "I need to go back and get my drum."

"We'll go back soon, Marjorie," she said and patted my leg. A loud ping came up through the wheel well. Then we were out of the dark where the sky was opening up, but still a deep blue. You could see how it was growing light at the edges of the flat land.

The nurse pulled the car to a stop and sat for a moment before setting the switches off. She reached back and pulled a blanket from the back seat. Now it was black in the car again, but she got out and came over to my side to help me out. She led me down the rest of the road. It was cold. The dew on the grass at the side of the road tugged at my gown and made the edges wet. The smell of the sea had deepened. It was in me now and I pulled away from the nurse and began walking on my own. She followed back a few steps and watched me. A little farther down the road she told me to go right onto a path. By now my ankles and shoes were soaked, my toes squished and were loose. I had blind trust in her - maybe because she was a woman or because of the warmth of her hands - I didn't remember her much from the past. The moon fell behind some far off hills.

A short distance away was a stand of trees that rose up into a hulking shape and stood apart from the sky, which had gone lighter still. The trees were black; the shape of them was like the great bow of a ship. As we got nearer they rose up ominously and frightened me so that I stopped.

"It's okay," the nurse said, coming forward and taking hold of my shoulders. She led me around to the front of the trees and then into the middle of them where there was a small clearing. She laid out the blanket and sat me down.

"Smell the eucalyptus?" The nurse took in a deep breath. "The trees are in bloom."

"My boys. Where are my boys?" Memories came back to me. Eucalyptus trees surrounded our home years ago.

"I don't know, Marjorie. I just found you, that's all."

"Where's my drum?"

"Don't know that either."

"Take me away."

"I can't do that, Marjorie. I was lucky enough to persuade them to do this with you. I have to take you back."

I went to stand up, but the nurse put her hand on my thigh. "Be still, dear."

Light began filtering through the trees. The nurse lay back on the blanket and I copied her. The sky turned cobalt blue above the trees, but the trees themselves were still dark. I began to make out detail, but only in shadow.

"Are you warm enough?" she asked. "I'll give you my sweater if you wish."

I kept still, transfixed on the awakening sky. I closed my eyes, drowsy from lying down and from the lingering effects of the pills they gave me and dozed.

When I woke, the sun had reached the tops of the trees. The sky beyond was light blue, but there were flecks of deep reds and orange flickering against it. The nurse was smiling and holding her hands up as if she were trying to catch something. The trees were now their gray-green. White tufts sprouting from pods made them sparkle as if they were lit up with Christmas lights. All around me were the disjointed fluttering of butterflies that had come to life in the sun. They flew up in clouds.

"They're Monarchs, Marjorie, come to be with us for a time."

"There're so many of them."

"Yes."

I looked lower on the trees and could see hundreds of butterflies coming slowly to life like waking children.

"They need the sun to power their wings," the nurse said, "Look how the tops of the trees have emptied and how full they are down here. It takes them a bit to wake up."

Butterflies landed on our blanket, on each of us. I held out my hand and one ambled into my palm. I studied it. The large wings were backlit and glowed. The butterfly was slowed down and fluttered only for balance. Its spindly feet attached themselves to my palm and its tentacles twitched. More butterflies fell down and covered us making us look like an oriental blanket - an intricate design of the colors of fire.

I awakened fully and began to cry. The nurse put her arm over my shoulder and we sat together under the canopy of the trees, the autumn-hued clouds of butterflies and came back into the world.

Later, the nurse took me back to the hospital and put me into bed where I slept without taking any pills. For several days she came to get me and take me out to a beach, a waterfall and a promontory where you could see the whole landscape. We sat for hours on the edges of the palisades and looked out over the ocean and talked or said nothing.

She told me she wanted to help me because she needed someone to save, that her husband was beyond it from drinking, but she held her own problems in as if in a safe and kept them there so that all of her attention went toward me.

I started savoring showers - I imagined the warm water feeling like sun on a butterfly's wing giving me strength to make my way out of the dark. Food had taste again - I'd roll a pea around on my tongue just to feel its texture. I waited at the window for the nurse to come take me away every day.

I became what they called "functional." They allowed me into the crafts room where I drew the ocean and mountains and all of the things I'd seen in the last few weeks. After a while they returned my belongings to me. They even gave me back my drum as long as I wouldn't beat it inside the hospital. I agreed just to have it hanging above me.

At the end of the summer Ann came to take me out. I was all ready to go. I'd combed my own hair, put on my own shoes and gathered a few things in a bag.

In the car she said, "I've got to leave now, Marjorie."

"Right now?" I asked.

"No, not right now, but soon. I'm going home to care for my parents who are getting old." I couldn't imagine her gone - not just yet. "They live far away."

After a moment I said, "They are lucky to have you take care of them." Ann smiled and relaxed until I said; "Everyone leaves."

Ann turned to look out her window. "I can't argue with that," she said.

We spent the day hiking in the mountains where we came upon a monastery. Men in robes, mostly Asian or white, shuffled by. Otherwise, it seemed the grounds were deserted. Ann and I climbed a hillside to a small hut that was hidden among scrub and pine. The clang of a bell echoed across the hillside and shuddered through me. Two monks, dressed in black with white collars like scarves, came out of the small hut and whisked by us without a word. Ann took my hand and led me inside and motioned for me to sit. She took my legs and crossed one over the other, brought my hands together, one hand surrounding a fist with the thumbs touching. She showed me how to sit, close my eyes, made me to breathe slowly and count my breaths.

Ann said, “If you ever start to feel like you’re going to panic or if you feel like people are trying to take things away from you, you find yourself a nice quiet spot like this and sit and meditate. Think of the good things that you and I have done together, all the good things in your life and you think about them over and over. It’s not hard and it’ll keep you safe and warm and looking to the future.”

After we sat, she led me up farther into the hills where we followed a small stream. I bent down to touch the warm water. Up ahead, off the trail we were following, clouds of steam rose from pools of water and caught the light. Moss hung down from oak trees and flat-leafed plants surrounded the pools. We’d left one world and entered another where everything was lush and green.

Ann removed her clothes and I did the same. She lowered herself into the water; first her feet then her knees, hips, stomach and breasts. I watched her intently like I was her student experiencing all of these new wonders of the world that I'd been apart from for so long.

As she sunk lower in the water, Ann let a long breath come from deep inside her and sat down up to her neck. She motioned for me to join her. We luxuriated in the warm pools until the steam lost the light and we could still make our way safely down the trail.

On the way back to the hospital she said, "I have one more surprise for you." She pulled around to the rear of the hospital and stopped the car. We sat and I think she was waiting for me to see something so she finally turned the engine off and got out of the car. I stayed inside and followed her with my eyes. She walked up to the back of a van - its blue color having faded and disappeared in places to reveal a white undercoat. I slowly recognized it to be my van. I got out of the car and went to it, stopping to see if it was really the same van, the one that had taken me away, carried my boys, been Michael's home, been mine.

"It's been sitting here all these years. I tried to start it, but I'm afraid it's going to take a little work, but I'll see that it's running before I leave."

"Why have you done all this Ann?"

"Because of all the women I've seen in and out of places like this or at the hospital because some man has abused them or left them or the circumstances of their lives have caused them despair - not one of them I really helped. Not one. I only did it because it was my job. When my husband left me, the only way to come out of all I was going through was to find one of you ladies and help. Maybe it's a selfish thing, maybe not, but that's all."

I went up to her and hugged her. "I'm still not all put back together. I want to be, but I don't think after this long I will be."

"All you can do is try," she said, bringing her head back to take me in. She smiled and began laughing. I joined her.

After Ann left, I had times where my mind cleared, but there were still times I teetered off. I learned to put myself to bed, sit and meditate like Ann showed me or make myself go to sleep.

I was released from the hospital. I could see tension lift from the nurse's faces, smiles creep up their shiny cheeks only to disappear when they found me back in their care after I was brought in off the streets again. They swept Big Sur in winter of my kind; they did it out of duty and humanity they said – but really only to take us in before they found one of us frozen in some campground or tossed up on the beach after having been caught by a wave.

Other sick people arrived following like lunks behind the same two officers who processed all of them through the gates that held us in during the cold months.

The front desk people knew to take my drum away, but I could keep an eye on my van out back that I kept running with handouts and the government check I received each month on account of my father being Native American. The government does strange things. Ann told me how to collect those checks – go to the post office, claim them, take them to the bank to cash. As the eighties unfolded the people at the hospital just wanted to get me out and show me how to stay out. Government hospitals couldn't afford to keep us anymore and we were loosed upon the streets. Every spring for a few years when the weather turned they let me out, gave me back my van keys and told me to have a nice summer – glad to have it peaceful again.

I'd go off into the parks, camp a night or two and stay down by the rivers. I'd head off up a dirt road sometimes and be lucky not to be chased off for a few days. When I was, I'd search out some spot along the road, always moving and trying not to run my van so much. When it broke down, Carl, one of the big orderlies from the hospital took a look at it and set it right again. He just loved cars is what he said and didn't mind working on it. I'd sit and stare, watching his hands and arms get dirty from the grease. He'd get me to turn it over, and the motor fired to life and he'd chuckle and say, "I just added some glue, that's all."

It didn't take long to disappear into the system. Once the cutbacks set in during the mid-eighties I was left on my own. Sometimes I'd see some of the other former patients on the highway, but I wouldn't say anything to them or acknowledge them. I felt separate now. I knew what to do for myself and how to keep moving to find the places I could get lost in.

26.
Nicholas

When I get back to Big Sur I find that Peter has all but disappeared. He hasn't been by to see our mother; Linda is frantic with worry. I even call out to the platform to see if he'd been at work, but they tell me he's been fired because he has missed two shifts. There are several messages on the machine: Lydia has called to explain herself and "to well, I just had to talk to someone." Patty is "overwhelmed with ingratitude from our client because it was she "who 'busted her butt' to get the goddamn newsletter out." Peter has left a message for me to call this man about a place for our mother to live, "and that's the best I could do, I'm sorry," he added and finally, the hospital who wanted to release her, but could find no one to release her to and would I please call as quickly as possible.

I took a few minutes to order things in my mind. I made a half-hearted attempt to call Matt. I let the phone ring three times and then hung up quickly just in case he caught it on the fourth or before the answering machine kicked in. I hadn't slept much even though I'd pulled off at a cheap motel in Santa Maria on the way up from Dad's. I laid awake most of the night. The hum of generators and car doors slamming kept me up and let my mind spin over the details of what had happened at my Dad's house earlier. I also kept feeling in my coat pocket where I'd put the check, not believing that I was holding so much money and trying to come up with an idea of what to do with it.

I was angry that Peter hadn't followed up on his promise to look in on her and had seemingly disappeared. Though he could lapse into silences and easily hang around the edges of people, he'd never just disappeared without telling someone at least - his ego wouldn't have allowed it. To leave Linda alone like he did up in that remote cabin was still very curious and contrary to what even Linda knew about him, for she knew more than anyone. She'd not seen him since just before I left for Los Angeles. She'd seen him on the phone with me and he'd got so agitated and distant that he'd gotten up out of the chair, slammed the receiver of the phone down so hard in its base that it cracked the plastic. "On top of that, he kissed me so rough when he left," she said, "that it drew blood on my lower lip."

So I was surprised by the cryptic message he'd left regarding a place to stay for Mom. He'd left the man's name and phone number, said to talk to him about a small cottage he had and would be willing to rent for cheap. I called and found out that it was up North of Big Sur, through a canyon that emptied into the flats on the other side of the St. Lucia Mountains. The cottage was clean and nice, however small, that his mother-in-law had stayed there for many years until recently when they had to put her in a home. I made an appointment to go see him that afternoon. I was hoping to check it out before I picked up Mom, but then the hospital called again and "could simply not hold her one more day under the insurance guidelines."

When I got there, she and a nurse were sitting quietly in the lobby. I went to her and touched her shoulder.

"We needed the extra bed," the nurse says by way of apology. I nod my head and look at my mother who has been watching me. She smiles and I am taken aback by a sudden feeling of grace and humility I feel toward her. I've learned that it couldn't have been simple for her to go up against people who didn't want her or someone like my father who was still as weak as a newborn, unformed and at odds with the world. I think that here is a man who really isn't a man and someone who never taught me to be a man and yet I have this instinct in me to care for people like an adult man should - like in the natural order of things. I wonder how it is that I've become caretaker for all of these people. Up until now I have never received anything back for it, not a thank you, not a cheap piece of paper that might have a scribbled "I love you" across it or a promise of someday just taking the time to be with me or fill me up like I think I want to be.

My mother looking at me right now though is enough. That's something isn't it? Isn't it supposed to be? My problem is that I'm not ready for this responsibility. I'm supposed to be figuring myself out. Not my mother who appears as helpless as a fallen bird or my brother whose disappearance is another one of his selfish acts or now Lydia who has called me "just to talk." I'm trying to figure out my own life: work, love, sex, and Matt. Matt - whom I love, yes, I'll say it. Deeply. Yes. Why does this come to me now? Is it my mother looking up at me, needing me? Is it my brother, who despite everything I love because of what we, brothers down to the core, had been through? Is it all the people in my life who've shaped me?

My mother tugs on my arm. She's ready to go and her shopping bags are full of her stuff. Some clothes, a couple of books she loves to read, which I find fascinating because maybe it has been her escape in life. We all need one of those. My use for books has been different. I've simply wanted to find things out. The stories and characters have meant nothing to me. It's their actions, where they lived and how they did things that always interested me. Maybe it's the way I learned how to behave toward others.

As we head out the front door she is carrying a wide flat drum. There is a long feather that dangles from it and beads in long strands that shake when she holds it up. Some might call it a tambourine, but it is larger and has a deeper sound that doesn't rattle or ping, but rather resonates and thunders. The moment we get outside she turns back to the hospital and beats the drum just once. The sound echoes back to us as she grabs my arm as I help her into the car, which I've parked in the red.

As we drive away, she says, "that's the last time I'll be in a hospital."

I believe her and don't say anything. I don't want to contradict her because most likely at some point she will be.

Farther away I can feel her relaxing more. I decide to take her down the long way around the Point and up through Big Sur Center before heading inland. I know she'll want to see the ocean and smell it before it disappears from her life for a while. It is like I'm reviewing her life for her by driving by all the things she's loved and been familiar with, showing her all the things she's going to miss when she dies. Is it a selfish act? Probably. I want to show her all the things that I love, too.

I swing by Matt's sister's house where I know he's staying just to see if his car is there, which it isn't. Now we head away and into the canyon that'll take her to her new home. I explain to her where she's going. I explain it to her like she's a child.

The farther we go into the canyon the more alert she becomes. She drums her fingers on her legs, turns her head to watch as we speed by the sandstone cliffs.

"You're in love," she says.

"I'm what?" I say and laugh because it is the most unexpected thing.

"You're in love," she says again. "I don't know how I know it, but I just know it." She laughs too and straightens up in her seat. Her finger thrumming gets louder, insistent like machinery. I'm hot now because I'd been thinking about Matt at the hospital.

"How do you know?" We passed one of those trading posts - a kind of store that appears so often up here - the carved totem poles, chain-saw statues of bears and eagles, neon blink of beer signs and the odd hitching posts that are guides for tourist's cars.

"I don't know.... I'm hungry," she says and stops her thrumming.

"How *did* you know?" I insist. Had someone told her about Matt and me? Who could that have been? Had Peter stopped by?

"I can see it in you, Nicholas, because I've seen it in me. I'm hungry, let's stop."

We stop in at a restaurant that is gearing down from the summer. It is noon and half the chairs are still upended on the tables. Two people sit at the bar with beers and a woman comes out of the kitchen to greet us. Mom takes a while to order after I tell her she could have anything she wants. "Anything?" she asks. She's giddy now from all the choices on the boards above the opening to the grill area. To make sure she asks me again. "Anything at all?" I look at her and laugh a little.

"Anything at all."

She settles on French fries, fried fish and onion rings. She's so happy now and I want to cry as I watch her bounce her focus from one menu board to another.

"It's a small thing to eat, but to eat whatever you want... now there's the prize," she says. She sits up at the counter so she can fidget with all of the counter things: napkin dispenser, squeeze bottles of ketchup and mustard, silverware in plastic cups, salt and pepper shakers. I'm watching her and this is when I decide what to do with the money. I'll just give it all to her. I couldn't accept any part of it and Peter certainly didn't help when I needed him. I'll figure a way to regulate it while giving her some options on what she wants to do with it. My father's writing of the check was the last selfish thing he could do to her - absolving his own weakness and complicity in the destruction of my mom. Why not give the money to her? At least she'd be comfortable for a while and I could see that she invests it and makes it work for her. I could split the cost of her rent, help her with food and provide her with things so she wouldn't have to spend the money, but instead let it grow. Again, too much to think about when all I want to do is take pleasure in the pleasure she's having in just enjoying her lunch.

Further into the drive my mother turns to me. I look quickly to her and quickly back to the road for I'm winding the car through the canyon as if I were trying to navigate a sidewinder's back. Her hair is fine now where it had been unwashed and coarse when I saw her at the station. It is now shiny, combed and set in a way that is becoming to her. The nurse had given her some makeup from her own collection of lipsticks and powders, but my mother, unaccustomed to such things anymore, had applied too much so that it smudged with the slightest touch and left marks on the sleeves of her sweater when she accidentally rubbed against it.

"I saw you once," she says, "I saw you watching me from the shoulder of the highway. I didn't know it was you at the time, but now I do." We come through the dark canyon and into the wide valley, which is gold and green where the crops are growing. Mom takes in a deep breath and sighs. "Oh, how beautiful this is," she says. Tears form in her eyes. She moves up in her seat and presses her forehead against the window glass as if to get closer or move out into the field.

"I'm sorry I didn't follow you that night." I say, "I wanted to, but you seemed..." I didn't know how she seemed - lost, happy, out of herself?

"I'm glad you didn't. Those are good times when the waves crash like that against those rocks. Good times. I went down there when the tide was up and the waves were strong because I knew that the spray could reach all the way to the top of the rocks and I could make it down far enough to get close and feel it."

"What was it like?" I ask.

"Being washed clean," she says and smiles. She is silent for a while as we head out into the flats. I take the directions from the dashboard and study them. She moves her face to the window to find the light. It beats down into the car and is trapped there though its shape moves over the interior - the seats, console and dash - and warms everything. I roll down the window and the heat of the afternoon fills the cabin and makes me drowsy.

The road becomes straight. The lulling slap of the tires makes us both burrow into our seats and settle in for the rest of the drive.

We get to the sign that says "Double Pine Ranch." From where we are you can't see the main house, but instead the road turns to gravel and is lined by a rotting, white rail fence. Some of its boards hang off one nail. Beyond the fence are fields of alfalfa waiting for their last autumn cut. When we reach the house chickens clatter away, a dog stands up out of a dead sleep to greet us. There is a tractor half-exposed in the sun protruding from a barn - two identical pick-up trucks are next to it. On their doors are logos: the legend, "Double Pine Ranch" is in black type over the green silhouettes of two pine trees hooked together at their base. In contrast to the fences, the main house is freshly painted. Clumps of pansies and Johnny-Jump-Ups potted in old oak planters sit at the bottoms of the joists that hold the sloping roof over the porch. On the left is the outer building I assume will be my mother's home for a while. It is clean, which pleases her, I think, because she steps out of the car and goes to it.

The front door opens and out comes Frank who I assume is the man I spoke to on the phone. He looks pleasant enough, gangly, but with a bell-shaped belly over blue jeans held in place by a frayed leather belt. Around his eyes are lines like tiny highways leading into piercing blue. I could see once that he was a handsome man, had probably been as self-confident as a bear, but now he's deferential to my mother and looks at her squarely. He decides that she's going to be just fine out here.

"I'm Frank," he says to her bending down to meet her. "Glad to have you here."

I feel my mother is returning to the way she was in the days when I was young. She gazes up at him and extends her hand, which he takes gently like he is holding a fall leaf.

Inside the small cabin my mother goes to each window and looks out. It doesn't matter how large the window is or whether it's just out of reach of her head because she gets up on her tip-toes or just gazes out of it as if, just by looking, she can bring the outside in.

Frank and I stand at the entrance and watch her.

He says, "My mother-in-law fixed this place up real nice and I just haven't had the heart to change it to suit my needs."

"It's perfect," mother says, "It's like you can see the whole world from in here."

"You're welcome to roam around the property as much as you want." he says, "I even have a patch of ground you can plant things in if you wish though we're heading into winter.

"I'll find something to plant," she says, "winter something." She turns to us and smiles. Frank begins to show her the heater controls and how to work everything. I go to the car and gather her shopping bags. I make a mental note to buy some clothes for her, take her shopping in a few days. I stand and wait at the car to give them a few moments to adjust to each other.

Frank comes out of the house. He's smiling, working his hands back into his pockets. "I think she's going to be fine here," he says, "she'll need some time I expect." He looks at me for agreement and I nod my head.

"She's had it rough," I say, "and it's going to be a while before she builds up trust. If you have any kind of trouble, I've written my numbers down for you here." I hand him a card, "work and home."

I loosen; the events of the past week have been hard on me. "Thanks for doing this for us. I hope it won't be a burden for you."

"Think nothing of it. It'll be nice to have the company again," he says, extending his hand, which I take. Frank ambles off to the barn, slaps the fender of the old tractor and disappears through the wide door.

My mother comes out of the cabin and stretches her arms out as if she wants to fly. She lets out a long loud sigh like a sleeping child would. Her whole body seems to expand and release. The sun is low as the afternoon wanes, but it is a brilliant orange. She has removed her shoes and her dress flows over her body like curtains, like waving laundry in the wind. She's pulled the pin out of her dark hair and now it falls straight down over her shoulders. I can see her now as a younger version of herself. I smile at the memory of her on the beach holding me in the air, the sun like it is now falling slowly behind her and me laughing at the thrill of being held up by her to see the whole natural world as she saw it.

We tend to her things. She takes her clothes from her paper bags, folds them and puts them in drawers. I go through the kitchen to see that everything works. I turn on the gas stove, check the temperature of the refrigerator and run the water to see that it is clear and free from rust. I see that she has things to cook and eat with, store leftovers in and cups to drink from. If nothing else, Peter has done well to find this place for our mother. I just wish he would come and help us and can't understand his reluctance to do so. I'm still angry with him, but this lucky find of a house pushes it back some.

On the way to find groceries my mother fidgets in the car, plays with the handle on the door, opens and closes the window. I'm afraid that she'll lapse into a spell or fit of some kind. I'm not prepared to deal with this sort of thing or to help her if she begins to empty all of her hurt out. I wouldn't begrudge her that.

"Everything is so new," she says. "Look at everything in this car. My van's so old, but I know every corner of it, every square inch. I don't know a thing in this car. Maybe that's good." She shakes her head, fingers the edge of the dashboard. "I thought I'd just live out the life I had left in that old van of mine. I wonder what happened to it. Some kid's probably got it somewhere. I don't mind that so much. It sort of fell into my lap anyway. Why shouldn't it fall into someone else's?"

"I suppose that would be fitting. Maybe we could find you something to replace it with."

"No, I don't want to drive anymore," she says, "not in something new like this." She laughs, "I wouldn't know where to begin with all these controls..."

"It's not so hard," I say, "just put in the key, turn it over. I .... It's just like any other car." A sign cautions us to slow down and I can see the edge of the town now. It always discourages me to edge out of the country into a town. The houses that begin them are always the most run-down, ghosted by plywood-covered windows and high grass running up their water-stained sides. As we go farther the buildings become newer - stucco, fresh paint, bright awnings - there are people on the sidewalks. Up ahead I recognize the name "Deacon's," which is the only market in Big Sur.

As I pull in my mother says, "You should stop watching me the way you are." She pats my leg, "I'm not going to do anything to embarrass you."

"I'm not watching you."

"Yes you are," she says, "I understand, but let's not have lies between us okay Nicholas?" She pushes the door open and then she's out and into the market as I sit in the car and breathe a sigh of relief and think that maybe everything will work out.

As we finish at the market, I remember the check Dad had given me. I tell my mother about it. Though a flick of her eyes tell me she's surprised, she pretends that she isn't and says, "that bastard should have done what's right a long time ago and it has nothing to do with money." Then I tell her about Lydia, Catherine and what happened at his house. Mostly, I'm exhausted and I begin to ramble and say things that maybe I shouldn't. Like how Grandfather had died and left everything to Dad and not to Grandmother, putting Dad right back in the middle of having to deal with her again. I told her of Melissa, her long stay at our house and how she'd finally made Dad break away from his mother and how Dad had really loved her all of these years.

"Nicholas, stop. It doesn't matter anymore does it?"

"It all matters." I say, a little hurt that she doesn't care to know.

"I've had all these years to think about it." She looks out her window as we slip out of town again and start heading through the fall fields. "I've spent more than twenty years wondering why everything happened like it did."

"Well, I haven't," I say, "all of this has just been thrust on me in the last couple of weeks. All of it! I've been the only one to try and make any sense of it." I'm blinded now to the road so I let the car just go or rather my subconscious take over the demands of driving.

"It's not so terrible, is it?" Her eyes are on me now. "Is it?"

"Yes, it is." I say, defeated and sad.

"Why?" she asks.

Why? Because I've lost the one thing in my life that really started to matter. I've lost Matt. If this hadn't come up we'd still be together, still working things out as we got used to each other. A year isn't enough time to learn about someone - even ten years. Or maybe you can never really know whom it is you decide to share your life with. Maybe you just go through it and bend around the obstacles together and hope that one or the other doesn't veer off into some unforeseen territory. My own parents veered badly, worse than most. It could happen to me as well, but I want that chance to try and do better.

I turn to my mother and say without anger and without any other feeling, “It just is, Mom, and it’s something I can’t talk about right now.” We make the turn off of the main highway back to the ranch in time for the falling dark to swirl in around us and allow us back into our own lives.

27.
Marjorie

This afternoon when I was dozing out in the field smelling the heavy sweetness of wheat grass and artichoke fields and watching blackbirds in great clumps swoop down to disappear among the old live oaks, I was lulled into a sense that I could stay like this for the rest of my days. I could lie out here in the heat or cold and enjoy the greens and browns of the Saint Lucia Mountains. The mountains that I have come to love on either side: one side that angles down into the Pacific, the other where I am now: the side that flattens out until you hit the foothills of the Sierras. Then the Sierras themselves - heaved in granite, which I haven't seen since I was a child. If I had the chance I'd go there.

I'm tired of the palisades, those long flat stretches of land where I've spent my days. I've come to learn that we as people can either live our lives on the flat reaches of them or head off into the mountains and rise up to meet ourselves. When our lives seem like they are no longer fit to live we could go to the edge of the palisade and allow ourselves to tumble down over the cliff and be swallowed whole into the great mouth of the ocean.

Out of my self-imposed stupor I heard a familiar engine sound. I'd taken a break from writing this letter to you and looked out over the grasses and rested on my two palms. I saw my beloved van coming down the road to me.

I sprang to my feet, knocked the hat I was wearing clear off my head and started toward the van. I waved wildly, but as I approached I saw who was driving and I caught myself, stood frozen on the road, my dress going out ahead of me waiting for me to catch up. I knew then. I knew who had come to me in the middle of the night, beaten me and left me for dead on the side of the road and stole my van.

As sure as I know the sky, the smell of the ocean and the shapes of trees, I remembered Peter's shape. I ran away from the van to my new home. I reached the front door, slammed it shut behind me and bolted the lock. I stood against the back of the door breathing heavily, hearing the van sputtering to a stop just outside. My heart beat wildly. My palms were flat against the door pushing it back against the latch. The car door opened, the metal whined as if it were being bent back and then forward. A footstep landed on gravel crunching the pebbles together.

Peter's voice came clearly through the door. "I've brought your van back. I've even fixed it up some." I kept silent. "I replaced the broken windows, the seatback that was bent. I've even tuned it up and put oil in it." I couldn't catch my breath. I began to cry. "I just filled it up so you won't have to worry about filling it up for a while."

I moved away from the door, turned and stared at it as if I could see Peter standing just beyond it.

"C'mon, Mom, you knew it was me all along." He tried the door and knocked on it. "You knew it was me. You just didn't want to admit it." He paced back and forth. "You were such an embarrassment. All those years carrying on. People laughing at you and shaking their heads. I couldn't take it anymore. It's a small town, Mom. People knew who you were, knew me."

I waited a moment and said quietly, "It was the only thing I had in the world, Peter. Why do you take everything from me?" I sank to the floor. I could hear Peter at the door, his breathing hard and labored.

In a whisper I heard, "I'm sorry." A loud moan came through the door and he began to pound it - the slap of his palm and the door banging against the jamb and the sound echoing through the empty room. The sound was full of the things Peter had done - lying at the trial, hating his father for making him do it and being ashamed of what I'd become. I wondered what he would do if he could take it all back. The sight of him at that trial was ingrained in my memory and would never leave, but I thought if there were one thing I could do now, one thing on the earth that I could contribute it would be saving Peter. But I moved away from the door and sat in the center of the room as if at an altar, cross-legged, staring at the latch and daring it to break. The pounding was insistent. Finally, I screamed at him to stop, but he kept pounding. My thought was to go to the phone and call the police, but I sat there dumbly in a state of shock, scared.

After a few more minutes I went to the door and in between hits I slid the bolt free of the jamb and turned the handle so that when the next hit came the door swung open and I stood there looking at him clearly for the first time since he was a boy as he fell forward on the landing.

He laid there for several moments in a daze and kept his face to the floor. When he pulled himself up on his haunches, I reached back slapped my hand across his face and knocked him over again. The force of my swing brought me down on top of him. The violence of what I'd done overtook me and I went off into another fit of crying. He cried too as we both lay there on the floor of the cabin.

For a long time we stayed like that. If you looked down you would have seen the two of us lying side by side, legs splayed out, both of us with our eyes wide open staring up at nothing trying to think of what to do next.

Peter spoke first, his voice thick and breaking like radio static. "I suppose I wanted that...wanted you to hit me like that. You can do it again if you want. You can hit me as hard as you want and as many times. I think I need to be knocked down some more. Maybe if you used something strong.... maybe if you took up a shovel then you and Nick won't hurt me anymore. Maybe that...."

His body shook. "Maybe I should just go off like you did and take the van and go. I wouldn't be able to mess up any more lives." I looked over at him. He'd hidden his eyes in the crook of his arm.

I moved closer to him and moved my mouth up to his ear. "It's over, Peter. All done. Everything that could happen has happened. Take the van if you want, but even I couldn't disappear like I want to. But it's yours if you want it." I kissed his cheek and tasted the salt from his tears. I'd gone dry by now; there was nothing I needed. It was Peter who needed to be absolved and, once again, I forgave him everything that he had done. It was easy. Maybe it's what a mother is supposed to do - forgive her children. Maybe it is what a mother needs. To be able to look at them and know that they are a part of you despite the pain they inflict. If there was one person who suffered more than I had, Nicholas, it was your brother.

In late fall the sun angles over the land sharp as knife blades. The summer days are a memory, but what the sun does is define the view, makes things clearer and easier to see.

When we finally went outside to walk along the road and talk, Peter told me about everything: the things you couldn't bring yourself to tell me or didn't know, his betrayal at the hands of your grandmother and father, his new wife, your half-sister, your life now. He rambled on about everything and as the sun edged closer to the mountains he turned to me and said, "I'm going to walk home from here." I told him I'd drive him and let him off below his house if that's what he wanted, but he refused.

He said, "No, I need to walk all the way home. It may take me 'til morning or I may just get tired of it and bum a ride, but I need to start out fresh. I don't know if you know what I mean, but I just need to start walking down this road and go home."

We stopped at the fence before the main highway. He turned to me, "I won't ever see you again, will I?"

"Why do you say that?"

"Just a hunch. It's okay. I'm sorry for everything I've done."

Peter started walking himself home. I watched him all the way until the only thing I could see was his speck. Because of the fading light he disappeared into the dark. I turned and headed back to the little house. I looked at the van in the driveway. It was old and tattered, but Peter had washed it and the windows were clean and clear. I went up to it and ran my hand along its side and looked in. He'd washed out the inside, hung new curtains behind the driver's seat and reupholstered the front seats. I opened the door and looked in the back. He'd built a platform with built-in storage boxes. He'd repainted the interior and put in new side paneling. It even smelled like eucalyptus, as he must have sprayed something inside. Seeing all the work he'd done touched me and made me giddy. I climbed into the van and lay in the back on the cushions he'd added. After a time, I decided what to do.

I love you Nicholas. I love your brother. I love the ocean and these mountains. I love everything that fills me up because so much has emptied me. I love the way the sky is after a rain. I love spring and the way it quietly takes over winter. I love how trees lose their leaves. I love the way some men look at women and how they look back. I love how memory works, how it lessens the worst of times and brightens the best.

I loved my old Indian father. I still have the feather he gave me: my one possession that has never been taken from me. I will leave it here on the table with this letter. It is still in fine shape and still takes on the weight of time. Keep it close.

I've collected my things in the van. I'm ready to go. I'm heading for the mountains away from the sea. I'm hoping for a brilliant sky tomorrow and bright, billowy clouds. That's the least of it. Take care of your brother and yourself. May you find love and hold on to it as hard as you can. It is worthwhile even when it gets bad at times. You need someone to forgive, always that. I hope you'll forgive me now as I leave you again. You need to lead your own life and not be concerned with my fitful mind. I'll make do, Nicholas. I always have.

28.
Nicholas

I hold the feather up in front of me as you would a sextant, fixing it first on the cottage as if I were taking measurements or giving a blessing. I might be doing the latter. My mother's letter has blinded me reading it in the sun as I have so it takes a moment for my eyes to adjust and see the fineness of the feather. It is beautiful and delicate. It must have taken great effort on her part to keep it in such shape over the years. Maybe it's because we tend to the things we cherish.

I've decided that this will be the last time I come here to look up and see where our troubles began. Maybe someday it will be taken over again by the woods or fall into the sea during some cataclysmic event to erase it from my memory. Or maybe it will, in time, be just another house along the road: a landmark to gauge my life by.

I have been sitting here for several hours reading her letter and remembering. I've formed my own thoughts about things. When I went to look in on her, only these pages and the feather were left. All of her things were gone. I suppose I could have called the police, filed a missing person's report. But I had a feeling that she wasn't lost, that she knew exactly where she was going. I was proved right by her letter and now I am alone again.

I walk around the cottage once more. I remembered everything now and what I hadn't known all these years has been filled in by everyone involved except for my grandmother who, had she'd been alive, would probably have brushed aside the whole affair as if it was just a small annoyance not to be bothered with.

When I come around the corner, Peter is standing there. He looks exhausted and hungry and his eyes are swollen and red. I walk up to him to take a closer look. There is a bruise where our mother hit him. It has gone black and blue. There is a stipple of red where the blood wants to come up through the skin. He looks at me and says, "Will you take me home, Nick? Can you do that, because I can't seem to find it right now."

"Linda called looking for you. She's worried sick, Peter."

"Hmmm, well." He hangs his head, walks over to the porch that juts out from the cottage and sits down.

"How'd you know I was up here?" Before he answers I remember my car parked along the highway. "Never mind." I sit down next to him and a funny thing happens. When our shoulders touch, I reach over and pull him closer to me and he just lets go. I sit there and don't say a word. I just let it work through him. When he settles he stands up and faces the cottage. He walks up to the windows and peers in.

"This place hasn't changed much," he says.

"Nope. Hardly at all," I say.

"Wouldn't it be nice to go back in there, turn on the TV and find "Wild Wild West" on and be in one of those shows where reality doesn't exist? We'd just turn off the TV and go to bed and in the morning we'd wake-up, get dressed and go running down to the ocean like we did."

"That would be nice," I said, "That would be perfect."

"Well, I guess we can't and that's that." Peter looks over at me. I can tell he wants to go inside, but we'd have to break a window to do so. "I don't think that's a good idea," I say.

"How'd you know what I was thinking?"

"Just do, I suppose." Then I laugh and he joins me. I'm tired and I can't be here anymore. I watch Peter. He's still looking inside, checks the door and comes back to where I am and sits down.

"You spoke to Dad?" he asks.

"Yeah. He gave us some money. It felt so strange taking it from him. I've never asked him for anything."

"What'd you do with it?" Peter doesn't care about the money. I can tell he just wants to know that I'll be okay while I take care of our mother, but I don't think he knows that she's gone.

"I gave it to Mom. All of it." I look for a reaction. He just nods his head as if it was the only thing to do.

"That's good," I say, then add, "You know she's left again." He isn't surprised and he doesn't say anything. He just gets up and motions for me to follow. We walk down the road and cross it and head down the trail we used to take to the beach. It is funny how I follow him still after all this. I figure I will follow him like this the rest of my life.

When we reach the cove the tide is out. The pools stretch out to the breaking waves reflecting the sky like windows. Peter looks at me, smiles and bends down to pick up a stick. Because he is so tired he needs support now as he makes his way out across the shoals.

Every so often he bends down to inspect something in the water and pokes an anemone. He makes them close up so they'll stop looking at him. His hand plunges into the water and comes out again. He's got a starfish. It's orange and gleaming, which he holds up for me to see. I smile and reach out to touch one of its arms and to feel its thousands of feet. They undulate back and forth, grab at the air and try desperately to hold onto something.

If we had been boys Peter would have thrown the starfish across the water as far as it would go, yelling and screaming as he brought his arm back so we would take notice of him. Now he turns the starfish over and brings it up to his face to smell it. He bends down to the pool and places it gently on the rock and smoothes each arm down until it is firmly back in place. He sits on his haunches a moment and watches the starfish reattach itself to the rock. He takes in the whole view of the ocean, the point south along the coast and swings slightly left to look up at the mountains.

"I love it here, Nick. I really do." He stands up, wipes his hands on his sweater, which is stretched and hanging from him. "Maybe mom will be happy now. Maybe not." I moved up next to him and we stand for a long time not saying anything.

You okay?" Peter asked.

"I'm beginning to be, I guess." After awhile the tide starts inching its way to us. The pools fill up with fresh seawater and bring new life.

"I'll follow you up," Peter says.

I turn and negotiate my way through the pools to the edge of the sand. The sound of the crashing waves becomes deafening. Each one pushes the tide farther in and, for some reason, I feel a need to rush back to the safety of the beach. When I look back Peter is still standing at the same spot, which makes me nervous. I remember Aunt Melissa. A wave comes up and swirls around his waist. I don't know whether to run back to him or stay put. I yell out after him, but he doesn't hear me. I begin to go after him. My feet are touching the ends of rocks, twisting around the edges, but holding firm, as I get closer. The curl of a wave rises; slowly it seems and rises higher and folds into white at its tip. From where I am it seems to tower over Peter, but it flattens out and rushes past him and over the pools and around my feet. Peter turns, sees me, but not the panic in my eyes and smiles. He's always at the edge willing himself into danger and out again. I'm not. I turn and head back to the beach and wait for him. When he reaches me, he turns away and stares off. He begins to shake and then a long winding wail comes streaming out of him. He's crying so hard now that he bends over to catch his breath and I cup my hand on his forehead to try and steady him. I support his back and massage it. I just let him go.

If someone had driven by an hour later they would have seen two grown men on the edge of the sand watching the world become new. They might have seen us holding onto each other or laughing madly at all that had happened to us. They might have seen my arm resting on Peter's shoulder. They'd never know that we had come close to the edge of the palisade contemplating jumping off. They'd never know that.

We head to Peter's house. On the way, I think about the family; how my father has slipped from our world, how my mother seems so much a part of it now even though she has left again. I think about running down the cliffs to the ocean in front of my father's house - running after Aunt Melissa and following Peter. How their lives paralleled each other - each trying to escape their pasts.

I'm reminded of the gifts that Aunt Melissa had given us. They were seemingly nonsensical and yet now I know that her perception of what we were like was only hers and the things she gave us simply were to make her happy, but in the giving of them she'd lost her way with us. Not me. I could have listened to her for hours telling me those stories. I could have listened to anyone then. I think that now my family will recede into the past. I have their gifts: a feather, a worn red book, a golden ring and the safe return of a starfish. At least I have those.

We find Linda waiting for us. She is upset and inconsolable, but she's quiet about it and just sits on the edge of the porch. I sit with her. My pants are wet and clinging to me. Peter comes slowly from the car and does an odd thing. He walks up to Linda and kneels in front of her and places his hands on the tops of her thighs and puts his head in the middle of them. I don't know whether to get up and leave or just stay put, but Linda reaches out to take my hand in hers. Her eyes are brimming with tears as she places her other hand on the top of Peter's head and strokes his hair. This is my gift I want to say to her, but I just squeeze her hand back.

The sun begins melting through the fog and steam rises from my wet legs and the ground around their cabin. The tree trunks and stumps begin to mist as well as the three of us sit in tableaux warming in the sun.

I see that wave again. I see the curl of it and the white lip wanting to lick Peter up into its hollowness. It is stuck there in my mind on play and rewind, play and rewind until I can stand it no longer. I decide to leave. Peter and Linda don't move. I tousle his hair and kiss Linda on the forehead. We look at each other; there are dark blue crescent moons under her eyes. She has been awake for hours and will be awake for hours more.

I tell them that I'll call later and reach over and kiss her again on the cheek. She closes her eyes when I do this, which is the first time I've seen them closed since we arrived.

I drive up into Big Sur Center. It's Saturday morning and the parking spaces in front of the stores are just filling up. There's Mrs. Hargrave pulling a lamp out of her station wagon to take to the hardware store to get fixed. There's Barry Moore going in to Jackie's Cafe for breakfast like he does every morning; weekenders mill around on the sidewalk wondering which way to go.

I take two turns back and forth along the highway driving slow as if looking for a place to pull in and park though I know I have no intention of stopping. I swing the car around and head off in the direction of Matt's sister's house. I turn down Cypress Lane like it's automatic, like the car knows the way and I'm just along for the ride. It is a strange thing to see and not see, to hear and not hear because now I'm in front of the house and I've forgotten where I've been and how I've gotten there only its been just a few minutes. I don't know how long I've been sitting in the car before there is a knock on the window and Matt's face is on the other side looking in.

His is an open and beautiful face. Eyes like lit lanterns you can see clear across a dark field. Only it's my dark field and those lights are beckoning and giving me direction. I finally see them. How they glow against the blackness, how warm they seem and how very close they are.

Acknowledgments

On the subject of Shamanism, Michael Harner's book, *"The Way of the Shaman"* was extremely helpful. On depression, William Styron's excellent, *"Darkness Visible,"* proved invaluable.

Details on the Big Sur were taken from many visits, however the landscape and town are wholly of the writer's imagination. Much of it was bent to serve the needs of the novel.

I would like to thank the writer, John Rechy, for the quality and generosity of his critique. Trusted readers, Louise Newman, Patrick Knisely, Jody Eng, Sue Scheibler and Adine Maron gave great insights into the manuscript. Tim Shawl gave me the kernel of an idea from which this novel was born, among many other things.

I would like to thank my Grandmother for her support and wisdom over many years. Joan Weiss Hollenbeck who opened up the world to me with visits to the Covina Valley Library. Finally, a feather to my mother for whom this book was written, who has since passed away.

Made in the USA
Columbia, SC
29 May 2018